THE
SINNERS
CLUB

Books by Kate Pearce

The House of Pleasure Series

SIMPLY SEXUAL

SIMPLY SINFUL

SIMPLY SHAMELESS

SIMPLY WICKED

SIMPLY INSATIABLE

SIMPLY FORBIDDEN

SIMPLY CARNAL

SIMPLY VORACIOUS

SIMPLY SCANDALOUS

Single Titles

RAW DESIRE

THE SINNERS CLUB

Anthologies

SOME LIKE IT ROUGH

LORDS OF PASSION

Published by Kensington Publishing Corporation

THE
SINNERS
CLUB

KATE
PEARCE

APHRODISIA

KENSINGTON PUBLISHING CORP.

www.kensingtonbooks.com

APHRODISIA BOOKS are published by

Kensington Publishing Corp.
119 West 40th Street
New York, NY 10018

All Kensington titles, imprints, and distributed lines are available at special quantity discounts for bulk purchases for sales promotion, premiums, fund-raising, educational, or institutional use.

Special book excerpts or customized printings can also be created to fit specific needs. For details, write or phone the office of the Kensington Special Sales Manager: Kensington Publishing Corp., 119 West 40th Street, New York, NY 10018. Attn. Special Sales Department. Phone: 1-800-221-2647.

Kensington and the K logo Reg. U.S. Pat. & TM Off.

ISBN-13: 978-0-7582-9017-5
ISBN-10: 0-7582-9017-9
First Kensington Trade Paperback Printing: January 2014

eISBN-13: 978-0-7582-9018-2
eISBN-10: 0-7582-9018-7
First Kensington Electronic Edition: January 2014

10 9 8 7 6 5 4 3 2 1

Printed in the United States of America

For the RWA special interest chapter, The Beaumonde,
who fills in the gaps of my Regency knowledge with
such amazing expertise and enthusiasm

1

London, 1827

Jack Lennox consulted his pocket watch and stared out of the grimy diamond-paned window at the street below. It was raining and most of the *beaumonde* had disappeared from the deluge, leaving only beggars, street vendors, and the occasional servant scurrying about his master's business.

He sighed, misting up the pockmarked glass, and turned to the man sitting in the cramped office behind him.

"Do you think Mr. McEwan will be much longer?"

The middle-aged clerk looked at Jack over the top of his spectacles. "As I said, Mr. Lennox, he will see you when he is ready."

"Is he with another client?"

"That's not for me to say, sir."

Jack got to his feet, dusting off his breeches. "Then perhaps I'll take my leave and ask Mr. McEwan to visit me when he *does* have the time."

"Oh no, sir!" The clerk also rose. "That's not necessary. I'll go and see if Mr. McEwan is available."

"At last," Jack muttered to himself as the hapless clerk scurried across the room and tapped on the closed door. A peremptory voice bade him enter, and he disappeared, shutting the door firmly behind him.

He obviously wasn't considered important enough to receive the full attention of the solicitor, but that might change. And he really was pressed for time. He had another appointment this morning, and was also expected by his newly married sister before she left on her honeymoon. She'd never forgive him if he didn't turn up.

The clerk reappeared and beckoned to Jack. "If you would be so kind, sir, Mr. McEwan will see you now."

"Thank you."

Jack entered the solicitor's office and was immediately struck by the sheer volume of books and parchments stacked on every available surface. In the midst of the towering piles of books was a desk, and behind it sat a large, fleshy man in an old-fashioned white-tie wig.

"Mr. McEwan?" Jack bowed. "It is a pleasure to finally meet you."

"Indeed, sir." The solicitor didn't rise and indicated the only uncluttered seat in the room. His accent held a hint of Scots. "Please sit down. I understand you believe you have a claim to the Lennox title and estates."

"I do." Jack extracted the sheaf of documents from his coat pocket. "My father, John, was the youngest son of the fifth earl. He ran away from home at the age of twenty to marry my mother, who was considered an unsuitable match. I have a record of my father's birth, his marriage lines, and details of my own birth."

"There *was* a successor to the title after your grandfather's death."

"One of my uncles, I presume?"

"The sixth earl was the *third* son of your grandfather. Two of the original heirs died during the war with France. At that point in time, there was no record of your birth, and he assumed the title without any issues."

"If he was my father's older brother, he was the obvious heir. Is he still alive?"

Mr. McEwan sighed. "We understand he recently died. It's all a bit of a muddle."

"My father was the fourth and last son, which means that if he was living, he would inherit the title now, yes?"

"If the sixth earl had no son."

"And did he?" Jack tried not to let his impatience show.

"Not as far as we know."

"Then my father would be next in line, and as I said, I am his only heir."

Mr. McEwan sifted through the pile of documents, his eyebrows raised. "You also have very influential friends, Mr. Lennox. I understand these documents were procured for you by Lord Keyes with the current government's approval."

Jack modestly inclined his head. "I have performed some services for the monarchy in the past."

"So I've heard." The solicitor sat back and viewed his potential new client. "When I was apprised of your claim, I took the liberty of instituting a search of the Lennox papers, which we hold as their family solicitors. If your documentation is authentic, you might well be the new Earl of Storr."

"Thank you."

"I will have to consider the matter carefully over the next few days. I have already consulted with the other trustees, and they are more than willing for me to make the final decision on this matter."

"I'm quite happy to wait for your verdict and at your convenience, Mr. McEwan."

The solicitor held up his hand. "There is a little more to it than that. You will need to petition the king, who will then turn the matter over to his attorney general for a writ of summons to take your seat in the House of Lords. As your father is deceased, we will require all the documentation you have brought with you, and those items that I can add from the family papers as evidence."

"I appreciate your help." Jack rose. "You have my direction. I'll await your response."

"There is one more thing, Mr. Lennox. Have you ever visited Pinchbeck Hall?"

"I don't believe so, sir. I know it is situated in the county of Lincoln."

"You should visit the place."

"Even before I am granted the title?"

"I would strongly advise it."

Jack hesitated, his hat in his hands. "Mr. McEwan, is there something you're not telling me?"

The solicitor fixed him with a baleful stare. "The deceased earl's will is missing from the family papers. I've also heard rumors that all is not right at Pinchbeck Hall."

"In what way? Is the place falling down? Has it been mismanaged?"

"On the contrary, sir. One *might* think that *someone* has been intent on feathering their own nest."

"And who might that be? The land agent, or an aggrieved cousin?"

Mr. McEwan folded his hands on his desk and looked down at them. "That I cannot say, Mr. Lennox. It is, after all, hearsay and gossip."

"Indeed." Jack contemplated the solicitor's bowed head. "If I should happen to visit the county of Lincoln, would you like me to get my hands on that will?"

"It would certainly be beneficial to the estate and to the speedy outcome of your claim." The solicitor permitted himself a small smile. "Good morning, Mr. Lennox."

"Sir."

Jack strolled out into the rain and hailed a hackney cab. It seemed as if he might have become involved in a mystery. . . . His spirits rose at the thought. Damn Mr. McEwan for suddenly turning coy and refusing to indulge in spreading idle gossip. Whatever was going on at Pinchbeck Hall certainly needed looking into, and Jack was the obvious choice to investigate. He was fairly sure that his claim to the title was unassailable. He might take a trip up to Lincolnshire in the near future to spy out the lay of the land, so to speak.

He smiled even as the rain drummed down on the roof of the cab. It wasn't far to his next destination at a discreet town house in Mayfair, but he was damned if he'd ruin his new boots by splashing through the puddles. After years of living on air and his wits, affording fashionable clothing was still something of a novelty. His pension from the Crown had been as unexpected as it was generous, and was quite separate from his expectations of the Storr estate. He doubted he'd ever develop the expensive tastes of the average young buck about Town. For one, he was too cynical, and for the other . . . he was handsome enough not to need all the embellishments of current fashion.

He imagined how his twin sister, Violet, would laugh at his preening self-conceit. But it was a fact. His beauty had endeared him to many and enabled him to carry out his nefarious activities in enemy France with wit and style and . . .

Damn, he missed that excitement.

The hackney drew up outside his destination, and he handed the driver a coin. The door was opened before he even had the chance to knock, and Ambrose, the distinguished soon-to-be-ex-manager of the House of Pleasure ushered him inside.

"Mr. Lennox, your sister is waiting for you in the family quarters at the rear of the house."

"Thank you." Jack removed his hat and gloves and followed Ambrose down the stairs and through to the large, warm kitchen in the basement. "And how is married life treating you, Ambrose?"

"Very well, sir. Emily and I are about to move into the master's rooms at the new school."

"Impressive." Jack paused to wait for his companion to catch up with him. "Will you miss the pleasure house?"

"It has been my home for many years, but it is hardly the place I would want to keep my wife or raise a family."

"I gather Madame Helene did just that."

Ambrose grinned. "On the contrary, she did everything to avoid bringing her children up here. They were all educated in France."

"Which explains both their excellent French and their volatile dispositions." Jack pushed open the kitchen door and surveyed the crowd of people milling around. "It seems as if the entire world have come to see Richard and Violet leave."

"Naturally. Despite the unusual circumstances, the Delornay-Ross families are very close."

"Jack!"

He turned to see his twin sister bearing down on him and accepted her embrace with enthusiasm. She wore a dark blue velvet pelisse and matching bonnet suitable for traveling, and sturdy black kid boots.

"I'm so glad you came."

"How could I miss it?" He looked carefully at her. "You are happy, love?"

Her blue eyes, the same sapphire shade as his own, filled with tears. "Never happier."

"Then I am content." He kissed her nose. "Where is your besotted bridegroom?"

She took his hand. "Richard's over here."

He allowed himself to be led over to Richard Ross and shook his hand. The possessive look on his new brother-in-law's face was enough to reassure him that the attraction between the couple was mutual. Even though the thought of being leg-shackled terrified *him*, he still wished them well.

The couple were escorted into their traveling carriage by the staff and family from the pleasure house, and set out for their bridal journey to the West Country. Apparently, Richard intended to buy property down there, having no wish to live at his father's palatial mansion in the countryside until he inherited the title and had no choice.

As he waved them off, Jack's thoughts turned back to his ancestral home. Would he soon visit as the acknowledged owner of both land and title? Having a home was something he'd dreamed about during his more terrifying moments in France. A dream that had seemed doomed to fail until he and Violet had met up with Richard and Lord Keyes again.

It was Richard who introduced him into the private world of the Sinners Club, and the motley collection of ex-spies and adventurers who made up its members. It was Lord Keyes who had assisted him in establishing his claim to the earldom in gratitude for his help with the double spy, Mr. Brown.

Fate was a fickle being. . . .

After saying farewell to Madame Helene, Jack walked around the corner into yet another of the immaculate tree-lined London squares and found the discreet entrance to the Sinners Club. He came into the lobby and closed the door carefully behind him. A man dressed in the club livery rose from his desk and bowed.

"Mr. Lennox. Mr. Fisher is awaiting you in his study."

"Thank you."

He knew his way to the private offices at the back of the Sinners Club, and had no hesitation in finding Fisher's rooms. The ground floor presented itself much like any other gentlemen's club. It was only if you knew the inner workings of the place that you realized the members were not quite like any other. For one, that membership included women, all social classes and all political leanings. The upper floors offered not only the opportunity to be involved in espionage at the highest level, but a freedom to explore one's sexuality that existed in very few clubs, especially in the heart of London where women were not usually allowed.

There were not many members present on such a rainy day, and Jack encountered no one he knew intimately. The scent of brandy and cigarillo smoke hung in the warm air, making him feel quite at home.

"Jack." Adam Fisher rose and held out his hand. "I'm glad to see you. Come and sit down. Can I get you a drink?"

He smiled at Adam, whose bland exterior hid an extremely complex and devilishly cunning brain. Not many people in London knew that along with Lord Keyes, Adam Fisher had been the mastermind behind some of the most daring spying activities in revolutionary France.

"A brandy would be welcome. I've just come from seeing my sister off on her wedding trip."

"From the pleasure house?"

"Yes. Richard was looking very pleased with himself."

"I'm sure he was. With the threat of Mr. Brown removed, he must feel much more secure with his new bride. As must you."

"I can't deny I'm glad Mr. Brown has been unmasked and defeated. I was able to go and see the Lennox solicitors this morning, and start the process for claiming the Storr title."

"And were they helpful?"

"They were." Jack accepted the glass of brandy with a grateful nod. "After all the information you have given me to prove my claim to the earldom, how could they not be?"

"It's the least we could do after that debacle with Mr. Brown." Adam took the seat opposite Jack by the fire. "We need more men like yourself in the House of Lords."

"Men who understand the dark side of foreign policy, and the underbelly of a great nation?"

"Indeed." Adam hesitated. "Are you intending to go to Lincolnshire and claim your estate?"

"I intended to wait until I had the title confirmed, why?"

"I was hoping you might consider a journey in the near future."

"What's wrong?"

Adam looked up. "It's Keyes."

"What about him?"

"He's still missing."

"Damn." Jack sipped his brandy. "Do you have any idea where he might be?"

"You know he disappeared a week or so ago?"

"Yes. Violet and I were worried he'd taken our chance to clear our name with him. At one point, we even suspected *him* of being Mr. Brown."

"Mr. Brown, or should I say Lord Denley, is dead now. Keyes wasn't involved with him in the slightest. We suspect foul play from other quarters."

"From what I've heard, Keyes did have a habit of sticking his nose in where it wasn't wanted. I'm fairly sure there are several people who might want to take revenge on him. Do you have any idea where he's gone?"

Adam sighed. "That's the problem. We've tried all the usual channels, and no one has seen or heard from him. There's been no ransom demand, or offer to exchange prisoners from any of our current enemies either." He hesitated. "Would you mind if I asked the Earl of Westbrook to join us and offer his opinion on the matter?"

"I have no objection. But I can't say I know the man."

Adam turned to ring the bell. "You probably don't, but he has an office here, as does his wife."

"His *wife?*"

"Didn't you know? He and the countess founded the Sinners in 1812. Lord Westbrook was alarmed at the number of his colleagues who received no official recognition from the government for the dangerous acts they committed to safeguard their nation's future. He wanted to offer them and their dependents a safe place, support in legal matters, money when needed, and a place to stay and enjoy their own kind."

"I thought that was your and Keyes's doing."

"No, we are mere inheritors of the day-to-day running of the place."

Jack rose as an older gentleman came through the door. He was still a handsome devil, his skin darker than normal and eyes the color of excellent whisky.

"Mr. Lennox?"

He sounded more English than he looked. Jack bowed. "My lord."

The man glanced at Adam and they all sat down again. "You are aware that Lord Keyes is still missing?"

"So Adam has just told me. How can I help you, sir, and, may I ask, what is your interest in this matter?"

"Ah, Mr. Lennox, you are as sharp as I was led to believe. You are an excellent choice for this adventure."

Jack couldn't help but notice the earl hadn't answered his question. "How do you think I can help?"

"Keyes has family in Lincolnshire. He usually avoids them like the plague."

"Ah, which is why you're both hoping I'd be going to visit Pinchbeck Hall."

Adam sat back and stretched his booted feet toward the fire. "I suspect that whatever happened, Keyes won't thank us for blundering in there and making an official fuss. His disappearance might not be connected to his work for his country at all. I trust your discretion in this matter."

"My discretion?" Jack fought a grin. "I'm a born hell-raiser, ask my sister."

"It is of no matter, if you aren't going to Lincolnshire anyway." Adam directed his next remark at the earl. "He intends to wait to visit Pinchbeck Hall until his title is confirmed."

"I understand. That is certainly the most prudent thing to do." The earl sighed. "It's a pity, but it can't be helped."

Prudent? Him?

Jack finished off his brandy and contemplated his empty glass as a flicker of excitement warmed his gut. Perhaps it was time to allow himself a last escapade before he settled down to the life of a landed peer. Didn't he *deserve* an adventure, and wouldn't it be amusing to descend on his inheritance without announcing his true purpose? He could see what was wrong at his ancestral home *and* help find Lord Keyes all in the same trip. He held out his glass.

"I think I might be going into Lincolnshire in the next few days after all. What exactly do I need to know about your missing colleague?"

2

The county of Lincolnshire was very flat. From his vantage point beside one of the cuts that came in from the cold North Sea, the view across the fens went on for miles. The sky was immense, a billowy mass of lowering gray clouds filled with the howl of a sharp easterly wind. His horse shifted its feet and threw back its head and Jack absentmindedly patted the animal. He'd heard tales that the ghosts of the drowned and the disappeared inhabited the fens, and with the wind screeching like a banshee in his ears, he might well believe it.

He nudged his horse down the barely perceptible incline away from the coast inland following a thin trail that ran parallel to the deep water-filled ditch. Far in the distance, he could see his destination, the squat tower of a church and a huddle of cottages and greenery around it. The host at the Golden Goose Inn on the previous night had told him that Kirkby la Thorpe—the village he sought—was in the Kesteven area of the county, east of the bigger town of Sleaford and on the Boston road. He wrapped his muffler more closely around his face and rammed his hat down on his head. He hoped to God this *was* his destination, as there was nothing else in sight. If he was mistaken, he might wander for days and be found raving mad in a ditch.

The distances were deceptive, and it took his horse far longer than he had anticipated to reach the edge of the small village, which barely qualified as such, apart from its too large church and old inn. The lights of the only hostelry, The Queens Head, appeared in the gathering dust, and Jack let out a relieved breath. The monarch whose faded redheaded portrait hung outside the inn was good Queen Bess. It was a fitting choice for a region that had lost its power when the old queen died and trade shifted to Liverpool, Bristol, and the New World to the west.

He rode into the stable yard and shouted for an ostler. A young boy appeared and obligingly held the horse's head as Jack dismounted.

"Do you have rooms to let, lad?" he asked, his voice cracked with cold and lack of use.

"Yes, sir. I'll take care of your horse. You go on in."

Jack bestowed a small coin on the boy and headed into the house, which was blessedly warm. The taproom appeared empty, but when he banged on the bar, a man who bore a striking resemblance to the boy who'd taken his horse emerged from the cellar and looked Jack over.

"What can I do for you, sir?"

"Good evening, my name is Smith. I'd like a room and a good dinner."

"That we can do, sir. Will Ferrers, landlord, at your service. Do ye have any baggage?"

Jack pointed outside. "It's with my horse."

"Tom will bring it in for ye then. Would ye like a drop of warm ginger punch before ye go up?"

"That would be most welcome. It is rather chilly out there."

The landlord warmed a bowl over the fire and the fragrant

scent of ginger, rum, and honey tantalized Jack's nose. Tom burst into the room with Jack's modest baggage and was bidden to take it up to the best bedchamber.

Jack followed soon after, a pitcher of warm punch and a flagon in one hand. At the top of the stairs, he bumped into a comely woman he assumed was the landlord's wife, which was a pity because he reckoned she'd make a cozy armful on a cold night.

"I've aired the bed for you, sir, and made up the fire." She hesitated by the open door. "Will you eat up here or come down to the parlor?"

"I'll come down." Jack bowed low, and her eyes widened. "Thank you, ma'am."

She patted her lush bosom. "I'm no ma'am, sir. I'm Mr. Ferrers's sister. His wife is busy in the kitchen cooking your dinner."

"How kind of her." Jack smiled slowly. "Then I will definitely come down so that I can give her my thanks."

She batted her eyelashes at him and proceeded down the stairs, her hips swinging while Jack watched appreciatively. His smile faded as soon as he shut the door and viewed his comfortable surroundings. He sternly reminded himself that in his current persona, he couldn't take advantage of any woman, even a willing one. It would not be in character.

With a groan he sat down and pulled off his boots unaided. As he hadn't traveled with a servant of any description, it was a good thing he was used to doing for himself. He poured a mug of the hot punch and drank it as quickly as he could, murmuring his appreciation as the spirits warmed and soothed the back of his throat.

Within half an hour he was in the best parlor in front of a crackling fire, eating a remarkably good dinner. The landlord offered him a decent bottle of claret and Jack accepted, with the proviso that his host join him. After a shared bottle, Mr. Ferrers was inclined to be more confiding, which suited Jack perfectly.

"So what brings ye to our village, sir?" Ferrers asked as he opened the second bottle.

"Business, Mr. Ferrers, business."

"Out here? Are you a land agent, or a buyer of wool?"

"No, I'm a private secretary."

"And what does that entail?"

Jack polished his spectacles. "I answer my employer's correspondence, help him write his speeches for the House of Lords, organize his staff at his various houses, and keep an eye on the butler and the household accounts."

"The man is too busy to see to these things himself, is he?"

"Indeed. My employer is an extremely active man in the government of this great nation."

"Does he have property around here, then?"

"I believe so. That is why I'm here."

Ferrers scratched his head. "Now, where would that be? There's the vicarage and the Grange on the hill, but apart from that . . ."

"The property is called Pinchbeck Hall. Do you know of it?"

"Pinchbeck Hall?" Ferrers shook his head. "Nay, that can't be right. That's the Earl of Storr's family seat. My cousin works up there as the housekeeper."

"Perhaps I work for the Earl of Storr?"

"Nay, how could ye? The man just died!" Ferrers roared with laughter and slapped his knee. "No disrespect to the old codger, mind."

"I am aware that the old earl passed away. I happen to represent the new earl."

His companion's jaw dropped. "The new one?"

"It is the way of the world, Mr. Ferrers. The old order passeth to make way for the new and all that."

"But—"

"I intend to present myself at the house tomorrow. Did you say that your cousin was still in residence? Perhaps she will be able to assist me in my perusal of the estate accounts, and give me a tour of the house."

"She is still there, sir, but so are the family."

"I'll deal with them when I see them. I have my instructions from the new earl. No one will be turned out, or left homeless."

"Well, I'm glad to hear that, sir, seeing as how things are up there." Ferrers frowned. "Are ye quite certain your employer is the new earl, sir?"

"Why do you ask?"

"Because I didn't think things had been settled yet."

"Indeed." Jack studied the landlord's dubious expression. "Is there another claimant to the title?"

"That's difficult to say yet, sir, isn't it?" Ferrers stood up and bowed. "I think I hear someone calling me in the public room. If you'll excuse me, I'll go and attend to his needs."

Jack contemplated the fire for a while and considered Ferrers's cryptic comments. There was definitely something not right up at Pinchbeck Hall, but he still wasn't clear exactly what was going on. Had somebody else claimed the title? Would he find an imposter in his place? His anticipatory smile turned into a yawn and he stood up. After his day in the saddle a good night's sleep seemed a just reward.

He made his way back up the stairs and found his door ajar and the very helpful Miss Ferrers turning down his bed. She smiled as he came into the room and he smiled back. Perhaps the new earl's private secretary deserved some reward for doing his duty after all. . . .

A cock crowed, waking Jack from his slumber, and he shouted down for some hot water. It didn't take him long to shave, dress, and pull on his newly polished boots. He descended into the parlor to devour a plate of ham and eggs while getting directions to Pinchbeck Hall. Within an hour he was on his way along the narrow country lanes with their high hedges.

The sun peeked out from behind the clouds bathing the sullen landscape with light and reminding him of the paintings he'd recently seen by a Mr. J.M.W. Turner at the Somerset House exhibition.

It didn't take him long to reach the walls of the estate and halt his horse. The high iron gates emblazoned with the Storr crest were open. The stone gatehouse appeared to be uninhabited but not neglected. Jack headed up the long elm tree–lined driveway, pausing occasionally to admire the view through the trees and try to catch a glimpse of the approaching house.

He spotted the high Tudor chimneys first and so wasn't surprised that the house turned out to be large and rambling in a typical black-and-white-timbered Elizabethan style. At one end stood a stone watchtower, which leaned awkwardly against the more traditional structure. It certainly wasn't a classically beautiful house in the current style, but it had a certain charm all its own. Despite its age, it looked to be well maintained, which confirmed Mr. McEwan's remarks about the estate being in excellent condition.

There was no one in sight. He rode up to the arched oak front door with its two sunken steps and dismounted before banging hard on the already dented wooden panels. He heard faint footsteps and the withdrawing of a creaking bolt. When the door opened, he fixed a pleasant smile on his face.

"Good morning, I've—"

The man who'd opened the door scowled at him, and flung the door wide. He wasn't dressed like a servant, and appeared to be a country gentleman.

"Come in."

Jack raised his eyebrows in mild surprise and followed the man into the hallway. The space was vast and betrayed its medieval origins with a high hammerbeam ceiling and rusted suits of armor. He wasn't given the opportunity to appreciate the sight for long as he remembered his primary business.

"May I ask whom I have the pleasure of speaking to, sir?"

The man swung around. "You should damn well know that before you come skulking up here with your lies."

Jack held his ground. "I assume Mr. Ferrers sent a message ahead of me, then?"

"Of course he did!"

"Which is supposed to account for your unpleasant reception?"

"You think I'm being unpleasant? Perhaps you might reconsider that after you meet my sister. Come into the drawing room." He stalked down the hallway, Jack at his heels, opened a door, and stepped inside. "The Countess of Storr."

Jack took off his hat and advanced toward the diminutive lady who reclined on the couch. She gave a little cry of distress and struggled to rise. It was Jack who reached her first and tenderly assisted her to sit up. He found himself looking into a pair of big brown eyes filled with a hint of wide-eyed terror and a suggestion of tears. Her face was heart-shaped and framed with artfully arranged golden curls.

"Oh my, have you come to throw me from my house in my condition?"

Jack forced his gaze from the beauty of her face, down over her fabulous bosom and finally to the swell of her belly clearly outlined against the black silk of her high-waisted gown.

"Ma'am?"

She clasped his hand in hers. "It's true, isn't it?"

Jack carefully disengaged himself from her frantic grasp and stepped back. "I have no idea whom I'm addressing, ma'am. Perhaps I should start by making myself known to you. I'm—"

"We know who you are." The male sibling interrupted Jack and came to stand by his sister's side. "You're an imposter."

Jack fought down an absurd desire to laugh. "I assure you, I am not. My name is John Smith."

"Then you are not the scoundrel who claims to be the new earl?" the woman whispered.

He bowed. "Didn't Mr. Ferrers tell you? I am the private secretary of the man who *expects* to be the next earl. May I respectfully inquire who you are?"

The lady glanced at her brother and exhaled. "Oh love, it's not as bad as we feared at all! I'm sure Mr. Smith is a reasonable man, and will soon understand why his employer is mistaken in his beliefs." She smiled brilliantly up at Jack. "Your employer cannot *possibly* be the new earl." Her hand curved over her belly.

"I'm not sure I understand, ma'am."

"I am the current, or should I say, *dowager*, Countess of Storr, and my child is not yet born." She raised her chin. "Your master cannot possibly claim the title until *my* child is delivered. And if it is a boy, as I believe it will be, then the title will never be your employer's."

Jack abruptly sat down.

"*You* are the Countess?"

"The Dowager Countess." She opened her eyes wide at him. "Obviously."

"The Lennox family solicitors made no mention of the last earl being married."

She bit her luscious lower lip. "I suspect that was Jasper's little joke. He was known to be rather secretive about such things." She reached out a hand to the auburn-haired man standing beside her. "My brother, Simon, has been a rock in this time of trial. I am so lucky to have him."

Simon's face softened as he looked down at his sister. Jack took stock of the tall redheaded man and the petite blond woman. They didn't look at all alike, but there was an obvious bond of affection between them. And why was he worrying about that when there were other, more important things to concern him? Like the fate of his inheritance? He hardened his resolve. He'd be damned if he'd let it slip away again.

"I'm fairly certain my employer, the Honorable Mr. Lennox, would expect me to inquire further as to this unexpected situation." He hesitated. "With all due respect, do you have copies of your marriage lines, my lady?"

Simon's expression darkened. "My sister doesn't have to prove anything to you! Ask anyone in the house! We have lived here for most of our lives, everyone knows us. You are the interloper here, sir, and don't you forget it."

The countess touched his sleeve. "It's all right, love. The quicker we can convince Mr. Smith of the legality of our situation, the quicker he can leave and post back down to London to break the news to his employer." She turned her charming smile on Jack. "Isn't that so, Mr. Smith? I'm sure you don't want to linger here if it is unnecessary."

Jack bowed. "I do have other business in the area to transact, so I don't consider my journey here a waste whatever the outcome. If you furnish me with evidence of your marriage, I can certainly take the particulars back to London with me."

"Then that is settled." The countess rose from her seat and held out her hand. "Will you care to stay for dinner? We keep country hours."

Hiding his surprise at this abrupt change of face, Jack nodded. "If that would not incommode you, my lady." He glanced down at his buckskin breeches. "I am hardly dressed for it."

She smiled. "We don't stand much on ceremony here. Before our repast, we might take advantage of the mildness of the weather, and enjoy a tour of the garden. You can then report back to your superior on the condition of the estate, and lay his fears for its survival at rest." She stroked her belly. "After my son is born, I suppose it is possible that your Mr. Lennox might be named as a guardian for the child alongside my brother."

"I would imagine that would be the case, my lady." In fact, Jack was pretty damn sure the previous earl would've insisted. "One would assume that despite your no doubt inestimable care, the deceased earl would like to keep the family involved with the upbringing of his offspring."

A look of slight revulsion marred the lady's perfect countenance, but it was quickly concealed by a bewitching smile. "My child will mean the world to me, I can assure you of that."

Jack bowed, took the countess's proffered hand, and kissed it.

A slight blush touched her porcelain skin, and she sighed. "You are indeed a gentleman, sir."

"The Honorable Mr. Lennox would employ nothing less, my lady."

"If you would care for some refreshment, I'll ask my housekeeper to wait on you while I go upstairs and put my cloak and bonnet on."

"Thank you, my lady." Jack obediently sat down again and watched as the pair made their way out of the salon and closed the door. Had he fallen into a Drury Lane farce or the pages of a gothic novel? He couldn't help grinning as he considered the "countess's" beautiful face and figure. In truth, he hadn't been so entertained for years. If she were married to the old earl, he'd eat his hat. He sat back and contemplated the afternoon ahead with considerable enjoyment.

Mary Lennox shut the door into her bedchamber and leaned against it, one hand clasped to her bosom.

"Oh my goodness! Do you think he believed us?"

Simon started to pace the carpet, his expression aggrieved. "I don't care whether he believed us or not. As I said, he's the interloper here, not us!"

"He was younger than I anticipated."

"Much younger." Simon stopped moving. "He seemed rather taken with you."

She shrugged. "I am remarkably good with men."

His smile flashed out, transforming his face. "I know. Do you want me to accompany you on your walk?"

"No, I think I can handle him. I'd prefer it if you went into the earl's study and tried to find the necessary documentation to convince him to leave."

"At least for a while." His glance rested on her belly. "At some point that child will have to be born."

"What if he won't leave? What if he wishes to stay until the succession is secured?"

"Then he stays, and we strive to convince him of our worth and bend him to our cause. Despite his gentlemanly appearance, he is still a paid employee and would probably be amenable to increasing his wealth."

"Who wouldn't be?" Mary asked. "Do you think we can convince him?"

He swept her a magnificent bow. "Why not? Our future happiness depends on it. And who is more persuasive than we are when prepared to risk anything?"

Mary took a deep, steadying breath. "You are right, as usual."

Simon walked toward her and planted a long, lingering kiss on her lips. "Of course I am. Now put on your prettiest bonnet and go and charm our guest into complete and willing submission."

Mary waited until Mr. Smith spotted her in the doorway before coming forward to greet him. It gave her time to study his serious expression, wire-rimmed spectacles, and black hair dusted with gray just at the temples. She guessed him to be somewhere in his thirties. He was dressed in a sober manner that befitted his position without much claim to fashion, but with impeccable taste. Beneath his garments, he appeared to be of medium height and lean build.

"My lady." He bowed.

"Mr. Smith."

She curtsied. His manners were faultless, as was his attempt to hide his reaction to her beauty. She knew she was beautiful.

It was something of a blessing and a curse in equal measures. But one had to use whatever weapons were available to get on in life, and she wouldn't shirk at using it now when her entire future was at stake.

He tucked her hand into the crook of his elbow and led her toward the front door. She tugged his coat sleeve, and he paused to look down at her.

"My lady?"

"We'd do better to start around the back of the house. The front door is seldom used these days."

"As you wish, my lady."

She led him through the maze of corridors and, avoiding the kitchen, led him out through the scullery into the walled garden beyond.

"Ah, this must be original to the house?" He looked around the tranquil walled space with its long mellow Elizabethan bricks and faded yellow and black border tiles.

"I believe it is. Most of the fruit and vegetables grown here are used to feed the family. Any excess is sold for profit at the market."

"You are obviously an efficient and economical housewife for the estate, my lady."

Mary fought a wince followed swiftly by a tremor of anxiety. He didn't need to know the source of her expertise, although she suspected that if he stayed in the area for long, one of the embittered Lennox cousins would tell him.

"I like to oversee the accounts personally, Mr. Smith. It certainly encourages honesty and efficiency."

"My employer is the same, my lady. He expects me to keep an eye on his household accounts as well as his business affairs. Unfortunately, his wife is not quite as economical as you are. She has a tendency to overspend her allowance every quarter on frivolities."

There was a note of censure in his voice, which bode well for their hopes of winning him to their side. It would gall anyone who had to earn an honest wage to see the way the rich wasted their money.

"That must put you in a difficult position."

He sighed as they continued to walk along the graveled pathway that led through the gardens and out into the park beyond. "Indeed it does. I have no wish to speak ill of my mistress, but one does become tired of being screeched at because her husband refuses to pay her gambling debts."

She patted his arm and waited as he closed the garden gate behind them. The sun came out and lengthened their shadows as they walked through an avenue of yew bushes.

"Do you have family in this area, Mr. Smith?"

"I'm not sure, my lady. I believe I might have some distant cousins here." He hesitated. "I do remember one family, the Keyes. Do you know of them?"

"I can't say that I do, but I must confess that with Jasper being so unwell, our social life had dwindled to almost nothing."

"Quite understandably. One of my tasks is to seek the Keyes family out, but it isn't urgent. My employer has some news for them on the matter of a missing inheritance."

"How exciting. Please don't hesitate to ask any of our staff here if they know of their whereabouts."

"Do you have relatives in the county, my lady?"

Mary kept smiling. "Not that I know of, Mr. Smith." And none that she would acknowledge even if she did. She steered the conversation into less choppy waters. "Did you grow up in London yourself, then, sir?"

"No, in France."

"That must have made it difficult for you during the last conflict."

"Not particularly, my lady. My allegiances were always with my mother country, although I do speak excellent French,

which is one of the reasons Mr. Lennox hired me to be his secretary."

"I'm sure there were many reasons, Mr. Smith." She
squeezed his arm. "You strike me as an extremely able and intelligent man."

"Thank you, my lady." He patted her hand in an absent
manner. "Is there a home farm?"

"There is." She stopped to point out the stone walls and
smoking chimney of the farm below. "It's down there and is
run by Ben Fakenham and his family."

"Do you currently have a land agent for the estate, or did
the earl manage such things himself?"

"My brother, Simon, is his land manager. He has all the relevant papers in the estate office up at the house. I'm certain he
would be delighted to share them with you."

"Are you quite sure, my lady? He didn't seem very pleased
to see me."

She smiled up at him, aware, not for the first time, of the intelligence lurking in the bright blue eyes behind his spectacles.
"He is rather protective of me. You cannot expect me to apologize for that. But once he sees that you mean me no harm, I'm
sure he'll be happy to show you anything you want."

"I am just doing my job, my lady."

She reached up and patted him on the cheek. "I know, Mr.
Smith, and I can see that you don't wish to hurt me at all." She
paused and slowly blinked at him. "You don't, do you?"

He met her gaze and then immediately looked away. "My
lady . . ."

She stepped away, confident in what she'd seen in that fleet-
ing moment, and continued to walk around the house. "The
park is stocked with game for all tastes and seasons, and there is
a trout stream down on the south boundary. If you wish to
speak to the head gamekeeper, that can be arranged."

"I doubt I'll have time for fishing, my lady."

Ah, he was back to being stuffy again. "The house looks quite beautiful from this angle, doesn't it? You can see the bones of the original structure, the addition of the state wing, and the improvements my husband's father made."

Mr. Smith paused beside her to look back at the house. "It is a remarkably appealing residence."

"I confess to being very fond of it myself." It was her home. Has he realized yet that she was prepared to fight to keep it with all the weapons at her disposal? "I'm glad you can appreciate it."

He bowed. "Considering the circumstances, you have been more than helpful, ma'am."

"Well, I understand how difficult this development might be for your employer, and I feel sorry that you are the one who must bring him such bad news." She hesitated and touched his arm. "He won't dismiss you, will he?"

"I don't think so, my lady. He isn't a tyrant."

"But his wife might use it as an excuse to be rid of you, might she not?" She attempted a laugh. "Oh, forgive me, Mr. Smith, this is hardly my business, is it?"

"Your concern does you credit, my lady."

"Oh, thank you," Mary sighed and batted her eyelashes at her companion. "I do so hate it when those who are born to privilege take advantage of those who serve them."

He smiled down at her and she was fascinated by the changes it made to his rather stern face. Even as she recalculated his attractiveness, the smile was gone, replaced by a stiff formality that reminded her of the earl's ancient butler, who luckily had expired the same week as his master.

The sun went behind the clouds, and a breeze tainted with a hint of threatened rain stirred the ribbons of her bonnet.

"Oh dear," she breathed. "We seem to have lost our good weather. Shall we return to the house?"

He offered her his arm again and she accepted, leaning

rather more heavily on him than was necessary, but anxious to remind him of her interesting condition. He conversed happily enough with her about the estate as they walked back toward the house, betraying none of the earnest interest she had aroused in him earlier. But she was content. She had stirred the coals and was content to let him smolder. Gauging a man's interest in her was second nature, and he was interested, she was sure about that. Whether it was enough to draw him into a stronger alliance with her and Simon was another matter, but time would tell.

She smiled dazzlingly at him. "Let me tell you more about the original house."

3

They were very good, even Jack could admit that as he sat back to admire his host and hostess at dinner. Both of them had faultless manners, were amusing dinner companions, and obviously were devoted to each other. In some ways they reminded him of his relationship with his twin, Violet. The "dowager," Mary Lennox, was also extremely beautiful and not averse to displaying her charms. She'd chosen to wear a thin silk dress in the palest gray that somehow managed to complement both her hair and her skin.

It was also exceedingly low-cut in the bodice, offering him a delightful view of her barely restrained breasts. At idle moments he found himself studying the perfection of her cleavage through the candlelight and imagining burying his face or his cock between those two plump mounds. . . .

"Don't you agree, Mr. Smith?"

Jack tore his gaze away from Mary and studied her brother, who had apparently asked a question. Simon was being remarkably amenable this evening, and displayed a sharp wit Jack could only respond to. It was a shame that the best of tricksters were so entertaining. He almost regretted that at some point he would have to bring the charade to an end. Fortunately for them, he wasn't done enjoying himself yet.

"I apologize, Mr. Picoult, I was woolgathering. What did you ask me?"

"Which is rather appropriate as I was merely commenting on the number of sheep we are able to graze per acre here in the county of Lincoln, and wondering how that compared to your employer's estates."

The countess rose to her feet with a chuckle. "If you are going to start discussing *sheep*, I shall leave you to your port and await you in the drawing room."

Both men stood as the lady departed. Simon dismissed the lone footman, walked over to the sideboard, and picked up the heavy tray of crystal decanters.

"What's your pleasure, Mr. Smith? Some port, or would you prefer a whisky?"

"Port will be fine, sir."

Simon placed the tray on the table and took the seat next to Jack.

"My sister says I should apologize for biting your head off when I first saw you." He ruffled his auburn hair with a rueful smile. "I have something of a temper."

"From what her ladyship told me, you are a very protective brother. I cannot find fault with that."

"Do you have sisters, Mr. Smith?"

"I have a twin sister."

"Then you understand my dilemma." Simon grimaced. "Mary is very beautiful. Unfortunately some men have been known to lose their heads over her."

"Even knowing she was married to the earl?"

"Even then, you'd be surprised at the stories I could tell you. Some of the Lennox family has been—"

"Yes?"

"Less than kind about my sister marrying a man old enough to be her father." Simon raised his candid gaze to Jack's. "But she held the earl in great affection, I can swear to that. She was the one who nursed him through his darkest hours when all the rest of them ran away in fear of infection."

Of course, a more cynical man might reply that any young woman who attracted an elderly earl's interest *would* hold him in affection. Jack didn't say it, because he was enjoying himself, and there was an uncomfortable element of truth to the man's words he found at odds with his first impressions.

"From all I have seen of the countess, she appears to have a good heart and a great sense of responsibility toward her family and the estate."

"She has." Simon poured them both a glass of port and held one out to Jack. "I'm glad you have the ability to see her true worth. She deserves to be admired and respected."

"Indeed."

Again that rang true. What had happened in the past to make the pair so supportive of each other? Again he was reminded of Violet. Or was it as simple as a beautiful woman needing her brother to protect her while she worked her charms on her elderly prospective bridegroom? Criminals often worked in pairs; one to draw the eye while the other committed the crime. He would do well to remember that as he dealt with his two adversaries. Things were rarely as simple as they seemed. He'd learned that to his cost many times.

"Are you anxious to go home, Mr. Smith?"

"Not particularly."

"You have no womenfolk awaiting your return?"

"No. My sister was recently married, and my stepmother doesn't live with me. I inhabit a bachelors' quarters near my employer's house."

In truth he didn't have a home at all. He'd never had a home. The house he currently lived in was borrowed from a family friend, and would have to be vacated in a matter of weeks. He wanted Pinchbeck Hall. Reminded of his resolution to oust the imposters, Jack considered Simon's choice of conversation anew.

"Excuse my interest, but you haven't chosen to marry?" Simon shoved his hand through his thick auburn hair. "My sister thinks that I should consider the advantages of the wedded state, but I find myself reluctant to commit myself."

"To one woman?"

Simon's enchanting smile emerged. "To any woman."

Jack held the man's gaze and considered all the very provocative replies he could make to that comment. In the end he merely smiled, and decided to turn the conversation into a safer channel. Had the siblings decided to see who could entice the staid Mr. Smith into bed first? It seemed highly likely. But if that were Simon's intention, he'd surely bring the matter up again.

"I've been meaning to ask you, Mr. Picoult, was the old earl buried in the parish church at St. Denys?"

"He was, Mr. Smith. Do you wish to visit his grave?"

"I will do so when I return to the Queen's Head. I believe the church is but a short walk from the inn."

"It is." Simon finished his port and seemed to hesitate. "Do you wish another glass, or would you prefer to join my sister in the drawing room?"

Jack smiled slowly at his host. He was experienced enough to know when another man was seeking his company and sometimes even why. "It *is* excellent port."

An answering smile lit Simon's brown eyes. "The earl was something of a collector of fine spirits and wines. The cellars are a marvel."

"Perhaps I should make time to investigate them before I leave Pinchbeck Hall."

"I'm convinced you should."

Jack finished off his port in one swallow while Simon regarded him intently.

"If you will permit." He put down his glass, his gaze on

Jack's mouth, and leaned in, swiping his thumb over his lip. "There's a drip."

He withdrew his thumb and licked the gleaming ruby port into his mouth, running his tongue around the tip of his thumb in a slow circle.

Well, well, how interesting . . . and how direct. Jack's cock twitched as he raised his gaze from Simon's thumb to his face. "Thank you."

"You are most welcome." Simon stood and brushed a far from innocent hand over the bulge in the front of his breeches. "Let me know if you find time to explore the cellars. They are well worth a visit."

Jack stood, too, allowing his companion a comprehensive glance at his own state of semi-arousal. "I must confess that I always enjoy the opportunity to sample new and untried pleasures. Such 'pleasures' and opportunities do not often cross my path."

Simon opened the door. "Mine either. My horizons have become rather provincial since my sister married the earl."

"Perhaps it is time for you to widen them again, Mr. Picoult." Jack stopped right alongside Simon. "What a shame I'll be leaving fairly shortly."

Simon reached out a leisurely hand and traced Jack's lower lip with his fingertip.

"More drips of port, Mr. Picoult?"

"No."

His breath hitched as Jack deliberately flicked his tongue over the gliding, roughened tip.

"Damn, I wish you were staying."

Jack leaned back against the door frame. "I don't think her ladyship would approve, do you?"

"She can be surprisingly accommodating."

"Accommodating enough to allow me to stay here while I finish my business at the estate, and my other commissions from my master?"

"If you like, I could suggest the convenience of the arrangement to her."

"And what will that cost me?"

Simon smiled. "A warm bed for the night?"

"But what about my room at the inn?"

"We can take care of that for you."

Jack sighed and pushed away from the door, deliberately pressing himself for an instant against the now fully erect Simon before pulling away. He put on his most stuffy and disagreeable voice. "I still don't think her ladyship would agree, and in truth, I—"

"Come now, there is no need to fret. You haven't committed yourself to anything but a bed for the night, and the lack of a long, cold ride back to the inn in the rain." Simon remained where he was, his breathing a little short, and his color high. Like any man who risked his life openly courting another, he had obviously learned to be wary. "It can't hurt for me to ask my sister about that."

Jack kept walking until he reached the double doors of the drawing room and opened them. The Dowager Countess was sitting by the fire, embroidering what looked like a baby's cap. Her golden head was bent to her task, giving him a view of her exquisite profile and the long, swan-like curve of her neck.

"Mr. Smith." She smiled up at Jack. "I was just wondering whether you meant to abandon me for the whole night."

He bowed. "We would never dream of doing that, my lady."

Even as he sat beside her and accepted the cup of tea she poured for him, he wondered if she knew about the sexual predilections of the brother who lounged at his ease opposite them. Because of the closeness between the siblings, he had to assume she did. Violet had certainly known that he would fuck anything. What would the countess feel if her brother took up with the new earl's supposed secretary? If he was correct, and they were both intent on seducing his support, would she consider it an advantage in the game they were playing? And what of the lures she had already cast out to him? Were the Picoults happy for either sibling to land the fish?

Jack sat back and sipped leisurely at his tea while the countess offered her brother a cup. What would she offer him next?

Simon winked at Mary as she passed him her tea and murmured, "He's not quite such a dry old stick after all."

"Sshh." She frowned at him, aware that Mr. Smith had an excellent sense of hearing and was sitting barely five foot away from them.

"In truth, I'd quite like a go at him." He raised his voice. "But *of course,* our esteemed guest should stay the night, dear sister, what an excellent idea." He looked over her shoulder at Mr. Smith. "I'm afraid it is too late to go over all the papers with you this evening. After all that port I'd probably not make much sense."

"It is of no matter," the secretary replied. "But do not feel as if you have to offer me hospitality. I do have a room ready for me at the inn."

Mary turned and went toward him, her hands outstretched. She'd be damned if Simon would take all the credit for their change of heart.

"We would love you to stay with us, Mr. Smith. It won't take but a moment to prepare a bedroom for you, and send a note to the Queen's Head to tell them you will return on the morrow."

He frowned. "If you are quite sure, my lady."

She took his hands in hers and squeezed them. "Absolutely, Mr. Smith. Jasper would never forgive me if I was less than hospitable to a man who represented another member of his family."

"To be honest, it would certainly be pleasant not to have to ride back in the rain. I am rather tired."

"I'm sure you are. After you have finished your tea, Simon

can escort you up to your bedchamber and lend you any necessities for a peaceful night's sleep."

"That is very kind of you both." He bent awkwardly and kissed her hand. "You truly are a gracious lady."

If only he knew. Mary turned away but not before she'd caught Simon's triumphant wink. "If you would excuse me for a moment, Mr. Smith, I must consult with my housekeeper."

She left the warm drawing room and made her way down to the servants' quarters. Simon caught her up on the backstairs.

"Nicely done, sister."

"Why did you ask him to stay?" she demanded.

"Because I thought it was a good idea. Can't you tell the man is lonely?"

"For you?"

"Maybe, I'm not sure."

"You'd bed him?"

Simon's expression sobered. "I'd bed the prime minister and the prince regent if it meant you and I survived. Mr. Smith is far more comely."

"Do you think he is interested?" She pouted. "I thought he was rather taken with me."

"I'm sure he is." He kissed her on the nose. "Mayhap he went to Eton and, like most of the male upper classes, is quite used to fucking men as well."

"Now you are making fun of me."

"No." He stepped away. "I've dealt with more than one titled lord who liked his own sex."

There was a harshness in his voice that made her reach out to cup his cheek. "Those days are long behind us."

"They are if we can continue this masquerade. If Mr. Smith wants a bit of rough, I'm quite willing to give it to him. And if he turns nasty on us, we'll have something to hold over him to ensure his future cooperation."

He turned and went back up the stairs, leaving Mary staring

after him. Was their unwelcome guest really attracted to Simon? If he were, she wouldn't begrudge either of them their sport. But she'd really believed he was ready to worship at her feet, not Simon's. . . .

She realized she'd been standing in front of the kitchen door for so long that she was getting cold. After a quick prayer, she pushed open the door and walked inside. Mrs. Lowden sat with the cook at the large kitchen table, sharing a jug of ale. The fire was banked up for the night, and the black leaded stove glowed a sullen red. At this time of night, the majority of the staff wasn't in evidence, having retired to bed in preparation for their early starts.

"What do you want, lass?"

Mary raised her chin. "I would like you to prepare a bed-chamber next to Mr. Picoult's for Mr. Smith."

The housekeeper sighed. "All right, then. I suppose you want it done now?"

"Yes, please."

Mrs. Lowden exchanged a look with the cook. "Yes, *milady*, certainly, *milady*."

The cook snorted with laughter she didn't even bother to conceal. Mary felt her cheeks heat.

"If you continue to treat me with such a lack of respect, I will turn you both off."

The cook's smile disappeared, and the housekeeper turned around to stare at Mary. "You'll do what, missy?"

"I'll turn you off. Do you think I can't do it? Jasper is dead now. I am the mistress of this house."

"Mistress indeed, my lady. If that Mr. Smith speaks true, you won't be in that position for long now, will you?"

"Whatever do you mean?"

"I hear he represents the new earl." Mrs. Lowden's smile wasn't pleasant. "When the new bloke finds out what you've done, you'll be the one being turned off, my lady, not us."

Mary glared at the grinning woman. "As that is not going to happen, I suggest you attend to your duties and mind your tongue!"

"Yes, milady."

"And be quick about it!"

Mary turned on her heel and stomped back up the stairs to the drawing room. At the doors, she paused long enough to take another deep breath and fix a pleasant smile on her face.

Both men looked up at her as she entered.

"It is all settled. My housekeeper, Mrs. Lowden, will prepare a room for you immediately."

"Thank you, my lady."

Mary sat opposite Mr. Smith and reached for her sewing. "Simon, I meant to ask you if you were acquainted with a family in the area named Keyes. Mr. Smith said he was seeking them."

"Keyes?" Simon looked thoughtful. "It does sound vaguely familiar. Perhaps I have encountered them at the county market or assizes."

"I understood them to live about twenty miles or so from here," Mr. Smith said. "I will have to inquire further."

"I'll ask the Fakenhams down at the home farm," Simon said. "They know everyone."

"I thought to ask the vicar of St. Deny's too."

Mary set another tiny stitch in the white satin. "That is an excellent idea. If you decide to stay with us while you search for this family, we can ask the Reverend Tyler to call one day and offer his services."

"Thank you, my lady." Mr. Smith attempted to conceal a yawn behind his hand. "I do apologize. It's been rather a long, tiring day."

Was he eager to go to bed because he was anticipating a visit from Simon, or was he as tired as he looked? Mary was unable to decide. She glanced up at her brother, who was watching Mr. Smith intently.

"Simon, do you want to show Mr. Smith to his room? He will be right next door to you."

"Of course I will." Simon came over and kissed her on the forehead. "Good night, love. Sleep well."

Mr. Smith approached her, too, and punctiliously kissed her hand. "My lady."

"Good night. Please ring the bell if you require any assistance from the staff and they will be happy to help you." At least she hoped they would. One could never tell these days. . . .

The men departed and Mary attempted to sew another seam, but gave up because of the poorness of the light. Should she attempt to ascertain if Mr. Smith really did have everything he needed, or should she leave that in the capable hands of her brother? She put away her sewing and decided to seek her own bed. If anything did happen, Simon was sure to tell her in the morning.

4

Jack took the candle Simon offered him and followed the broad back of the land agent up another flight of stairs and then another. Simon took a turn to the left and headed down a wide corridor lined with dark paneling and hunting pictures. Their gigantic shadows flickered up the walls and around the corners ahead of them as if announcing their presence.

"Are we in the attics?"

Simon glanced over his shoulder at Jack and smiled. "No, there's another floor of those above for the servants. We're in the bachelors' quarters in the old stone tower."

"Away from temptation."

"You could say that." Simon stopped and waited for Jack to come alongside him. He held up his candle. "My room is to the right, and yours is on the left."

He unlatched the door on the left to reveal a turned-down four-poster bed and a warm, crackling fire. "It seems that Mrs. Lowden has already been in to attend to your needs."

Jack walked into the surprisingly large room, which was dominated by the tapestried bed. "This is excellent and very kind of you both."

Simon shrugged. "My sister and I are glad of the company." He pointed at the dresser, where a jug of still steaming water and a bowl sat ready. "There's water there to wash in. If you leave your boots outside the door, they'll be cleaned for you."

"Thank you." Jack crossed over to the window to close the curtains. "Good night, Mr. Picoult."

"Good night, Mr. Smith. If you need anything in the night, please don't hesitate to seek me out. There's a dressing room between us. I'll leave both the doors unlocked."

"Thank you again."

Simon nodded and went out through the main door, shutting it carefully behind him. Jack remained staring thoughtfully at the space his companion had recently occupied. Had he been issued an invitation to investigate the unlocked doors, or was Simon merely being a good host? Would bedding one of his potential adversaries help or hinder his cause? If they thought he was on their side, wouldn't it be easier to bring them down from within?

Jack sighed, shrugged out of his coat and waistcoat, and hung them on the back of the chair by the fire. In truth, he wouldn't mind bedding either of the Picoults. They were both enticing in their own ways, and it wouldn't be the first time he'd been involved in a threesome. . . .

A tap on the interior door concealed in the round wall of the tower drew his attention. He went over and unlocked the latch, swinging the door wide to reveal Simon in his shirtsleeves. He held something out to Jack.

"I thought you might require a nightshirt or a cap."

Jack slowly let out his breath. "That's very thoughtful of you, but I prefer to sleep in the nude."

Simon's eyes widened. "That's rather unusual."

"You have to remember, I was brought up in France," Jack

said almost apologetically. "It does make me rather unconventional."

"You didn't attend school in England?"

"Sometimes." Jack loved spinning a convincing tale. "My father was a baronet and I was his third son. I attended a minor public school from the age of fourteen until I was eighteen."

"Like Eton?"

"As I said, not quite that high-flying, but a fee-paying institution nonetheless."

Simon licked his lips. "Is it true, what they say about such schools?"

"Is what true?"

"That the younger boys had to fag for the older ones, and carry out their every wish?"

"It was not unheard of, even at the school I attended."

"Did you, were you—?"

"Did I fag for someone?" Jack smiled. "Indeed I did."

"Were you treated well?"

He leaned his head back against the door frame and stared into Simon's eyes. "Do you mean, was I fucked by him?"

"Yes."

Jack removed the modest jet pin from his serviceable cravat and started to unwind the linen from around his throat. "I was required to serve one of the senior prefects who had a reputation as a ruthless boxer and was a much-admired athlete. I must admit I was rather concerned about his *size*."

"His size."

Simon's gaze was riveted on Jack's hands. "I was neither as tall nor as strong as I am now. I feared he might overpower me and force me."

"And did he?"

"No, he was far more subtle than that." Jack took the nightclothes out of Simon's unresisting hands and let them fall to the floor. "One night, after I'd finished serving dinner to him, he offered me a drink of whisky. I'd never touched the stuff, and I didn't realize quite how powerfully it would affect my senses."

"He took advantage of you when you were *drunk?*"

"Oh no." Jack smiled. "He started talking to me about women. Not *ladies,* you understand, but about the sort of women men of his class and even mine consider fair game. Servants, barmaids, and dairymaids—you know the kind of girl. One who wouldn't be averse to a roll in the hay for a few coins, no questions asked, or give a gentleman any 'trouble'."

Simon's mouth firmed into a straight, forbidding line. "I know the kind of man who thinks like that."

Jack took note of his companion's strong reaction and filed it in his memory for further thought before returning to the far more interesting business of seduction.

"I don't like the aristocracy much myself these days, but you have to remember that I was young then, and eager to impress this sprig of nobility with my worldliness and masculinity. And, in truth, as he talked about having such a woman, fucking such a woman, my cock started to grow." He reached down to cradle the growing bulge in his soft buckskin breeches. "I was drunk enough not to know how to hide it, or how to extricate myself from the situation. I'm sure you know how it is. And, as I could see that his cock was also erect, I assumed I was behaving in an appropriate manner."

He reached out and touched the front of Simon's breeches. "You understand, I think?"

Simon pressed his hand over Jack's and held it firmly against him. "I believe I do."

"The prefect suggested we both stroke ourselves to release, and again, I was too intimidated to argue with him, so I did what he told me." Jack shifted his grip on Simon's cock, rubbing his thumb roughly up and down the length until the other man shuddered. "It's not as though every boy, or man for that matter, hasn't shared such a moment with a friend."

"Indeed." Simon moved closer and cupped Jack's cock and balls, closing his fingers around them with gentle strength. "What man hasn't helped out a friend?"

"Before I knew it, the prefect had his hand on my shaft, and I had my hand on his, and we were shoving our cocks together into the slick wetness of our pre-cum and our thrusting fingers and—" Jack groaned as Simon attacked his breeches and then his own, baring them both and wrapping his large hand around both their throbbing lengths.

"And what?"

Simon was breathing as hard as he was, both their gazes directed downward to the erotic sight of Simon's fingers enclosing both of their lengths. Jack added his own.

"And don't stop."

They worked together in silence, hands locked together in an ancient rhythm, bodies aligned, faces tightening with pleasure as they took each other's full measure and climaxed together in shuddering ecstasy.

Simon's head was on Jack's shoulder as he struggled to breathe. "God . . ."

Jack bit his throat. "I haven't finished telling you the story of my seduction yet."

"There's more?"

He slid his hand down past Simon's balls and stroked the skin of his taint.

"Ah, that's good, I—"

"While I was still recovering, he touched me, here, his finger wet from our joint climax, rubbing and circling until I was groaning and moving against him. I didn't even care when I felt his finger rimming my arsehole, venturing inside. . . ." Jack suited the words to his actions, as Simon's cock started to fill out again. "Do you like that as much as I did?"

"Yes." Simon groaned. "Give me more."

Jack bit his ear. "That's exactly what I said." He wrapped one hand around his own cock, and pushed the tip of his finger further inside Simon. "But unlike my prefect, I don't want to hurt you by doing this dry."

"It's all right. I like it." He groaned and flexed his inner muscles, drawing Jack in deeper.

"I'd much rather strip you naked and fuck you on my bed," Jack murmured.

"Are you sure? Most men like the idea of having another man like this."

"So do I." Jack eased his finger deeper to the knuckle and Simon gasped. Temptation throbbed in Jack's skull, and in his cock to take what was being offered, to mount the other man and have him at his mercy.

"I'd like to fuck you raw, but I'm not going to." He kissed the side of his throat. "Do you have any oil?"

Simon sighed. "Yes. In the drawer beside the bed."

"In your room or this one?"

"Both."

"You often invite potential bedfellows to stay the night, then?"

"If I can." Simon's grin was as disarming as it was unexpected. "As I said, it gets very lonely out here in the wilds of Lincolnshire sometimes. Will you strip for me too?"

Jack pulled his shirt over his head. "Naturally. As I said, I usually sleep naked." He stepped out of his breeches and small-clothes and took off his stockings. "Now you."

Simon followed suit, baring his well-muscled chest and arms to Jack's appreciative gaze. "You are very well made, Mr. Picoult."

"As are you, Mr. Smith."

Jack rubbed his stomach. "Unfortunately, at my age I am going to seed."

"Don't say seed." Simon fell to his knees in front of Jack and kissed his way across from Jack's hipbone to the very tip of his cock. "Don't say it unless I can sample it."

"Be my guest. We have all night. I can wait to have you for a little while longer."

Simon circled his tongue around Jack's wet crown, gently easing down the foreskin to expose the whole of the throbbing, heated head. He licked up the pre-cum, swirling it over his lips as if tasting the finest brandy.

"I've missed this. I never thought I would."

Jack slid his fingers into the other man's thick auburn hair and pressed his cock hard against Simon's lips. "Take me inside. Take my seed, suck me dry."

Simon's groan of compliance vibrated against Jack's shaft, making his hips thrust forward until he filled Simon's mouth and he began sucking. Jack tightened his grip in his hair, shuddering as his companion wrapped his arm around his hip, his hand palming Jack's arse, and pulled him in closer.

To his surprise, his climax was just as quick and explosive as the first one and Simon took every drop, swallowing him down and then licking him clean. It had been a long time for Jack too. He'd forgotten the power of a man's mouth on him, the struggle for dominance and the lack of need for caution with a strong male body that equaled his own.

He reached down, drew Simon to his feet, and led him over to the vast bed.

"Lie down on your back."

"If that is your pleasure, Mr. Smith."

"It is." Simon's cock was still hard and Jack studied it with lascivious intent. "You may call me Jack if you wish."

"Jack and not John?"

"Never John." He blew softly on the other man's crown. "I prefer Jack. Now place your hands behind your head, and don't touch me until I give you leave."

Simon instantly obeyed, his breathing ragged, the taut muscles of his abdomen gleaming with exertion. Jack knelt on the bed and trailed his fingers over his companion's nipples until they tightened. He kissed his way down over the hard chest and concave stomach, pausing to bite and nip at a jutting hipbone and the concave arch of the muscle below. He paused only long enough to check the drawers next to the bed, and found a vial of unscented oil, which he carefully uncorked.

"Spread your legs."

Jack crawled between them and studied the upthrust of Simon's big, thick cock, which was surrounded by dark auburn hair. Droplets of pre-cum slid down his shaft shining in the candlelight.

"Impressive."

"Thank you."

Jack slid a pillow under Simon's buttocks, raising his hips slightly, and moved closer, one finger now coated with clear oil. He stroked his finger from the root of Simon's cock down to his anus, back and forth, back and forth, adding more oil as he went, rimming the puckered hole until Simon was pushing up into the rhythm, offering his arse to Jack in an instinctive way that made Jack's cock come to life again.

"Please," Simon murmured.

"Please, what?" Jack leaned in, delicately licking the collection of pre-cum gathered on Simon's crown into his mouth, and then licking him again just to watch him shiver.

"I want your cock."

"Eventually."

Jack was enjoying himself far too much to want to rush. He'd often got into difficulties with previous missions because he forgot himself in the sheer pleasure of another naked body, the scent, the play of muscle in the candlelight, the *need*. . . .

"My finger, first." He slid one oiled finger inside and eased it slowly deeper. Holding it steady, he looked down into Simon's eyes and planted the tip of his tongue in the slit of his cock.

"Ah, God . . ."

While he flicked his tongue deep, he slid his finger in and out of Simon's arse until he was clenching his internal muscles around Jack's finger and rocking his hips into the motion. Jack added another finger and then another, his gaze alternating between watching the play of his fingers and licking and nibbling at Simon's exposed crown.

"Jack . . ."

"What is it?"

"*Please.* I want your cock in me. I need—"

"Patience, my friend. You'll thank me when you eventually come, I swear it."

Balancing carefully, he continued thrusting his fingers into Simon's arse and tonguing the head of his cock and wrapped his other hand around the base of his partner's shaft, squeezing tight.

"*Jack.*"

He changed position, moving from Simon's side to between his legs, his own cock now slick and hard again. Keeping one hand around Simon's cock he removed his fingers and positioned himself at the other man's entrance.

"You'll take me now, hard and fast if that's how I want it, and you won't come until I tell you to."

Simon groaned as Jack pressed forward the head of his cock, sliding easily into the well-oiled hole. Jack momentarily closed his eyes as his rigid flesh was surrounded by heat and tightness, and God . . . He started to thrust, needing the friction, the slap of skin against skin, the sense that he'd never have enough of this particular man's smell and taste. Pressure gathered in the small of his back and in his balls and he released his hard grip on Simon's stiff length.

"Come with me. Now."

He shoved one last time and closed his eyes as his come jutted out deep in the other man's arse, leaving him spent, and then collapsed over Simon's still-shaking torso. Simon's hand came up to cradle his head, and the warm stickiness of come between them melded their skin together.

Eventually, Jack managed to lever himself up onto his elbows and found his new lover staring quietly up at him.

"Thank you, Mr. Smith. That was . . ." Simon hesitated. "Extraordinary."

"I'll do better when I'm not so tired." Jack rolled off Simon and onto his back. "If the occasion should ever arise, of course."

Simon's chuckle was low and comforting. "I would be honored to share your bed again."

Jack turned his head and smiled at his companion. "Then perhaps I *should* stay here rather than at the inn, as you suggested."

"I'm sure my sister will agree."

"She won't mind?"

"You staying, or this?"

"Either."

"She won't mind. She loves me."

"My sister is the same. She despairs of me ever settling down, though."

"If your inclination is to bed another man rather than marry a woman, it does present some difficulty."

"To be perfectly honest, Simon, I am happy to bed men and women."

"You are?"

He hesitated. "Does that offend you?"

"Not at all." Simon reached out a lazy hand and stroked Jack's hip. "I can perform perfectly well with a woman too."

They smiled at each other in perfect accord and then Jack yawned.

Simon sat up and swung his long legs over the side of the bed. "I should leave you. You must be tired after your journey."

Jack watched with pleasure as Simon strode toward the collection of their hastily abandoned clothes and extracted his garments. He didn't bother to dress and just bundled everything up in his arms.

"Thank you."

Jack nodded. "It was a pleasure."

"One that I would be more than willing to repeat." Simon jerked his head at the tower door. "You know where I am if you need me."

"I do."

Simon retreated after a last smile, leaving Jack staring up at the ceiling, his body pliant and humming with the echoes of pleasure. As sensation retreated, common sense returned and he considered what he now knew. Simon was no stranger to a man's touch and had willingly allowed Jack to take the lead in their encounter. He obviously hadn't attended public school, so where had he picked up the "English habit" as the French called it? It was possible that a female lover had introduced him to it, but he sensed there was something more. That Simon hadn't always offered such services willingly . . . and if that was the case, how did that impact his sister, the supposedly virtuous and aristocratic Dowager Countess of Storr?

Jack washed in the now cold water, pulled back the covers, and got into bed as tiredness overtook him. Tomorrow he would probably discover that the Picoults had no evidence to support their claims to the earldom. What would they do then? Did Simon believe that by bedding Jack he'd created an ally to deceive the new earl?

Jack's sense of well-being dissipated completely.

No one was going to deprive him of his inheritance this time. He'd wandered for too long. Now that his sister had found happiness, the lack of a place to call home had finally become plain to him. If the Picoults thought he could be bought that easily, with *sex,* they were due for a terrible disappointment.

Mary knocked gently on Simon's bedroom door and held her breath until he opened it and beckoned her inside.

"Is Mr. Smith here?" she whispered.

"No, he's asleep in his own bed."

"Then you didn't—?" Simon smiled at her and she blushed. "Of course you did. You're still naked and you smell of sex."

He turned away from her and went to wash, sluicing quantities of cold water and soap down his chest to pool at his feet.

"Damn, that's cold." He took the drying cloth she offered him and rubbed vigorously at his chest and torso.

Mary walked closer and placed her hand on his upper arm. "Well?"

"Well what?"

"Was he grateful for the attention?"

"You mean, was he willing to fuck another man? He was, my love, and very experienced at it too."

"Oh." She pouted.

"Are you jealous that I got to see him naked first, to suck his cock, and have him sucking mine?" He caught her hand and placed it on his already rising shaft. "You are, aren't you?"

She squeezed him hard and his breath hissed out.

"Be careful with that."

"Why? You've done what you needed with it tonight, haven't you?"

He smiled down into her eyes. "That depends."

"You are irrepressible!"

"I know and that's why you like me." He pushed against her

palm, his crown now slick and throbbing against her skin. "Do you want me to tell you about it?"

Before she could protest, he picked her up and deposited her on his lap on the chair by the fire. She tried to pull out of his grasp, but he held her steady, one warm hand cradling her hip, the other blocking her escape on the arm of the chair.

"What's wrong?"

"What if he wakes up and comes looking for you?"

"Then we'd hear him, you could make a run for it, and I— well, I'd be a very well-satisfied man."

"He was really that proficient?"

"Mary, he had all the skills of a professional, and I should know."

"Do you think he has *lied* to us?"

"I'm not sure. His knowledge of the Lennox estate and the fact that he brought a letter of recommendation from Mr. McEwan would suggest that he is what he says he is." He kissed her shoulder, pushing her shawl away to expose her simple nightgown. "He *did* spend much of his life in France, which might explain a lot."

"That's true." Mary shoved ineffectually at his head as he continued to kiss his way down her arm. "Perhaps it would be better to let him stay here while he finishes his various tasks so that we can gather a better sense of him."

"Oh, he is more than willing to stay." He nuzzled her breast. "He wants me."

"So you said." His chuckle was muffled against the swell of her breast. "I am not jealous."

"Methinks you are, but whether of me or him, I'm not sure." His mouth closed over her covered nipple and sucked hard. Even as her body heated she yanked on his hair.

"Ouch!" He looked up, his expression aggrieved. "What?"

"This is hardly the time for *that*."

"Why not?" He slid one hand down the front of her nightgown and cupped her breast, his thumb unerringly finding her nipple.

"He might come in!"

"He's already come, my darling." He kissed her. "In my mouth, in my hand, and in my arse. I reckon we're safe for a while."

"You let him fuck you?"

He shrugged with lazy grace. "It seemed the right thing to do."

Mary pulled back so that she could see his face. "You don't like to be fucked."

He sighed. "I know, and yet somehow, this seemed right. He suggested it and I . . . was more than willing to let him." He briefly closed his eyes. "And it was worth it. He used his mouth and fingers on me until I was begging for his cock."

She brushed a finger over his mouth. "You begged?"

He shifted beneath her, and she was aware of the swell of his shaft pulsing against the thin fabric covering her thigh.

"I told you he was exceptional."

"And now I *am* jealous."

He pinched her chin. "If he does wake up and desire me again, do you want to stay and watch?"

"Why would you think I'd be interested in such a thing?"

"Because I know you. I can smell your arousal already." His hand snaked around her thigh and delved between her legs. "Damnation, you're wet." He stood in one easy motion and brought her over to the bed. "Let me see you."

"Simon—"

"Let me show you what he did to me." He dropped her onto her back and spread her legs wide, wedging his shoulders between them. "He used his tongue on my prick while he rimmed and played with my arse."

He bent over her and his tongue stabbed at her clit, circling and licking it until it was as swollen and stiff as a man's cock. She slid a hand into his hair and tried not to moan too loudly as he continued the sweet torment. His finger slid inside her slick cunt and she took him gladly, accepted more until he was thrusting with all four fingers in and out of her.

"He wouldn't let me come." He raised his head, panting to stare up at her. "It was the most beautiful torment imaginable." He looked down at her sex and licked his lips. "I'll let you come now, though. I want to see you. I almost wish he'd walk through that door and see you too."

That thought was enough to send Mary spiraling into a climax. He kept her coming, using his mouth and fingers to prolong her pleasure and then finally gentled her down. He kissed her thigh and her knee and slowly lowered her nightgown.

"Will you stay?"

"No. It wouldn't be proper."

He wiped his hand over his mouth as if relishing her taste. "*Proper?* After that?"

"Don't be disrespectful."

"Yes, my lady." He bowed elaborately. "I *apologize,* my lady. Let me know when you next require your unworthy serf to use his mouth on you, and I'll be instantly at your service."

"Don't." She struggled to sit up. "I've enough sly comments from the rest of the staff to deal with without you starting."

His smile disappeared. "Mary, I didn't mean anything by it. You know that. I'll always support you." He held out his hand. "Forgive me?"

She went into his arms and he held her tight.

"I'm the one who should be apologizing. I don't know what's wrong with me at the moment."

"Well, you are with child, love."

She scowled up at him. "And you are incorrigible."

He kissed her forehead. "I think you mentioned that already. I know Mr. Smith's descent on us wasn't quite unexpected, but it is still stressful for you."

"Yes." She breathed in the scent of his skin, the smell of herself, and the faint, not entirely unappealing scent of Mr. Smith. "I should be relieved that you have engaged him as an ally."

"I haven't done anything yet."

"You've bedded him."

His smile was full of wickedness. "But I fear that is only half the story, love. I think you'll have to consider bedding Mr. Smith yourself."

5

Jack crunched through a piece of toast and took another from the piled plate in the center of the table. Apart from a footman stationed by the door, he was the only occupant of the dreary breakfast parlor. It was another gloomy day. He was beginning to wonder if the sun ever shone in Lincolnshire or if it sulked permanently behind a veil of clouds. He almost missed France and the warmth of the south.

If he wasn't mistaken, his hostess had visited her brother's bedchamber the previous night, perhaps to get a report of his success or lack of it. He hoped he'd proved satisfactory. He'd enjoyed the encounter with Simon more than he had anticipated and wouldn't object to having him again. It was a shame that it was unlikely. Once the Picoults failed to prove Mary was married to the earl, Jack would either have to leave or reveal his true purpose and kick them out. Neither scenario meant Simon Picoult would feel inclined to share his bed again.

It really was a pity. . . .

"Do you want some more eggs, sir?"

A tall, angular woman stood at the open door, her hands folded at the waist.

"No thank you." Jack smiled. "Are you the innkeeper's cousin, Mrs. Lowden, the housekeeper here?"

"I am, sir."

"Your cousin said you had been with the Storr family for many years."

"Indeed, rose from parlor maid to housekeeper too."

"So you've known the Dowager Countess for a while then."

An expression of wariness crossed the housekeeper's face. "You might say that."

"Did she grow up in this neighborhood, or did the earl meet her elsewhere?"

"He brought her and that brother of hers back from goodness knows where and installed them at the house. She was about fourteen, I think."

"Oh, I didn't realize that the Picoults had lived here for so long. That's quite unusual, isn't it?"

"I suppose it is, sir."

Jack tried again. "I must confess that I'm unsure of how long the late earl's marriage lasted." He smiled deprecatingly. "In fact, I wasn't even aware he'd married so late in life. My employer was expecting to inherit the title."

"So I heard."

Jack waited patiently as a myriad of expressions chased themselves over Mrs. Lowden's face.

" 'Twas a bit of a surprise to us here too."

"Really? Why was that?"

"Well, she's so much younger than him, and why did he bother? It wasn't as if he needed to make it all legal or anything."

"Perhaps he thought of the child," Jack said delicately.

"I suppose that might be part of it. He was a God-fearing man and near meeting his Maker." She stared critically at Jack as if assessing his longevity. "That's enough to make any man consider the wickedness of his ways, isn't it?"

"Indeed." Jack slowly shook his head. "Those are wise words for any Christian to live by, Mrs. Lowden."

"Well, then. I'll leave you to your breakfast."

"Thank you."

So the beautiful Miss Picoult had been the earl's mistress before she had "married" him, had she? Was that why he'd brought her and Simon back to Pinchbeck Hall? It seemed horribly likely, and made the idea of the old earl stooping to marry such a woman even more improbable. He spared a thought for any beautiful woman forced into such a situation and wondered what had happened to Mary and her brother to make them accept the earl's offer. Had bringing her brother been Mary's condition for accepting carte blanche from a man three times her age?

The door opened, and the Dowager Countess herself came through. She wore a black muslin dress and a demure gray fichu that covered her ample bosom and was held together with a jet and silver brooch. Her bright hair was partially covered with a dainty white lace cape, which gave her the appearance of an innocent Quaker miss or, perhaps, a nun.

Appreciating her artistry, Jack stood and hurried to pull out a chair for her. She sank down into the seat in a cloud of soft scent and fluttering thanks.

"Good morning, Mr. Smith. I trust you slept well?"

"Very well, my lady. It must be all this fresh country air."

"I'm delighted to hear it." Her smile held no trace of triumph or smugness. Had Simon told her what they'd done? One had to assume so. "Some of our guests find it altogether too quiet."

Her refined accent was perfect. He could detect no hint of provincialism or carefully hidden working-class roots. But if she really was born a lady, how was it that her brother hadn't been sent away to school? And how had they ended up living at Pinchbeck Hall?

"Is Mr. Picoult not joining us?"

She poured herself some tea and looked over at him. "He's already eaten. He's waiting for us in the earl's study with the necessary papers."

"Then I'd better finish my repast."

She reached over and touched his sleeve. "There's no hurry. I'll be a while myself yet. My appetite is increasing by the day."

"Well, you are eating for two, my lady."

A faint hint of pink caressed her cheeks. "It is a burden I carry most gratefully, sir."

Jack returned his attention to his plate and contemplated his rapidly congealing eggs. If his fate depended on bringing an heir into the world, he would be damned careful about his health as well. He wondered what would happen when Simon couldn't produce the necessary documentation. Would they have had time to forge it, or would they attempt to appeal to his better nature and bribe their way out of the situation with his help?

He was almost looking forward to seeing what the inventive Picoult siblings would come up with. With that thought, he finished his eggs and drank another cup of coffee while the dowager nibbled at a piece of toast. For someone who claimed she had a hearty appetite, she seemed surprisingly off her food. But if she feared being unmasked as a charlatan shortly after her repast, perhaps she had reason to be picky.

He waited patiently until she finished her lackluster meal and dabbed at her lush mouth with her napkin. Even as she started to rise, he was on his feet ready to pull her chair out and offer her his escort.

"Thank you."

She glanced up at him and smiled and he readily smiled back.

"Shall we adjourn to the study?" Jack asked. "I fear to keep your brother waiting for too long. He must have many other duties to attend to around the estate."

"He certainly works hard."

"When did he decide that he wanted to be a land agent?"

"When he realized he wanted to make his own way in the world and not be dependent on the whims and goodwill of others."

There was a hard note in her voice that made Jack pay close attention.

"No man likes to be beholden to another for his coin."

"Or woman. But that is usually our fate, isn't it? We are ordered around by our male relatives as if we are truly chattel."

"You did not wish to wed the earl?"

They'd reached the study door and she paused to look up at him. "I was honored to marry him, Mr. Smith. Whatever anyone else might tell you, that is the truth."

Her gaze was steady and he could sense no hint of deceit in it.

"Then the earl was a very lucky man indeed."

He opened the door and they both walked through. Simon sat at the desk, which was covered in important-looking documents. Sunlight streamed through the window behind him, making red lights dance in his auburn hair.

"Mr. Smith. How pleasant to see you again."

Jack ushered the dowager into a chair and inclined his head to his new lover. "Mr. Picoult, always a pleasure."

He took the chair next to the countess and focused his entire attention on the man behind the desk.

Simon cleared his throat. "I have two items that may be of interest to the Lennox solicitors in London." He picked up one of the pieces of parchment, which was covered in elaborate wax seals and appeared to be several pages in length. "This is the late earl's final will and testament." He selected something else. "And these are his marriage lines to my sister."

Jack stared at the official-looking documents for longer than was polite. "May I inspect them?"

"Of course, Mr. Smith."

He rose to his feet and crossed over to the desk. With his past, if either of the documents were rushed forgeries, he would be able to spot them easily. Having a feckless father had taught him much about the ways of the underworld. Simon handed him the marriage certificate and Jack read it through very carefully, his indignation rising by the second. If it was a forgery it was impossible to tell. It stated very clearly that Mary Elizabeth Picoult (spinster) had married the sixth Earl of Storr six months previously, which meant that any male child she delivered would be considered the earl's legitimate heir. . . .

"Why didn't the earl send this marriage certificate to his solicitor in London?"

"I don't think he was that eager for the news to be spread around."

Jack looked up. "That's hardly like broadcasting it from the town crier, is it? Informing one's solicitor of one's marriages is a legal necessity that would have saved my employer and me much false hope and anxiety."

"I beg your pardon? You doubted the validity of my marriage?"

He turned to Mary Picoult, who wasn't looking quite as amiable anymore. In truth, she looked positively furious.

"I didn't say that, my lady. I just wondered why the old earl chose not to share this happy news."

"Perhaps he knew what your employer's reaction would be!"

While inside he raged at the vagaries of fate, Jack kept his expression as neutral as possible. "We can hardly speculate on my employer's reaction, can we? He is still unaware that his claim has been challenged."

"Something that you can remedy on your return, Mr. Smith," Simon intervened. "I've prepared a copy of the marriage lines for you to take with you, and have a signed statement from the local vicar to confirm my sister was married in a private ceremony to the earl in St. Deny's church."

"I notice that you are one of the witnesses, Mr. Picoult."

"It was my privilege to do so." Simon bowed to his sister. "Do you wish to examine the earl's last will and testament as well?"

"I suppose I should."

Simon vacated his chair and waved Jack into it with a gracious gesture that set his teeth on edge.

"Go ahead. It is rather a lengthy document. Would you prefer it if we left you alone to peruse it?"

"I'd rather you stayed, Mr. Picoult. I might have some further questions." He smiled at Mary, the apparently legitimate Dowager Countess of Storr. "If you don't wish to stay as well, my lady?"

Mary rose. "I trust my brother to represent my interests fairly in this matter, and I must see to my household."

Both men rose as she swept out of the room. Jack resumed reading while Simon sat and stared out of the window, one hand tapping against his thigh. The clock on the mantelpiece ticked merrily in the silence, and the fire crackled, sending out puffs of warmth into the chill. Eventually Jack sat back.

"This will was made the night the earl died."

"Yes."

"And you and Mrs. Lowden witnessed it."

"We did."

Jack stared down at the closely written pages. "I should imagine you were *privileged* to do this for your sister as well. Did you write the whole thing too?"

"What do you mean?" Simon started to rise.

"Well, someone did, and if the earl was dying one might assume that such a task was beyond him and fell to you."

"I wrote down his words, yes, but he read through them before he signed. What exactly are you trying to suggest?"

Jack whipped off his glasses. "Nothing, Mr. Picoult. I'm just trying to understand the sequence of events."

"It's not that difficult, Mr. Smith. After the earl married Mary, he decided to change his will. He sent down to London for the last version, read it through, and told me which parts he wished to alter. When he was taken by a sudden illness, he insisted that we finish the new draft and get it signed and witnessed before he died."

"To ensure that his new, young wife would be sufficiently protected for the rest of her days."

"What else would you expect? He was truly enamored of her."

"So I hear." He glanced down at the text. "I doubt the rest of the Lennox family are going to feel quite so kindly toward her when they find out they are getting nothing."

Simon shrugged. "They hate us anyway. They refused to receive my sister after her marriage and made several very public remarks about her and the earl, which ensured that the local gentry shunned us as well."

"How uncharitable."

"One of them even thought he was in line for the title!"

"Which one?"

"George Mainwaring. He lives at the Grange on the opposite edge of the village. His mother was the previous earl's aunt."

"Which makes him ineligible as long as there are male heirs." Jack paused. "If your sister has a male child, the title will be secure beyond doubt."

"Exactly." Simon shifted restlessly in his seat and avoided Jack's gaze. "It is something of a slender hope to rest one's future on, though, isn't it?"

Jack glanced down at the closely written pages in front of him. "But according to the will, the countess will receive a pension for life even if she delivers a girl. Surely that is enough?"

"It will have to be." Simon stood and paced over to the window, presenting Jack with his broad back. "One has to wonder if that comes to pass, whether the new earl will allow her to stay at Pinchbeck Hall or expect her to move out."

"It *is* customary for a dowager to move into a smaller property on the estate." Jack studied Simon's averted face. "With all due respect, Mr. Picoult, I don't quite understand your concern for your sister's welfare. Whatever happens, she will not be left destitute."

Simon turned, walked back over to Jack, and perched on the edge of the desk.

"You consider me too apprehensive?"

"I must confess that I do."

He sighed. "To be perfectly frank, Mr. Smith, the Lennox family hates my sister and wants her gone. I fear they will do anything to dispute the marriage and the earl's last will, leaving my sister with nothing."

"It is often the case that a new young wife puts a cat among the pigeons as the saying goes, disrupting certainties and changing the dynastic implications of inheritance. But from what I can see, the marriage was legal." Jack hesitated. "Unless there is something more to this?"

"No, the marriage is legal. But as it was carried out in secret, there are those who might choose to contest it out of spite, malice, and greed."

"I see what you mean." Jack contemplated his companion. "Surely it would be in your sister's best interests to get this document safely to the Lennox solicitors so that if such claims do arise, they will be able to refute them for her in their professional capacity?"

"That's exactly what I said to the old earl." Simon grimaced. "But I think he liked the idea of his relatives finding out everything was legal and above-board after he'd died, when there was nothing they could do about it."

"Except take the dowager and the estate to court."

"He didn't think they would do that to the fine name of Lennox."

"Then he obviously doesn't understand the nature of greed."

"I agree."

The two men stared at each other for a long moment. "I can take the will and the original marriage lines back with me to London when I leave here," Jack offered.

"Why not the copies?"

"Because the solicitors will prefer the originals."

"Are you hoping they'll be fakes? What if your employer decides that is the case, takes Mary to court, and we lose everything?"

"My employer would never do that, Mr. Picoult. I swear it. Even if any irregularities were discovered, he would never leave one of his family destitute. Your sister would always be provided for and treated with the utmost respect."

"And what of the child?"

"What of him?"

"If it's a boy, why shouldn't he be entitled to his inheritance? It's not just about dispossessing Mary, is it? What about her son?"

"You sound rather agitated, Mr. Picoult. Has anyone suggested that the child shouldn't inherit even if he is a male?"

"There are always those who gossip, Mr. Smith, and when the gossip comes from the earl's own family, there are many who choose to listen to it, and believe it."

Was there already chatter as to the child's father? Jack eyed Simon speculatively.

"Which is surely another reason to get the Lennox solicitors on your side. With them fully aware of the facts and in possession of the late earl's will, they will stand behind you, *especially* if the countess gives birth to a male heir."

Simon sighed and stretched out his legs. "I suppose you are right, although the thought of relinquishing my hold on all the proof that we have is downright terrifying."

"I can understand that. Perhaps you might consider traveling down with me to London so that you could keep hold of the documents and deliver them to Mr. McEwan yourself?"

"I can't leave Mary in her condition." Simon shook his head. "She needs me."

Jack held Simon's gaze. "As I said, I would be more than willing to take the documents for you."

"I know that."

"But you don't feel that you can trust me yet?"

Simon's smile was wry. "I don't trust anyone."

"Why is that?"

"Because I've been betrayed by those who should've had my best interests at heart before."

"In what way?"

Simon stood up and walked toward the door. "In ways that need not concern you, Mr. Smith. Let's just say that I've learned my lessons well and I won't allow myself to be taken in again." He hesitated, his hand on the latch. "Do you wish to speak to my sister again?"

"Not at this point. But I would appreciate some more time to go through these documents."

"Be my guest." Simon bowed. "I'll return after I've visited the home farm to see how you are getting along."

"Thank you."

Jack waited until he heard Simon's footsteps fade away and then got up and helped himself to a large glass of brandy. *Damnation!* If Mary Lennox did have a son, Jack's title hopes would instantly disappear. Considering how recently he'd found out about his heritage, he was surprised by how much that idea depressed him. He'd never known his father came from aristocratic stock. They'd traveled together through

France, using their wits, his father's luck with cards, and their more secret spying activities to finance their erratic lifestyle. He'd often been in danger, not known where his next meal would be coming from, or had to worry that his father wouldn't return.

It wasn't until after his father's death, when he'd been sent to his French grandmother's house, that he'd even remembered he had a twin sister and a family. Those things had become infinitely precious to him in the last chaotic years of the war. Facing death at the hands of Mr. Brown had concentrated his thoughts wonderfully. He'd never understood his sister's need for security until then and now he craved it.

With a sigh, he turned his attention back to the documents in front of him and painstakingly started to read.

"Well?"

Simon closed the door into the drawing room and leaned against it.

"He's reading through them again."

Mary stood and started pacing the room, her black lace handkerchief twisted in her fingers.

"He's not convinced they are legal, is he?"

"That's not the impression he gave me." Simon took a seat by the fire and stretched out his booted feet to the blaze. "In fact, he seemed most sympathetic to our plight and willing to help in any way he could."

"Any way?" Mary stopped in front of him. "Do you think he'll support us against his own employer? Are you mad? Did one night in his bed curdle your brain?"

"Mary, he is a very thorough and upright man. He might not be corruptible, but having met us, I doubt he'll readily accept any lies the rest of the Lennox clan tell him."

"I'll believe that when I see it."

He reached out and tugged at her skirt. "Would I lie to you about something so important?"

"No." She looked away. "I'm just so worried. Why did the earl have to die so quickly after our marriage?"

"You're forgetting that he only agreed to marry you because he knew he was dying. If he'd remained hale and hearty, we'd both be out on our ears already, George Mainwaring would've seen to that."

She shivered. "I hate that man. He has cold, clammy hands and they inadvertently land on me in the most inappropriate of places."

"That's because he thinks you're a whore."

"I am."

He stared at her. "No more than me, love. We've done what we've had to do to survive. I'm not ashamed of myself, are you?"

"No." She took a deep breath. "What do you think Mr. Smith will do next?"

"I should imagine he'll want to speak to the vicar, and the rest of the Lennox family."

"Should we let him?"

"Why not? It's not as though we can stop him anyway. I've already warned him that our reception in the family has been frosty at best."

"And what do you want me to do?"

"Continue to charm him. It can't hurt."

"While you continue to bed him."

He headed for the door. "You can always join us if you like." He winked at her. "I know you've always liked a three-some."

"But I'm pregnant."

"Which means he won't expect anything from you that you're not willing to give." He blew her a kiss. "Think on it. I've got to go down to the home farm and find out the where-abouts of the Keyes family for our guest."

"Then I'd better go and see how he is."

"That's my girl."

Mary waited until he'd left before leaving the drawing room

and heading down to the study. She'd always hated the earl's study. Being sent to see him always meant she was in trouble or that Simon was. He'd always made her witness her brother's punishments, sometimes made Simon take hers too . . . not that he had minded. Ever since they met, Simon had been willing to do anything for her.

She knocked politely on the door and went in. Mr. Smith was still sitting at the desk, his gaze lowered as he focused a magnifying glass on the text of the will.

"Have you found anything incriminating yet?"

Her words came out more sharply than she had anticipated and his head shot up. He rose hurriedly to his feet and bowed.

"My lady, I didn't hear you come in."

"I did knock."

"I was somewhat engrossed."

"Naturally." She took a seat in front of him and waited until he sank back down into his chair.

He took off his spectacles and stared down at them. "I perceive that I owe you an apology."

"Why ever would you think that?"

His smile was devastating and without his spectacles his eyes gleamed like sapphires.

"Your arctic tone?"

"You will have to forgive me. This whole situation is incredibly difficult for us."

"Your brother said that the rest of the Lennox family don't like you."

"He's correct."

"Why is that?"

"Because in their opinion no aristocrat should stoop to marry a women he has already bought and paid for."

"One might say that every woman is bought and paid for regardless of her social class. We touched on that subject yesterday, did we not?" He replaced his spectacles. "Not that I would blame any woman for attempting to make the best of her opportunities."

"Most men of your class would."

"My class? My dear countess, I work for my living. I'm no idle aristocrat."

"Yet you were born into relative prosperity."

"I was born in France. My parents made a runaway match of it."

"Apparently, my parents forgot to attend to the social niceties like marriage."

"Ah."

"What does that mean?"

He smiled again. "Luckily for my mother, she managed to get her marriage lines drawn up before his family found out. Is that why you consented to marry the old earl? Did you not wish your own child to suffer a similar fate?"

"I didn't say I'd suffered, sir."

He shrugged. "The stigma of being a bastard never quite goes away, does it?"

She stared at him for a long moment as she strove to get her feelings under control. He was far cleverer than she'd anticipated.

"I'm not here to discuss my past, Mr. Smith. I only came to see if there was anything I could assist you with in your further inquiries."

"That's very gracious of you, my lady. Would you happen to know if Mr. George Mainwaring is in residence at this time of the year?"

"I believe he is."

"Then I will send a note requesting an audience with him."

"He'll be delighted to see you."

He sat back in the chair and regarded her. "You don't like him?"

"He makes my skin crawl."

"Then I won't invite him to meet me here, then."

"I wouldn't let him over my threshold, nor would he come." She gathered her skirts in one hand and stood up. "Simon has gone down to the home farm. He will be back for dinner. If you wish to send a note to George, may I suggest you leave it on the small table in the hallway and one of the grooms will take it round for you."

"Thank you, my lady."

She smiled. "You are more than welcome, Mr. Smith." She had reached the door before he spoke again.

"If you were the product of a misalliance, my lady, was Simon one too?"

"I hardly think that is any of your business." She froze with her hand on the latch.

"You are quite correct, my lady. I apologize again."

She said nothing more and escaped through the door to the sanctity of her bedchamber. Perhaps Simon was right and she did need to further embroil Mr. Smith in their toils.

6

Jack finished writing his note to George Mainwaring and after a glance at the clock, decided to take it down to the kitchen himself and renew his acquaintance with the dour Mrs. Lowden. He suspected she had quite a few opinions about the old earl and the Picoults, and since she'd also witnessed the late earl's will, she might be willing to give him her views on that matter too.

Note in hand, he went down the backstairs and by dint of following the smell of roasting beef, found the kitchen. The cook was busy shouting at various members of the staff and stood at the stove with her back turned to the door. Mrs. Lowden sat at the table, counting silverware and writing in what appeared to be the household accounts book.

Jack approached the table and smiled down at the housekeeper.

"My apologies for disturbing your work, but I wanted to have this note delivered and wasn't quite sure whom to entrust it to."

She patted the bench next to her and Jack obediently sat down.

"It's for Mr. George Mainwaring. Do you think one of the grooms could take it over for me?"

She took the letter. "You're not as daft as you look, are you, Mr. Smith? If you'd given this to her ladyship it would've ended up in the fire."

"I gather there is some friction between the two branches of the family."

"Friction? That's a mighty fine word for it. I've never seen such a lot of whining and wailing ninnies as if it was the second coming of the Lord."

"I suppose it is always difficult when a man marries late in life."

"Practically on his deathbed, methinks." She glanced up at Jack. "I've known that girl for years, and I never thought he'd marry her."

"She has lived here that long?"

"Aye, she and Simon came together. The earl came home with them one day and told me to make up rooms for them and to treat them like family." She sniffed. "Two more frightened children I'd never seen, but they soon got over that, forgot where they'd come from, and started treating this place like home."

"And where exactly did they come from?"

He was rewarded by a sharp look.

"What's that got to do with you?"

Jack smiled engagingly. "You're right, I'm being terribly nosy. It's just such an unusual story, isn't it?"

"I suppose so," Mrs. Lowden said. She wrote something in the book and moved on to counting the soup spoons.

"Do you like Mr. Mainwaring?"

"Not that it's my place to say so, sir, but no, I don't. He's much too free with his hands, that one. It upsets my staff."

"I'm sure it would." He paused. "Is that why you signed the earl's will, to keep him out of Pinchbeck Hall and safeguard it for the countess and her brother?"

She stood up. "It's what one might call the lesser of two evils, now, isn't it, Mr. Smith? Now, I'm sure you need to get ready for dinner and I must get on."

"Of course, Mrs. Lowden. Thank you for your help."

Jack bowed and headed out of the crowded, steamy kitchen with much to think about. The housekeeper was as sharp as a pin and thankfully not averse to speaking her mind. Playing the part of a secretary meant he was able to move between the world of the aristocracy and the hoi polloi with much greater ease. He was also accepted more readily by both sides and could play the common man or the bored peer as necessary to gain a confidence.

Of course, Mrs. Lowden had somewhat of a sour disposition and saw fault in everyone. He paused at his bedchamber door. Where *had* the earl found Simon and Mary? If he knew that, he might be able to find out exactly who they were. And he wanted to unravel that mystery. If the Picoults had arrived at Pinchbeck Hall as children, they were unlikely to be common tricksters as he had originally thought. But what were they? Genuine souls in danger of being dispossessed, or persuaders of old men to do stupid things? He still couldn't decide.

With a sigh of frustration he went into his bedchamber to find that his bags had arrived from the inn as promised. Someone had pressed his other coat and hung his shirt and spare cravats in the cavernous walnut clothes press. Even if the water in the jug was cold, it was a relief to be able to change out of his well-worn clothes and have a thorough wash.

As he pinned his new cravat in place, the clock on the mantelpiece chimed the hour and he headed back down for dinner. Would Simon expect his company again, or should he pretend to be tired and retire early? He'd enjoyed the man rather more than he'd anticipated. He went down the stairs and saw one of the footmen opening the door into the dining room, his hands full of covered silver platters. His stomach growled in anticipation. Why shouldn't a man feed all his appetites? Surely even a harried secretary like Mr. Smith deserved to be satisfied every once in a while?

He turned left to the drawing room, where he could already hear voices, and smiled. Tomorrow he'd have to face the vicar and Mr. Mainwaring. If Mr. Picoult desired his company tonight, he certainly wasn't going to say no.

"More brandy, Mr. Smith?"

Jack pretended to yawn and stretched out his legs. "No thank you. I think I'll retire for the night."

"It's all this fresh Lincolnshire air."

"And the exercise." He smiled directly into Simon's eyes. "Not that I didn't enjoy every last delightful moment of it."

His companion licked his lips. "If you should wake during the night and desire some company, I do keep very late hours. You'll probably find me awake and eager to assist you in any endeavor you might have."

"I'll bear it in mind." Jack rose and bowed. "I'll just take my leave of your sister and then I'll head upstairs."

"Good night, Mr. Smith."

"Good night."

Jack made his bow to the countess and then went to his room and slowly undressed, anticipation already streaming through him, evident in the blunt thrust of his cock. He slowly ran a hand up and down his shaft and shuddered as he imagined Simon's mouth and hands on him. Without a stitch of clothing on, he unlocked the door between his and Simon's rooms and went through. There was no one there yet, so he took a moment to examine the somewhat Spartan surroundings. There were no family portraits, or obvious keepsakes, but then he hadn't really expected to find any. He suspected that, like him, Simon was not a man who gave up his secrets easily.

He crossed over to the bed, which was the twin of his, and drew back the covers. Under one of the pillows he discovered a small leather-bound book and settled back against the pillows to examine it. The first page was inscribed.

"To S from J." Jack murmured. "I wonder who J was?"

The book was a series of erotic images from the Orient of men and women in erotic sexual positions of all kinds. Jack smiled and settled in to flick through the pages, one hand wrapped around his cock as he appreciated the finer details of the etchings.

A slight sound made him look up to see Simon at the side of the bed.

"Mr. Picoult. What an interesting book."

Simon's gaze flicked down to Jack's now erect cock. "You seem to be enjoying it, sir."

"Who wouldn't?" He turned the book toward Simon. "Which is your favorite illustration?"

"This one."

Jack studied the picture. "A man on his knees sucking another man's shaft, another behind him fucking his arse, and a woman beneath him taking his cock in her cunt. That's your favorite?"

"If I was the man in the middle."

"Being used in every way a man can?"

Simon's hand trembled on the book. "Yes."

Jack sighed. "I only wish there were three of me. I was rather hoping I'd be the one being fucked tonight, but I'm quite willing to change my mind."

"Why are you in my bed?" Simon asked.

Jack opened his eyes wide. "Didn't I just tell you? Didn't you offer me your companionship earlier, or was I simply mistaken?"

"Oh no, you weren't wrong. I want you." Simon matched his words by bending his head and licking the wet crown of Jack's cock. "I want to suck this and then I want to fuck you."

"Oh good," Jack breathed. "I do so hate it when I'm *de trop*."

Simon's chuckle reverberated around Jack's shaft as he drew it deep into his mouth. With a sigh, Jack slid a hand into Simon's hair and let himself be sucked dry.

A little while later, they'd both shed their clothes and Jack was on his knees, grasping one of the bedposts as Simon moved behind him, his oiled cock pressing and sliding between Jack's buttocks as he nibbled and licked at his throat and ear.

"Fuck me, then."

"As you said, Mr. Smith, patience is a virtue. I need to get more oil." His weight shifted on the mattress behind Jack. "Don't move."

Jack had no intention of going anywhere while the pleasurable sensations of being about to be fucked flooded through him, and he wanted it, now, wanted it hard and deep.

"Come on."

"Oh, don't worry, Mr. Smith. I'll make you come and then I'll lick you clean."

Simon's hand came to rest on Jack's hip and then slid around to grip his shaft. "You're nice and big for me."

"Naturally." His breath hitched as Simon slid one finger deep in his arse. "Ah, that's good. Give me more."

Simon obliged and soon Jack felt the head of his companion's broad cock pressing hard against his arsehole and arched his hips.

"Yes."

"Yes, what, Mr. Smith?"

"If you please."

Simon gave a satisfied grunt as he pushed deeper. "Better?"

"More."

"As you wish." Simon eased back and then shoved his entire length inside in one strong thrust.

"God." Jack breathed hard through his nose as he fought to accommodate so much cock. "You're big."

"Just how you like it, yes?"

"I always enjoy a challenge."

Simon bit his shoulder and then seemed to freeze. The fragrance of lavender teased Jack's nostrils and he opened his eyes to see the Dowager Countess pressed against the door, one hand covering her mouth as she stared at them.

"Mary?" Simon croaked.

The countess slowly lowered her hand. She was dressed in a soft muslin nightgown and wrapped in a shawl that fell almost to the ground.

"The door wasn't locked. I didn't realize you were"—Her throat worked convulsively—*"busy."*

"I forgot to lock it when I came in, Mr. Smith was already in my bed naked."

Her gaze swept over Jack, who was still on his knees, his shaft grasped in Simon's hand and his arse full of Simon's cock, a position that his lover seemed unwilling to relinquish.

"That might make you forget anything."

Jack finally managed to speak. "You have caught me at a disadvantage, my lady."

"Oh, not at all. Simon had already told me about last night." She came closer and his cock twitched within her sibling's hard grasp. "Don't let me stop you."

She sat on a chair at the foot of the bed a mere foot from Jack and looked up expectantly.

"You're not shocked, my lady?"

She shrugged and the shoulder of her gown fell away to reveal the rounded swell of her breast. This close, he could see the dark circle of her tight nipple through the thin muslin.

"Everyone has their needs, Mr. Smith. Unfortunately, since I am now a widow, I have to live vicariously through my brother."

She leaned forward. "I want to see Simon fuck you. I want to see you come."

Inside him Simon's cock seemed to grow even bigger and Jack rocked back into the rigid hardness, tightening his muscles until his partner groaned along with him.

"Then watch, love." Simon started to move, his hips pistoning into Jack's, his hand tight on his cock controlling him as surely as a bridled horse. Jack tried not to close his eyes as he watched the countess, the way her hand crept inside her bodice to fondle her own nipple. He wanted that in his mouth, sucking it hard; he wanted his shaft in her cunt, making her climax along with them.

"Do you want his cock, Mary?" Jack tried to jerk his head back to look at Simon, but the angle was too acute. Simon drew Jack's length away from his belly. "Do you want her to suck you, Jack?"

"God, yes."

"He likes a woman's touch. He'd love your mouth on him."

She angled her head to one side. "Would you enjoy that, Mr. Smith?"

"Only if you wish it, my lady."

She rose and crossed the small space between them, her lips pursed as she studied the thick, pulsing length of his cock. Letting her shawl drop to the ground, she leaned forward and licked very delicately at the pre-cum on his crown and then wiggled her tongue into his slit making him yelp with the pleasure of it.

Simon's hand tightened around the base of his shaft.

"Not yet, Mr. Smith. You bide still until Mary's had her fun with you. She doesn't get the chance to lick a real live cock very often. We can wait."

He watched in helpless fascination as she continued to flick and lick her way over and under his straining cock. She sucked his crown into her mouth and played with it, making him yearn to push his hips back and thrust deep, but Simon wouldn't allow it. Jack was held captive between his strong body and the delicately probing tongue of the countess. Not that he minded; he could take such exquisite torture forever.

She drew back and cupped her breasts, allowing his now dripping shaft to tunnel between them. Every time she pushed him up between her breasts, she licked him and he started to groan and strain against the pleasure, aware of Simon starting to rock into him, of both of them losing their fragile control.

"Please, my lady, take me deep, finish me."

She stopped touching him entirely and he almost groaned at the loss.

With a glance at her brother, she wrapped her hand around Jack's cock just above Simon's. "Come then, both of you."

Simon started to move hard and fast, letting Jack's cock slip more easily through his fingers. The countess sucked the rest of him into her mouth and held tight as the two men climaxed in shuddering waves. As his seed pumped out, she drew back and watched his come flood helplessly over her hand and her brother's.

Without a word, she bent her head and started licking him clean, her rough tongue making him shiver as she traversed his now sensitive cock and balls. Simon eased free and got off the bed to wash, bringing water and soap back to Jack, who was still trapped by the countess's fingers and mouth.

The water felt cold against his heated, pummeled skin as Simon carefully washed him. The countess sat back and watched, her gaze fixed on Simon's hand as he swirled the washcloth over Jack's now flaccid cock.

"That was very nice."

Jack eyed her carefully but she didn't sound like a woman who intended to throw him out on his ear the next morning. She sounded almost pleased with herself. But then why would she not? He was now doubly compromised by the siblings and hopelessly enmeshed in their peculiar relationship and love life. He fought a grin. They probably thought they had him tied to them for life, but they had no idea that scandal was his lifeblood. Sometimes it was good to be wicked.

Mary bent to retrieve her forgotten shawl, allowing Mr. Smith an excellent view of her bosom. Her heart beat strongly against her skin and she was still warm.

"Oh dear," she sighed.

"What is it, my lady?"

She touched her finger between her breasts and then licked it into her mouth. "I'm all sticky too."

Mr. Smith glanced back at Simon, who was smiling appreciatively. "I'd be more than willing to help you with that, my lady, if your brother permits."

Simon waved his hand. "Be my guest?"

Still naked, Mr. Smith climbed off the bed and came toward her. She took a moment to appreciate his lean strength, the firm muscles in his thighs and the already increasing length of his cock.

"Would you care to sit down, my lady?"

She sat and waited to see what he would do next. Simon handed him a fresh bowl of water and a clean drying cloth. Mr. Smith came to kneel at her feet.

"Might I beg a favor of you first?"

She fluttered her eyelashes at him. "What is it?"

"May I use my tongue on you, before I use the cloth?"

Her nipples hardened in anticipation and she sank back into the cushions with a sigh. She undid the drawstring at the neck of her nightgown. "Yes please, Mr. Smith. That would be delightful."

She shivered as he delicately drew the fabric away from her breasts, uncovering them completely. For a moment, he did nothing but stare at them before slowly licking his lips. Her nipples ached for his mouth and she drew a deep, tremulous breath.

With a soft sound, he reached forward and cupped her breast. His tongue flicked out and skimmed over her nipple and then around it, making her shiver. He continued to lick at her, his tongue agile as he worked his way around her flesh, dipping between her breasts spreading his time between the two needy points of her nipples.

"Ah, Mr. Smith, that's—"

He nuzzled her skin, sucking her into his mouth and she dissolved into a puddle of desire. She became aware of Simon kneeling by Mr. Smith's side, his hand inching up her night-dress spreading her knees wide to reveal her needy sex.

"She's wet here, Mr. Smith. Do you want to lick her clean here as well?" Simon asked.

"God, yes," Mr. Smith breathed.

He lowered his head, his wide shoulders pushing her thighs apart. Simon rose to his feet and came to stand behind her, his hands dropping to her shoulders.

"Play with your breasts, Mary. Pinch them hard. Mr. Smith will like it."

She obediently cupped her breasts, her fingers unerringly finding her nipples just as Mr. Smith's warm mouth sucked at her clit. Her hips surged forward into the heaven of his tongue and teeth and she writhed against him.

"Oh God."

As Mr. Smith played and sucked at her lower lips, Simon kissed her mouth, stifling her cries as she neared a climax. So wet now, she could hear herself, but she didn't care.

Without warning, Mr. Smith slid one finger deep inside her and curled it around. With a muffled cry she climaxed, her inner muscles squeezing his finger as he continued to draw spasms of pleasure from her clit.

"That's nice, love," Simon murmured. "God, he looks fine between your legs, making you come, making you scream."

She lay back against the cushions and Mr. Smith raised his head. His mouth was wet with her juices, his eyes a vivid, narrowed blue.

"I fear I made you even wetter, my lady."

She smiled at him. "I appreciate your efforts on my behalf, sir."

He smoothed a hand over his now erect cock. "It was my pleasure."

Simon moved from his station at Mary's head and knelt beside Mr. Smith. "And now you have left us both hard and wanting more."

"There is a solution to that." She sat forward and grasped a cock in each hand. "It's the least I can do."

She started moving her hands, watched the men's expressions focus on her fingers and on each other's cocks.

"Hold them together." Simon murmured. "Use both hands."

They faced each other, their cocks touching, their shoulders inches apart and Mary wrapped both hands around them, working them together, pushing wet, straining flesh against flesh until they both started to come, Simon's head falling to rest on Mr. Smith's shoulder as he shuddered out a last spasm of seed. She wondered what it would feel like to take them both in her mouth, whether it was even possible. . . .

With a sigh, Mr. Smith eased out of their complicated embrace.

"Thank you both for an excellent evening. It was most unexpected, but memorable nonetheless."

"We should be thanking you, Mr. Smith." Simon drew away too. "Let me just put on my robe, and I'll escort Mary back to her room. Was there something in particular you wanted to speak to me about, love?"

Mary made herself respectable again and stood. Her legs still felt a little wobbly. Despite his quiet exterior, Mr. Smith was certainly an inventive and creative lover. "I can't quite remember."

Simon grinned at her as Mr. Smith made his excuses and retreated to his own room. "I'm not surprised. That was rather fun, wasn't it?"

"Fun?" She let him escort her back to the countess's apartments and made him come into her bedroom with her. "It was a dangerous thing to do. You shouldn't have kissed me like that."

His smile was lascivious. "Because he'll think we're too close?"

"There are enough rumors out there already without you adding to them."

He advanced toward her. "You're just angry because you didn't get properly fucked."

"I am not! I'm—"

He caught hold of her hand and yanked her against his chest. "Yes, you are. But don't worry." He lifted her against him and backed her toward the bed. "We can soon take care of that."

7

Jack finished a leisurely breakfast without seeing either his host or his hostess and walked down to the stables to inquire as to whether he needed a horse to get to the Grange. He'd received a prompt, if curt reply to his note from Mr. George Mainwaring and was ordered to present himself at ten in the morning at the Grange. Considering the inevitable inclement weather, the head groom recommended a horse, and Jack set out at a slow pace, which was all the old hack would allow.

He didn't mind dawdling. It gave him time to think over the extraordinary events of the previous day, and especially the night. Mary and Simon Picoult had the most unusual relationship he had ever encountered between two siblings. He was not easily shocked, and knew how it felt to have his relationship with his own sister brought under close scrutiny, but he'd never felt any lust for Violet. He was completely sure that she would have gutted him with his own knife if he'd kissed her the way Simon had kissed Mary last night.

A reluctant smile curved his lips. Maybe they'd thought he wouldn't notice . . . even so, it was an incredible risk to take in front of a stranger. As everything that had happened had been at Simon's instigation, he obviously wasn't as quiet as Jack had suspected. In fact, he might even be as sexually imaginative as Jack. Violet would find that highly amusing. Jack found it remarkably stimulating.

His horse tossed his head as a partridge flew up from the undergrowth and Jack had to grab the reins. He needed to concentrate and forget the Picoults while he considered how to deal with the interview ahead. In his coat pocket, he had two letters he'd written before breakfast and deemed too unsafe to leave at Pinchbeck Hall. One was to Mr. McEwan in London asking some questions about the previous version of the earl's will, and the other to Adam at the Sinners Club asking for help in identifying the Picoults. He'd also added a note about his lack of progress looking for Lord Keyes, but he hoped that would change after he'd spoken to the vicar.

He crossed through the village green, passed the inn and the ancient church, and headed toward an imposing house mounted on a hill overlooking the small village. The gates weren't manned, so he dismounted to open them and remembered to fasten them securely behind him before he proceeded up the main driveway. In his travels, he'd discovered that countrymen of any nationality became very irate if you left the gates open.

He followed the narrow shady driveway up to the house and discovered it was a modern square stucco box in the Palladian style. A path led around the side of the house and he followed it to the stables, which were older and less well maintained than the gleaming façade of the house. He left his horse with a groom and walked back around to knock on the front door.

After what seemed like forever, the door opened and an elderly butler stared at Jack.

"Your business, sir?"

"Good morning, I'm Mr. John Smith. I have an appointment with Mr. George Mainwaring."

"Indeed, sir. The master is expecting you." He stepped back

and allowed Jack over the threshold. "You may await him in his study."

Jack followed the butler down a long hallway lined with remarkably gloomy portraits and dreary landscapes and was left in a book-filled room that smelled of wet dog and pipe smoke. He strolled across to the fireplace to study the family portraits that hung over the mantelpiece, his hands clasped behind his back.

He didn't recognize anyone in the largest of the pictures and assumed they must all be Mainwarings. Even if the painter had been kind, they were hardly an attractive family. A smaller painting caught his eye and he leaned in close to observe the details. As a child, he'd seen a miniature of his paternal grandmother, and reckoned the central figure had to be her. How the picture had ended up in George Mainwaring's house rather than Pinchbeck Hall, he couldn't imagine.

He examined the faces of the four children in the picture, his gaze finally focusing on the angelic toddler with the black curls and bright blue eyes who must have been his father. The other children had the fair hair, round faces, and slightly protruding eyes of their father, his grandfather, who stood glowering down at them at the back of the group. Looking at the picture, it wasn't surprising that his parent had never felt he'd fitted in and had eloped as soon as he was old enough. He wondered whether there were any other portraits of his father at Pinchbeck Hall. He was said to look very like him. Would the Picoults make that connection? They certainly hadn't done so yet. . . .

"Dull and worthy indeed," Jack murmured, remembering his father's summary of his family.

"I beg your pardon?"

He swung around to see the current master of the house frowning back at him. George Mainwaring was short, rotund, and wore the belligerent expression of a pug dog bested in a fight.

"Mr. Mainwaring?" Jack bowed low. "Your obedient servant, Mr. John Smith."

"Aye, I know who you are. Sit down, man."

Jack took the seat in front of the desk and waited for Mr. Mainwaring to do the same.

"I appreciate your willingness to see me at such short notice, sir."

"Well, as to that, I'm pleased that someone in London has finally taken note of what is going on up here."

"My employer, the honorable Mr. John Lennox, asked me to visit Pinchbeck Hall to ascertain what state it was in. Unfortunately neither he, nor the Lennox solicitors were aware that everything had changed and that the last earl had married."

"Married?" Mr. Mainwaring snorted. "I doubt that, young man. Why buy the cow when you've already sampled the milk for free?"

"Be that as it may, sir, I have seen the marriage lines and they appear to be genuine."

"I don't believe that for a second." Mr. Mainwaring pointed a stubby finger at Jack. "And what's more, I'm sure your employer won't thank you for thinking that either."

"Obviously, you are correct. My employer expects to inherit the title. He will not be pleased by this news at all."

"And that's another thing. Who exactly is this 'John Lennox'? I've never heard of him. Maybe he's in league with those bloody Picoults to stop me inheriting what should rightfully be mine."

"With all due respect, Mr. Mainwaring, I cannot see how you could inherit under the present laws of this land. A male heir always takes precedence over the female line. My employer is the eldest son of the fourth son of your maternal grandfather."

"So he says."

"The Lennox solicitors believe his claim is valid."

"So *you* say."

Jack forced down his irritation. "If the current countess is carrying a male heir, all this conjecture will be meaningless anyway. Her son will inherit the title directly from his father, the late earl."

Mr. Mainwaring stood and started pacing, his face lined and glowering. "I'd swear on my mother's grave that marriage isn't valid. Why would he marry the little trollop?"

"I cannot speculate on the matter, sir, not having known the late earl myself."

"There must be a way to pay them off." Mr. Mainwaring swiveled around to stare at Jack. "I'd rather your master got everything than *that woman*. Do you think he'd split the costs with me and take them to court?"

"To dispute the current countess's claims to be married and carrying the earl's heir?"

"That's right. Do you think your master would consider it?"

"I could certainly write and ask him, sir. But how do you intend to proceed? Do you have proof that the marriage isn't real?"

"I know the Picoults are scum and that's enough for me. I'm working on finding out the rest. These things take time, lad, but I'm getting close to the truth." He paused. "It won't take you long to discover that everyone around here thinks those two are far too friendly for siblings." He winked at Jack. "I'm sure we could find someone to swear that the babe she carries isn't the earl's at all, but her brother's."

"You're suggesting they are physically intimate?"

An image seared through Jack's mind of the extremely familiar kiss he'd witnessed just a few hours ago.

"Aye, or we can pray that the child pops out with red hair just like his father's." Mr. Mainwaring's chuckle was distinctly unkind.

"But if the marriage *is* legal, it doesn't matter what gossip says, does it? Any child born within that union is deemed legitimate and is heir to whatever his father's name entitles him."

Mr. Mainwaring sat down again. "Listen, Mr. Smith. You just tell your employer that if he's of a mind to it, I'm willing to work with him to get rid of the Picoults once and for all."

"May I ask why you dislike them so much?"

"From the age of fourteen, that woman has tried to seduce every man she's met with an eye to marriage. It didn't matter how old or how young they were, she'd try and get her claws into them." He mopped his perspiring forehead with a large handkerchief. "It's not surprising, though, is it? You can haul a person out of the gutter, but they'll never have true class, will they?"

"I suppose not. Is that where the late earl found the Picoults?"

"He brought them back from a trip to London like a pair of puppies, and we all know what a den of iniquity that place is."

"Indeed. Surely the earl is to be congratulated for his charitable act rather than condemned?"

"There was nothing charitable about Uncle Jasper. He brought those guttersnipes back with him for a reason. No doubt that girl was putting her lures out even then."

Jack rose before he said something he'd regret. "Thank you for your time. I'll write to my employer, Mr. Mainwaring, and ask for his thoughts on your suggestions."

"You do that, Mr. Smith."

"If you need to speak to me, I'll be staying at Pinchbeck Hall for the next few days while I finish up my business in this area."

"Making sure those Picoults haven't stolen your employer blind." He nodded. "I've been wondering about that myself. She declined my help after the funeral. Said her brother would manage everything. I bet he will too."

"From what I can see, the estate appears to be in excellent

order." And now he was defending the Picoults. That probably wasn't wise.

"More cream to skim off the top when they realize they game is up and they run." He pointed his finger at Jack again. "You watch them carefully, mark my words."

"I will, sir." Jack bowed. "I wish you a good morning."

"And to you, sir."

Before Jack could take his leave, the door to the study opened and a tall woman, accompanied by a younger, paler version of herself, entered the room.

"Ah, my wife, Mrs. Victoria Mainwaring, and my eldest daughter." Mr. Mainwaring nodded at Jack. "This is Mr. John Smith, secretary to a Mr. Jack Lennox who claims to be the next Earl of Storr."

Jack bowed low. "A pleasure, ma'am, Miss Mainwaring."

"Indeed. Would you like some tea, Mr. Smith?"

"That's very kind of you, Mrs. Mainwaring, but—"

Mr. Mainwaring waved a hand at him. "Oh, go on, lad, stay for some tea and entertain my lady for a few minutes."

Jack gracefully acquiesced and was escorted into the drawing room, which had been decorated in chilly tones of blue and silver that made him feel most unwelcome. To his surprise, Mr. Mainwaring hadn't accompanied them. He took a seat on the hard couch and eyed his hostess and her unsmiling daughter. The tea tray was already present, and he accepted a cup of lukewarm tea from Miss Mainwaring and wrapped a hand around it for the warmth.

"You are from London, then, Mr. Smith?"

"Yes, Mrs. Mainwaring, although I—"

"It is an unpleasant city. I try not to go there unless I absolutely have to." She turned her penetrating gaze fully on Jack. "Did my husband make our position about those upstart Picoults clear to you?"

"I believe he did, ma'am."

"They need to be stopped." Her mouth settled into a thin, forbidding line. "As I'm sure my husband mentioned, we would rather your employer inherited than the Picoults."

"They seem to be universally disliked, ma'am."

"By anyone who matters. The common folk love them, but that's because they come from nothing."

"So I understand." Jack sipped his watery tea. "By all accounts, Mr. Simon Picoult seems to have run the estate rather well."

"For his sister's gain."

"I don't think that's quite fair, Mama. Mr. Picoult can hardly be blamed for his sister's choices, can he?" Miss Mainwaring's voice was quiet but firm, and her cheeks were pink.

"Don't be ridiculous, Margaret. Mr. Picoult is in league with his sister. Just because he has a pleasant way with him doesn't mean he isn't a rogue."

Jack fought a grin. "Your mother does have a point, Miss Mainwaring. Remember, a rogue lives off his ability to be charming."

She turned to him. "I didn't mean it like that. He certainly isn't a rake. I meant that he is a good man."

Jack smiled into her eyes. "You are obviously a woman of substance, Miss Mainwaring, and one who follows her Christian duty not to judge her fellow men."

She raised her eyebrows. "I still don't think he is as bad as my parents make him out to be."

Mrs. Mainwaring shook her head. "You are very young, my dear. When you meet a true gentleman, like Mr. Smith's employer, you will realize the error of your ways and understand that Mr. Picoult is socially and morally unacceptable. Is Mr. Lennox married, Mr. Smith?"

"Mama!" Margaret's color grew even higher.

"He is, and the proud father of two sons and a daughter."

"Oh." Mrs. Mainwaring pouted a little. "I suppose his sons are still young, are they?"

"Still in the nursery." Jack put his cup down on the table and rose to his feet while Miss Mainwaring glared at her mother. "Thank you so much for the tea. I have another appointment at the vicarage, and I must be on my way."

"It was a pleasure to meet you, Mr. Smith. If your employer does come into the title, I assume you will be moving into Pinchbeck Hall with him to take care of his affairs?"

"We haven't discussed the matter, ma'am, but I think it likely."

"Are *you* married, Mr. Smith?"

He thought he heard a muffled groan from Miss Mainwaring behind him.

"No, Mrs. Mainwaring, I am not."

Her smile this time was gracious. "Then we must hope that your employer's claim to the title prospers, and look forward to welcoming you to our neighborhood."

"Thank you, ma'am, Miss Mainwaring."

He bowed again, and headed for the door before she could start inquiring as to his family and potential income. As he closed the door, Miss Mainwaring started to berate her mother and he allowed himself to smile. Matchmaking mothers really were the devil.

Jack marched out into the sunlight and let out his breath. What an unpleasant, bitter individual Mr. Mainwaring was, his sour mouth and narrowed eyes mirroring his unpleasant interior. A man who saw no good in anyone but himself. No wonder the Picoults didn't like him. Jack hadn't taken to him either. The only person of worth he'd met was the eldest Miss Mainwaring.

But George Mainwaring was a local landowner, and probably much respected in the area, which gave him considerable power. The Picoults had nobody but each other and a reputation that was becoming worse every time Jack asked after them.

He walked around to get his horse and rode down to the village and into the stable yard at the inn. The taproom was empty, but Jack could hear the landlord shouting something out from the cellar below so he waited patiently. After a minute or so, Will Ferrers appeared, a barrel balanced on his shoulder, which he deposited with a thud on the wood plank floor.

"Mr. Smith, are ye off down to London then, sir?"

"Good morning, Mr. Ferrers." Jack smiled at the landlord. "I'm not leaving yet, but as I'm staying up at Pinchbeck Hall, I did want to pay for my first night's accommodation before I forgot."

"That's good of ye, sir. Would ye care for a pint of ale while you're here?"

"Yes, please. I also have a favor to ask you." He waited while Ferrers poured him some ale. "I have two letters that need to go to London on the next direct mail coach that passes through here. I'll give you enough coin to cover their passage."

"That will be first thing tomorrow morning, then, sir." Ferrers topped up Jack's tankard.

"That's soon enough." Jack put down some coins to cover the ale. "May I also borrow a pen and ink? I have to add something to one of the letters before it goes."

"Be my guest, Mr. Smith. There's pen and paper in the best parlor at the back of the house."

Jack picked up his ale, slid off the stool, and followed Ferrers into the small, dark parlor, where a desk stood in solitary splendor against the wall.

"Thank you."

He waited until his host had departed, and retrieved the two letters he'd already written from his coat pocket. He needed to add a note to the Lennox solicitor to ascertain the exact nature of George Mainwaring's claim on the title and whether it was feasible that he could inherit. Each peerage was different, and subject to various restrictions and allowances, depending on the age of the title and the particular family's ability to keep the title alive despite the distressing ability of male heirs to die without issue.

There was something about George Mainwaring's dislike of the Picoults that was deeply vindictive and personal. If Mary had spurned his advances, would that be enough to damn her in his eyes forever? Jack suspected George had a great ability to bear a grudge. And it wasn't as if Mary were the only person who disliked the man. Mrs. Lowden hadn't had a good word to say about him either.

Still thinking, Jack resealed his letter and took them both back through to the bar, where Ferrers was arranging and polishing the pewter tankards.

"Here are the letters, Mr. Ferrers." Jack put a gold sovereign down on top of them. "And hopefully this will cover my bill and their passage to London."

"That should be fine, sir. How did ye find them up at the hall, then, all well?"

"Indeed. I met your cousin, Mrs. Lowden. She has taken excellent care of the house."

"Sarah? Aye, she loves that place more than she loves her family."

"She has children?"

"No, she's never married, sir. She's a bit too sour and forthright for most men's tastes around here. Although she did take care of the Picoults when they arrived at the park."

"They've lived there awhile I gather."

"About ten years or so, I'd say."

"And one of them married the earl." Jack fixed the landlord with a piercing stare.

Ferrers shrugged his wide shoulders. "Well, I didn't think it was my place to tell ye that, sir. Unlike many in this village, I don't mind the Picoults. They were friends with my children, and I never saw any harm in them. 'Twas a bit of a surprise when the old earl married the girl, mind you. I don't think any of us imagined him doing that."

"Maybe he did it because she was carrying his child?" Jack suggested.

"Aye." Ferrers nodded slowly. "If it kept the title out of Mr. Mainwaring's hands, then he might have gone for it."

"Mr. Mainwaring isn't terribly popular in the village, I gather?"

"He's the local magistrate. The common folk have no cause to love him. He's known as a harsh man."

"I met him this morning, and I'd certainly agree with that. He seems convinced that he should've inherited the title."

"But he didn't know about your employer now, did he?" Ferrers smile was slow in coming, but full of dry satisfaction. "I remember his father as a lad. A right little scamp he was. Always in trouble."

"So my employer has told me." Jack put down his tankard. "Well, I must be going. I have to speak to the vicar as well."

"Ye should find him at home at this time of day, sir."

"Then I'll be off directly. Thank you for all your help, Mr. Ferrers!"

Jack made his escape, and leaving his horse at the inn, crossed the road and went over to the massive church. Its size seemed vastly out of proportion to the population in the village until one remembered the past greatness of the wool towns. In the shadow of the main tower sat a small stone house bearing a sign that read Vicarage of St. Deny's.

He went up the path through a beautifully laid-out garden and knocked on the door. It opened immediately. He was ushered inside by a smiling maid who left him in the front parlor while she went to summon the vicar. The surprisingly sunny nature of the room was in direct contrast to the icy grandeur of the Grange and far more appealing.

The man who appeared at the doorway was in his mid-fifties, and had direct gray eyes and surprisingly white hair.

"You must be the visitor who has set the whole village in a flutter. I'm Colin Tyler, the current vicar. Please do take a seat."

"Mr. Smith, secretary to the Honorable Mr. John Lennox." Jack shook the proffered hand. "I hardly intended to send the village into a twitter. I had no idea when I arrived here that things had changed so significantly at Pinchbeck Hall."

"I believe that came as a surprise to many people."

Jack studied the calm face of the vicar. "I understand that you officiated at the marriage of the late earl and Miss Picoult."

"I assume the countess showed you the copy of the marriage lines?"

Jack nodded. "I also have a signed letter stating that there were no legal impediments you were aware of at the time of the marriage. I'll be taking the information back to the Lennox solicitors in London."

"Naturally. Please, sit." The vicar gestured at a chair and joined Jack by the fire.

"Forgive me for asking you this, sir, but do you have any idea why the marriage was kept secret?"

"I should've thought that was obvious." He sat back in his chair and studied Jack. "Neither the earl nor his bride wanted to incur the wrath of the Mainwaring branch of the family."

"But surely you can see that such secrecy only adds to the oddity of the union, and increases suspicion that something underhanded was going on?"

"Such a scenario would certainly be in your best interest, or should I say in your employer's best interest, wouldn't it?"

"Mr. Tyler, unlike most of the people I've met, you seem like the Picoults. Why is that?"

"Because I'm a man of God?"

"I apologize, that was rather a stupid question, wasn't it?

I'm just struggling to understand why two people can evoke such opposing feelings within the same community."

"Because some of the people in this village have no Christian charity, and no ability to value those who, despite their appalling start in life, have striven to succeed."

"Some might consider their means of striving to be suspect, sir."

"But they don't know the truth."

"And you do?"

Mr. Tyler dropped his gaze to his clasped hands. "I hold many confidences. I'm sure you're not expecting me to divulge the details."

"With all due respect, you are not a Roman Catholic priest."

"I still believe in the sanctity of the confessional, Mr. Smith. I cannot divulge that which has been told to me by someone in the belief that I will not betray their confidence."

Jack sighed. "Sir, I am merely trying to understand what has happened, so that I can present a good account of myself to my employer when I return to London. Surely you can appreciate that?"

"I suppose it depends on whether you consider your employer a good man. I knew Mr. Lennox's father, you see." He smiled. "We went to school together. John was a charming, feckless fellow who hated authority, and escaped his duty to his family as soon as he was able."

"You liked him, despite that?"

"He was impossible not to like. He had that indefinable ability to charm the birds out of the trees. As far as I remember, he'd give you the shirt off his back, and he never willingly hurt anyone."

"His son is very like him."

"Feckless and irresponsible?"

"No. Unlike his father, my employer is ready to settle down and accept his responsibilities to his estates and his title."

"Responsibilities that he now might not have?"

Jack held the vicar's wide gray gaze. "He is scarcely dependent on that income or identity, sir. He is well-occupied both at court and in the governance of this country."

"Then he is certainly not like his father."

There was a tap on the door, and the maidservant came in with a tray of tea and biscuits, and placed it on the table next to the vicar.

"My wife is out visiting the sick, so I'll man the teapot. She will be disappointed to have missed you."

"I'm not leaving the village quite yet. I have some other commissions from my employer to carry out in the surrounding area. In fact, you might be able to help me with one of them."

"I'm all ears, Mr. Smith."

Jack accepted yet another cup of tea. "I'm searching for the family home of a man called Keyes."

"There are many families with that name in this area. Can you be more specific?"

"The family I seek is landed gentry."

"Oh, *that* Lord Keyes, the courtesy title the heir of the Marquis of Alford holds."

"That's the one."

"The family don't use the Keyes estate anymore. I don't believe it's grand enough for the current marquis."

"Is it still habitable?"

"Oh yes, there are several Keyes relatives who inhabit the current house, and stop it from falling down. I don't think the current heir has ever visited it, though."

"My employer's solicitors in London asked me to ascertain if the house was occupied, because they believe there is a small bequest due one of the family. I was hoping to visit the house and see if the beneficiary was still living there. Is it far from here?"

"It's about twenty-five miles away in the village of Lindsey St. Joan. It's the original medieval manor and still the largest estate in the village. You can't miss it."

"Thank you." Jack finished his tea, and the vicar refilled his cup. "If the weather improves, I should be able to visit the house, and be back within a day or so."

"I doubt the weather will improve much, but the roads out toward the coast are better than most, so you should make good time. Ask Simon Picoult to draw you a map. He has a good eye for such things." The vicar handed Jack the plate of shortbread biscuits. "Eat up."

Jack bit into the buttery flaky biscuit and almost sighed with pleasure.

"They are good, aren't they? My cook used to work up at Pinchbeck Hall before she quarreled with Mrs. Lowden. I believe she trained in France."

"Please give her my compliments."

His host put the plate on the table beside Jack. "Help yourself. My wife will never forgive me if I don't ply you with refreshments until you are unable to move an inch."

"You are being remarkably hospitable toward a man you suggested was setting the village in turmoil."

"I believe in giving everyone a fair chance, Mr. Smith." He hesitated. "And somehow, I sense your sympathies are more in line with the Picoults than the Mainwarings."

"My sympathies and my livelihood lie with my employer. I am in an impossible situation."

"Because you like the Picoults."

"I . . . admire anyone who has had to fight for what they want, and to be perfectly frank, I suspect the Picoults are simply doing their best to survive a very difficult situation. Unfortunately, I have to go back to London and face my employer and his solicitors, who will not welcome this news at all. I also have to tell them that Mr. Mainwaring is willing to contribute to a lawsuit against the current Dowager Countess."

"Is he now?" The vicar frowned. "I didn't think he'd take it this far."

"His dislike of Mary Lennox seems deeply rooted."

"That's because despite all his ham-handed efforts, she has never shown the slightest interest in him."

"That's rather an unchristian remark, vicar."

His smile was wry. "I said I aspire to live a good Christian life. I don't always succeed."

Jack ate another biscuit and then reluctantly dusted off the crumbs and rose to his feet.

"You have been very helpful, Mr. Tyler."

"And you have been remarkably honest with me."

Jack grimaced. "As honest as I am capable of being at the moment."

"I'm so glad you said that." The vicar angled his head to study Jack's features. "You look a lot like him, you know."

"I beg your pardon?"

"Your father."

"I—"

"Mr. Smith, I spent several years living cheek by jowl with John Lennox. He wrote to me before he died, and told me that he had married and had a son. Did you think I wouldn't recognize his offspring? Now, perhaps you'd like to sit back down and tell me exactly what is going on."

8

Having tried to explain himself, and extracted a promise from the vicar not to reveal his identity to anyone, unless it was absolutely necessary, Jack made his way back to Pinchbeck Hall. The Picoults were certainly a dividing force in the community, but despite everything, his sympathies definitely lay with them, and it wasn't just because he'd fucked Simon and almost bedded his sister.

But what of his own claim to the title? He'd fallen in love with the house on sight and could see himself settling in the area. But despite everything, he wouldn't conspire with the likes of George Mainwaring to deprive the rightful heir of his title. If the child were a girl, he'd do everything in his power to ensure that Mary Lennox and her brother were comfortably situated for life. If it was a boy . . . well, he still had his pension from the Crown, and he could set up home anywhere the fancy took him.

He left his horse in the capable hands of one of the grooms and walked through the back of the house to the old earl's study. Was there a portrait gallery at Pinchbeck Hall? He didn't want to ask Mary in case she insisted on taking him to see it. If there was a picture of his father as a young man on the wall, she was likely to make a connection that might lead to awkward questions and definitely complicate matters. For a moment, he regretted his impulse not to don a disguise. The vicar hadn't approved of his explanation for his deceit, and he suspected the Picoults would be furious. But it was too late to admit to his trickery now. He'd simply have to carry on.

The door to the study was closed, so he knocked softly on it. When no one answered, he put his head around the door. The room was empty, so he advanced cautiously toward the desk. There was no sign of the earl's will, or the marriage lines either. He surveyed the desk and discovered the drawers were all locked.

"May I help you with something, Mr. Smith?"

He looked up, and smiled at Simon Picoult, who had come quietly into the room.

"Yes, please, I was looking for a fresh piece of paper and some ink. I have a letter to write to the Lennox family solicitors."

Simon produced a key from his pocket and opened the first drawer. "Here you are. Do you need sealing wax as well?"

Jack sat down. "Yes, thank you."

"It's getting rather dark. Let me get you some more light." Simon lit a candle from the embers of the fire and brought it over to Jack. "Did you have an interesting day?"

"I met the Mainwaring family this morning." He looked up at Simon. "They don't like you or your sister very much at all, do they?"

"I told you that." Simon sat on the edge of the desk, a frown on his face. "George has been trying to get into Mary's bed since she arrived here."

"He said she was the one who'd been attempting to get her claws into him."

Simon's expression darkened. "As if she would, after everything she went through—"

Jack waited, but unfortunately his companion decided to keep a tighter grip on his unruly tongue. "You do have a champion in that household, though."

"Really? Somehow I doubt it."

"Miss Margaret was convinced that you are a good man."

Simon's smile was derisive. "She said that about me?"

"Several times, even when her mother and I tried to dissuade her."

"You told her I wasn't a good man?"

"I simply said that her mother was right and that an accomplished rake would be very charming *indeed*."

His companion grinned. "You are a complete hand, you know? Who else did you see?"

"The vicar. He had a far higher opinion of both of you."

"Mr. Tyler is a good man. He tutored me with his own children, and kept me on when none of the public schools would accept me as a pupil."

"Oh, I wondered why you'd suggested you didn't go to school."

"Because everyone thought I was a Lennox by-blow. A rumor spread about by the Mainwarings and the Huddlestons, of course."

"Who are the Huddlestons?"

"The earl's eldest daughter married one of them. Detestable people."

"And you're quite sure you aren't the earl's bastard?"

"I bloody hope not." Simon got off the desk and walked toward the fire and poked it unnecessarily.

Jack returned his attention to his letter and ignored Simon, who was prowling around the desk. It appeared that he wouldn't be getting any easy answers to his questions.

"I found out where the Keyes family home is, so I'm passing the information on to Mr. McEwan."

"Oh, that's encouraging. Where exactly is it?"

"About twenty-five miles from here on the coast at Lindsey St. Joan. Do you know the area?"

"I certainly know the location of the village. We get some of our fresh fish directly from the fleet there."

Jack finished his letter and blotted the ink. "Do you think you could draw me a map of how to get there? I suspect I'll have to visit in person to give the good news. My employer will certainly expect it."

"I could come with you, if you like?"

"I thought you didn't want to leave your sister alone at this time?"

"One night isn't the same as a three- or four-day trip to London."

"When exactly is the baby due?"

Simon shrugged. "I'm not sure. You'll have to ask Mary. I'm not an expert in such matters."

"Few men are. If she is willing to let you accompany me, I'd be glad of your company."

Simon smiled slowly at him. "I must warn you that the only inn on the way there is devilishly small and often overcrowded. We might have to share a bed."

"At least we'll be warm."

"Aye, and close." Simon reached out and cupped Jack's chin. "I'd like that."

Jack turned his head and licked Simon's callused thumb, making him groan. "A tight fit, I reckon, the two of us together, don't you think?"

"Tight and hard and wet—"

Jack bit down on the fleshy part of his lover's finger. "Indeed."

The clock chimed five times and Simon moved away. "Dinner will be ready soon. Do you need to wash off the dirt from the roads?"

Jack glanced ruefully down at his mud-splattered buckskin breeches. "I certainly do."

"I could help you."

"And then we'd both be late for dinner, and your sister would not be pleased with us."

"We could make it up to her later."

"Don't tempt me." Jack deliberately stepped into the other man until their cocks rubbed against each other. "You're hard already."

"As are you."

Jack leaned in even closer and licked a sultry path along Simon's lower lip. "If I let you wash me, I'd still be wet and I'd still be dirty."

"So would I."

"Not if I didn't let you come, if I made you watch and kept you waiting for it and begging for it all through dinner, until I was ready."

Simon's pupils dilated. "And what if I came anyway?"

"Then I'd get you hard again and keep you that way while I punished you for disobeying me." He bit down on Simon's lip until his lover shuddered and his cock jerked against Jack's. "Is that what you want?"

"I—"

Jack stepped away and headed for the door. "I'll see you at dinner then." He smiled as he ran lightly up the stairs, his cock throbbing with anticipation. Would Simon follow him, or would he wait until after dinner as ordered? Each scenario had distinct possibilities, but Jack hoped Simon would be patient. He needed a few minutes to find a good place to hide the key he'd taken from the desk drawer while he'd distracted his lover.

He wouldn't need it for long, just time enough to search the desk drawers for the wills later that night. He'd put the key back in the lock before Simon even remembered it was gone.

Half an hour later, after easing himself with the aid of a wet washcloth and his fist, he arrived back downstairs to find Simon and Mary awaiting him in the drawing room. He bowed to the Dowager Countess, who was looking rather beautiful in soft black silk and chiffon cut low on the bosom. Her golden curls were arranged artfully in a knot on the top of her head and cascaded down to her shoulders. One luscious lock curled over her bosom as if placed there by an artist.

"Mr. Smith, how was your day?"

He came over to kiss her hand. "Rather busy, my lady, but I did make some progress in my inquiries."

"I understand you met Mr. Mainwaring."

"I did." He sat down next to her on the couch. "He seems determined to drag the matter through the courts, although I did advise him that such cases are rarely successful. The English establishment is generally unwilling to tamper with the rights of an established family line without overwhelming evidence of deception or criminal activity."

She placed her hand on his knee. "I'm so glad you told him that. Do you think it did any good?"

"To be honest, I don't. He seems fairly determined to bring you and your brother down at any cost."

The countess's beautiful eyes filled with tears. Jack watched, fascinated, as one single teardrop rolled artistically down her cheek.

"Oh, he is such a *tiresome* man."

The footman announced dinner and Jack offered Mary Lennox his arm and escorted her into the small family dining room. Simon followed, and after the covers were removed, he told the remaining servants they could leave them to serve themselves.

Due to his ravenous appetite, Jack waited until the end of the meal to continue the conversation.

"Mr. Mainwaring is certainly used to getting his own way."

"I know. He's managed to turn the whole neighborhood against us!"

"Not quite everyone, my lady. The vicar spoke very highly of you both."

She sighed and contemplated the food on her plate. "Mr. Tyler is a staunch ally, as is his wife, but everyone else who matters thinks we are interlopers and have taken advantage of an old man."

"Surely you knew that such a marriage was bound to cause confusion and gossip amongst your peers?"

"They've been gossiping about us ever since we arrived. I didn't think my marrying Jasper would cause such an uproar, or I wouldn't have agreed to it."

Jack studied Mary carefully but she appeared to be quite sincere. "The *earl* suggested the marriage to you?"

"Of course he did!"

"Because you were carrying a child?"

"What exactly are you implying, Mr. Smith?"

Jack took a sip of his wine. "To be frank, gossip has it that the child is your brother's, and that the two of you forced the earl to marry you to hide your incestuous relationship."

Mary's mouth formed a perfect O and she glanced imploringly at her brother. "Simon! Tell him it isn't true!"

"I'll swear on the Good Book that child isn't mine."

To Jack's surprise, Simon was chuckling.

"Do you find this amusing, Mr. Picoult? Your reputation is threatened, as is that of your sister, and the potential heir to an earldom. Surely it is no laughing matter?"

From the way Simon jumped and winced, Jack could only surmise Mary had kicked him hard under the table.

"Of course it isn't. I'm just amused at the speed the gossips manufactured such a ridiculous tissue of lies."

"Not so ridiculous if Mr. Mainwaring believes he can prove it."

"He can't." Simon snapped his fingers. "It's impossible."

Jack regarded him evenly. "Servants can be bought, Mr. Picoult, as can false witnesses, you know that. I myself have been witness to behavior between the two of you that would be considered scandalous if not verging on incestuous."

Mary Lennox pushed back her chair and Jack automatically stood too. She came toward him and he braced himself for a blow.

"Did you think our behavior was *scandalous?*"

"He kissed you."

"So? Do you not kiss your sister?"

"Not quite like that."

She licked her lips. "But I like him to kiss me."

His cock hardened in a single aching rush. "I noticed."

"Jasper didn't like to kiss."

Jack's gaze flew past Mary to Simon, who was watching them intently.

He smiled at Jack. "She's right. He didn't. She had to get her kisses from someone, and who better than me?"

Mary had to distract Mr. Smith before he began to ask questions that she and Simon were unwilling, or unable, to answer. She focused her gaze on her prey until he stopped staring at Simon and looked only at her.

"Simon said you wished to play with him again tonight. May I watch?"

"I—"

"He didn't do what you told him to do. I found him playing

with his cock and coming into his hand. Aren't you going to punish him for that?"

He stared at her for a long moment as if deliberating whether he was willing to be distracted. "What do you think would be a suitable punishment for him, my lady?"

Thank the Lord; he was as sexually avaricious as Simon. She bit down on her lip. "I think we should tie him up and make him watch us."

"Do what, my lady?"

"Fuck of course." She opened her eyes wide at him. "Don't you want to?"

"Here, my lady?"

It was remarkably hard to shake his composure. Normally she would consider that a dare, but with matters as they stood, she had no time to enjoy the sexual challenge. "We will retire to Simon's room. He has all the necessary equipment there."

"Equipment for what?"

"You know, rope and gags and other useful items for ensuring a man cannot come unless he's allowed to. That was your plan, wasn't it?"

He bowed. "Then perhaps we should go our separate ways and meet again in a few minutes in Simon's room."

"Agreed."

She made sure he left first, and then turned to Simon, who was regarding her with a somewhat quizzical expression.

She raised her chin. "I had no choice. He was beginning to ask such awkward questions."

"That you decided to sacrifice me to the lions?"

She touched his arm. "You don't mind, do you? If it is still distasteful, I'll think of something else."

"No, I've always liked being tied up, you know that." He kissed her nose. "I suspect I might even enjoy myself. Mr. Smith is very skilled."

"Surprisingly so for a man with such a stuffy exterior."

"Still waters run deep, my dear. Look at the old earl." He patted her cheek. "Also be careful."

"I am being careful. What are you worried about?"

"I still don't think Mr. Smith is being entirely honest with us about his purpose here."

She turned back. "Why?"

"He seems rather too interested in our past. He's been questioning the servants about where we came from, and when we arrived here."

"I wouldn't expect anything less from a man of his intelligence. I don't think he liked George Mainwaring at all, which is good. But he's still in the pay of the potential new earl. He's not going to throw in his lot with us completely, is he?"

"Maybe we should tie him up and attempt to extract *his* secrets."

Mary opened the door. "I suspect he'd enjoy the experience far too much, and not reveal anything at all. He is something of an enigma, isn't he?"

"He certainly is, but heed my words and be *careful*."

She returned to her bedchamber and, with the help of her maid, changed out of her formal dress and into a loose gown with ribbon fastenings and lace. She kept her corset and shift on as well as her stockings and garters. Men seemed to like that, and she wanted to distract Mr. Smith's attention from her belly as much as possible. Covering everything in a thick robe, she stole down the corridor to the bachelors' quarters and let herself in to Simon's bedroom. He'd already stoked up the fire and stood beside it, his gaze fixed on Mr. Smith, who sat in one of the large wingchairs facing him.

"Ah, my lady." Their guest rose to his feet and bowed. "Shall we have him strip for us, first?"

"That would be an excellent place to start." Mary took off her outer robe and glided toward him, aware of his intent gaze dropping to her bosom and the sheen of her skin beneath the thin silk of her frivolous nightgown. "Do you want me to fetch the ropes and the other items?"

"Let's start with the ropes. We can decide what we need once he's suitably restrained."

A tremor ran through Simon's solid frame as Mary found the drawer full of ropes and laid them on the bed.

Mr. Smith patted his knee. "Will you sit with me?"

She obliged, settling herself with deliberate slowness against the hard planes of his stomach and the even stiffer bulge of his cock. He'd taken off his coat, cravat, and waistcoat, and wore just his shirt and breeches.

"Disrobe, Mr. Picoult, and do it slowly."

Simon stared straight ahead and started to take off his clothes, dropping each layer to the floor until he was down to his breeches and shirt.

"I see you're hard again, Mr. Picoult."

"Yes."

"Yes, *sir*."

Mary shivered at the deliciously hard note in Mr. Smith's command. He slid his hand around her waist, drawing her back against him; his thumb nudged the underside of her breast and she wiggled.

He bit her ear. "Wait until we have your brother settled, and then I'll see you are well satisfied too."

"Yes, sir," she breathed, and he kissed her throat.

"Continue, Mr. Picoult. I didn't tell you to stop. Your breeches and then your shirt."

Simon complied, his breath hissing out as he eased the buttons of his placket open against the heavy swell of his trapped shaft.

"He's beautiful, isn't he?" she whispered to Mr. Smith.

"Indeed he is."

For a moment they just stared at the naked man who stood in front of them, his hands fisted at his sides, his cock curving up and inward toward his tightly muscled belly.

"I'm surprised you can fit him all in your mouth, my lady. I found him large for me."

"Practice, Mr. Smith. If you want something badly enough, you'll make room for it."

Under her bottom, his cock kicked up. "I'll hold you to that, my lady."

She smiled. "I hope you do. I've spent several hours recently wondering whether I could manage you both in my mouth."

His lips descended over hers and he kissed her with a savagery that made her instantly wet. When he tore his mouth away from hers, he was breathing hard.

"One thing at a time. Let's deal with Mr. Picoult first."

Despite her concerns of not being able to manage him, she was glad she could affect him so strongly. It made her feel powerful.

"Get up on the bed, Mr. Picoult."

Simon obliged, his muscled limbs gleaming in the candlelight.

"Kneel between the two end posts of the bed, please and stretch out your arms." Mr. Smith looked at Mary. "Which ropes do you think will be best to secure his wrists to the posts?"

She slid off his lap and went over to the pile. "These silk ones." She held up a matching pair. "They are strong but they don't mark the skin."

He glanced at her and nodded, but didn't comment on her choice or her obvious knowledge. She gave him one of the ropes and followed his lead as to how he wanted to tie the knots. Simon waited patiently, his breathing erratic, his cock already wet with pre-cum.

When he was satisfied with the tension in the ropes, Mr. Smith turned his attention to the chest of drawers.

"There are more items here?"

"Yes." She opened one of the drawers at random. "What do you want?"

"A cock ring."

She shut the drawer and opened another. "Metal or leather?"

"You have both?"

"Naturally."

He moved to look over her shoulder, his breath stirring her hair. "Leather can be pulled tighter and causes less damage."

She handed him the leather contraption, and he spent a moment familiarizing himself with the buckles and straps. She liked watching his hands work; they were extraordinarily strong and graceful.

He swung around to Simon, who was watching them avidly, and strolled across to him.

"Have you worn this before?"

"Yes, sir."

"Did you like it?" He wrapped the first circle of leather around the base of Simon's cock and looped the narrower straps around his balls, bringing all the elements together. "I'm going to make it tight and if you complain or start to come, I'm going to go up another notch so you'll beg for release."

He fed the strap through the buckle and started to tighten it. Simon's hands clenched into fists as his captured balls were drawn up against the thick leather band around the base of his cock. His shaft was swollen and thick, wetness streaming from the now uncovered crown of his cock.

Mr. Smith's mouth hovered over the slit for a second before his tongue came out to taste the pre-cum. Mary leaned in as well, breathing in the well-remembered scent of leather and sex.

"What else?" Mr. Smith looked at her. "Something for his arse, perhaps?"

She nodded and led him back to the armoire, opening a drawer that contained a variety of phalluses in various sizes in jade and stone and leather. He selected a thick leather one, and held it out to Mary.

"You have oil, too?"

"Yes." She stroked her finger along the leather. "This is quite big."

"Should it be bigger?"

"No, it's perfect."

Her gaze flew up to discover his blue eyes were narrowed with lust. He looked nothing like the quiet, well-mannered secretary of a potential earl now. Reaching out, she removed his glasses from his nose and tucked them in his pocket, which only added to his allure.

"We wouldn't want these getting in the way, would we?"

He smiled at her and she couldn't look away. "Thank you. Do call me Jack."

"If you will call me Mary."

She was the first to move away and busy herself finding a vial of oil. She placed it in Jack's hand. He climbed onto the bed behind Simon and ran his finger down the bound man's spine and between his buttocks.

Simon's eyes half-closed, and he arched his back.

"Do you want your arse filled with this nice, thick phallus, Mr. Picoult?"

"Yes, please, sir."

Mary held her breath as he poured some oil onto his fingers and they disappeared between the cheeks of Simon's arse.

"Ah, that's good . . ."

"I didn't say you could speak, Mr. Picoult." Jack picked up the leather phallus and coated it with oil. "If you do it again, I'll have to gag you. Don't come."

Mary realized she was still holding her breath as Jack slowly eased the thick leather into Simon. She knew how it would feel, the sense of pressure, the hugeness, the sense of being stuffed full to bursting. She cupped her breast and pinched her nipple hard. Jack glanced at her but didn't comment as he focused on sliding the whole phallus into Simon's arse and securing it with leather straps.

"What do you think, Mary?"

She moved to stand directly beside Jack. "He looks . . . full."

"I believe he is." He held out his hand to her. "Shall we continue?"

She waited until he climbed off the bed and walked around to view Simon from the front, his tightly strapped shaft and balls and outstretched arms. His chest was heaving as if he'd been running.

Jack maneuvered a chair to sit right in front of Simon and then sat in it, taking Mary down on his lap. He spread his knees wide, spreading hers with them, and undid the ribbons that held the front of her gown together with practiced, deft fingers. He drew up her shift to expose her sex. The cold air on her already heated, throbbing flesh made her shiver as he cupped her mound.

"Will you play with your breasts, while I play with you?"

"Yes."

Simon shifted slightly and licked his lips, his gaze drawn to Jack's hand between her legs. She smiled at him and circled her hips, pressing her swollen bud against Jack's hard palm. He murmured his appreciation, his fingers caressing her folds, teasing and tempting her needy flesh until she was wet and open.

"Please," she whispered, her fingers plucking hard at her nipples.

He obliged and slid two fingers deep through her slick heat, his thumb planted on her bud as he worked her. She tilted her hips trying to find her satisfaction, her knees wide, her whole sex exposed to both men. Jack added more fingers and increased the strength of his thrust and withdrawal, until she felt a wave of heat crash into her, making her spasm and tremble into ecstasy.

"That's nice, my lady." He kissed her throat. "Did you like that, Mr. Picoult?"

"God, yes."

"You'll like this even more." He lifted Mary until her feet were planted on either side of his thighs. "Take my cock, now, and do it slowly so our captive can see your cunt swallow every inch."

He held both his cock and her steady as she slowly impaled herself on his impressively long and thick length. She started coming even before he was fully sheathed, but he didn't stop, he just kept pressing onward making her climax last forever. When she was settled over him, one of his hands returned to her clit and the other to her breasts.

"Does she like to be pinched, Mr. Picoult?"

"Yes."

"Hard?"

"*Yes.*"

Mary squirmed as his fingers plucked at her nipple and her bud.

"You'll be sore tomorrow, but I like to think that every time you notice the tenderness you'll remember sitting on my cock like this, feeling the pleasure and pain of it and wanting more."

Another climax crashed over her and she gasped.

"Ride me, then, my lady. Make me come hard."

She didn't need a second invitation. Fixing her gaze on Simon, she started to rock back and forth, lifting herself and falling back down until she was gasping for breath, for it to end, for—*God,* she ground herself down on his willing cock, milking his length as he wrapped an arm around her hips in an iron grip and held her captive while he pumped into her.

* * *

"Thank you."

Jack kissed the side of Mary's throat and drew her gown around her. To his secret amusement, she seemed incapable of movement. Had he satisfied her that well? He certainly hoped so. He carefully lifted her away from him and stood up, placing her back in the chair. He fastened the top button of his breeches over his still throbbing cock and turned to Simon.

"I wish I could lift her up so that you could lick her clean."

Simon shuddered, his gaze fixed on Jack. His tongue moistened his lips, but he didn't say anything. Jack moved closer and brushed his fingers over Simon's mouth until he opened it.

"But you can still taste her. Suck them clean."

While Simon worked, he used his other hand to play with his lover's nipples, pinching them until they were as tight and needy as Mary's. He glanced back at the chair where Mary still sat watching them both.

"We still haven't finished punishing him yet, have we?"

She smiled lazily at him. "You don't think watching us and not coming was enough?"

"Not really. I suspect he enjoyed it." He turned back to Simon. "Didn't you? Shouldn't you be punished for that too?"

Simon met his gaze and then immediately looked down. "Yes, sir."

Jack smiled, walked over to the chest of drawers and began looking through the lowest drawer. He found what he expected and drew two of them out.

"Whip or crop, Mr. Picoult?"

His captive's gaze remained on the floor, but his body quivered with what Jack knew must be anticipation rather than fear. He'd met men like Simon Picoult before, men who craved the pain and pleasure of punishment, who needed such roughness to enjoy it. And Jack prided himself on never having shied away from giving any man or woman what they truly desired.

"Mr. Picoult?"

"Crop," he whispered.

Mary stirred in her chair, her expression strained. She spoke urgently to her brother as if Jack weren't even there. "Simon, are you sure? You don't have to—"

"I want it, Mary. Can't you see that? I *need* it."

She swallowed hard and subsided into the chair. "If you are sure."

His smile was breathtaking. "I am."

Jack discarded the thin whip and advanced on his captive. He hoped Mary would stay to witness his mastery of her brother. It would make things so much easier.

He touched the rounded end of the crop to Simon's sternum and slowly brought it down to his flat stomach. With all his concentration, Jack wove a trail around Simon's hips and down his thighs, just touching him with the leather, soft against hard muscle, supple leather against heated skin.

He drew the crop up the inside of Simon's thighs, making his breath hitch, Jack paused to probe the still erect shaft and Simon groaned. The leather cock ring was darkened now with the pre-cum that streamed out of him. Jack eased the head of the crop down Simon's shaft, between his tightly strapped balls, and rubbed it hard against his taint.

"God." Simon jerked forward, the muscles in his arms straining against his bonds.

"Be quiet, or I'll gag you and leave you like this."

Jack waited, and with a visible effort, Simon slowed his breathing and gathered his control.

"Good." He stroked the crop against Simon's soft skin once more and then stepped away. "How many strokes do you think you deserve?"

"I—don't know, sir. Whatever you decide."

Jack smiled. "A dozen, then? Without you coming, or complaining?"

Simon nodded, his lower lip already held between his teeth. Jack turned to Mary, who was still looking anxious.

"You think that's too many?"

She managed to shrug. "It is your decision."

Despite her airy words, her hands were fisted in her gown and she looked ready to fly to Simon's aid if he so much as whimpered. Jack admired that. He knew Violet would've done the same for him.

The muscled globes of Simon's arse beckoned him, their smoothness interrupted only by the leather bindings and the thick leather phallus stuffed between them. Jack stroked the end of the crop as he considered where to start. Six on each buttock, or should he alternate? He drew back his arm. He'd always liked the element of surprise. . . .

Simon made no sound after the first four blows, and Jack stood back to admire the slight red lines on his skin. Four more and his captive was arching his back and panting, his skin gleaming with sweat as he took each deliberately placed blow. Jack walked around and took Simon's chin in his hand, forcing his gaze up to meet his. It was as he'd suspected; Simon was in another place entirely, his body now compliant to Jack's touch, the pain inextricably linked to the pleasure.

"Four more to go, Mr. Picoult. Where would you like those?"

Simon blinked at him. His lower lip was bitten ragged and Jack couldn't resist kissing him hard. He'd like to see that swollen, bloody mouth around his cock, sucking him dry, would like to see both of the Picoults on their knees taking turns to service him.

"Where, Mr. Picoult? On your cock?"

He sensed Mary stirring behind him; would she come to her brother's defense and offer herself in his place? Jack didn't want to give her the opportunity. He brought the crop up and rubbed it against Simon's mouth until he groaned.

"If you won't tell me, I'll have to do what I want then."

He flicked the crop against his thigh as he considered Simon's quivering, expectant flesh. Seeing all this gloriously exposed male skin made his own cock ache like the devil. He wanted to fuck Simon more than he wanted to complete his plan. Carefully adding two more quick strokes on Simon's buttocks, he waited until his captive went still. With a sigh, Jack undid the single button now holding his breeches up and freed his cock. He was in charge. Simon would let him do anything he wanted.

He climbed up behind the other man and, without offering any explanation, extracted the phallus and drove his own cock home in its place.

"God—" Simon's cry was abruptly cut off as Jack started moving. The oil made his arse surprisingly easy to fill, and he thrust his whole length in and out, slamming into Simon's reddened buttocks with every lunge of his hips until he had to climax. Breathing hard, he slid out and wiped himself on the bed covers. Simon was shaking now, his whole body trembling with suppressed need.

Jack picked up the crop and pushed Simon's knees farther apart, making him arch his back and offer up his arse even more. With great care he smacked the crop once on the now tender skin of his lover's well-ploughed hole and soft taint.

Simon cried out and Jack got off the bed and walked around to face him. His lover's gaze was hazy, his mind somewhere Jack didn't want to contemplate. But he was where Jack needed him, totally under his control.

"Mr. Picoult. One smack of this crop against your cock and you'll be coming whether you want to or not."

Simon didn't answer, or raise his head. Jack grabbed hold of his hair and made him look into his eyes.

"Yes or no?"

"I want—"

Jack smiled. "All you have to do is answer one question, and I'll make this the best sexual experience of your life."

"Simon," Mary whispered.

Jack held Simon's gaze. "I'll give it to you hard, just how you like it, and afterward I'll lick you clean."

Desire flared in Simon's gaze. "What do you want to ask me?"

Jack picked up the crop. Simon's gaze followed it like a lover's. "Mary isn't your sister, is she?" Simon grimaced as Jack gently placed the tip of the crop on the crown of his cock. "You want to come, don't you? You want to please me?"

"God, *please,* I *need* this. Mary, I'm sorry, but—"

Jack's arm shot out as Mary launched herself from the chair and held her back. "Say it."

"No, she's not my sister."

"Damn you!" Mary shouted. Before Jack could stop her, she ran for the door.

Jack drew the crop back and delivered one short tap to Simon's cock. "Thank you."

"Jack—"

He dropped the whip and wrapped Simon in his arms while he kept coming and coming into Jack's hand. He ended up cradling Simon's head on his shoulder as the other man shuddered and shook like a babe. After releasing his bound wrists, he carefully unbuckled the cock rings, and made Simon lie back in bed while he washed him clean both with soap and water and then with his mouth.

"Sore," Simon murmured.

"I'm sure you are. I'd suggest sleeping on your side." Jack drew the covers up over Simon's naked body.

"I can't sleep. I have to find Mary, you don't understand . . ."

"I'll find her and make sure she's safe, I promise you." Jack smoothed Simon's damp auburn hair behind his ear and kissed his forehead. "Now sleep."

Simon was snoring within less than a minute. Jack had seen

such behavior before, at the pleasure house, from those who took their pleasure in the more dangerous forms of sex. It seemed a pit of exhaustion usually followed the height of ecstasy. He could understand it, even if he didn't crave such excesses himself.

He left a candle burning by Simon's bedside, and went back into his room to wash more thoroughly and find his dressing gown. Simon was right about one thing. Mary Lennox was not going to be pleased about what had happened at all.

The tap on the door was not unexpected. The fact that her visitor was Jack Smith was.

"I didn't give you leave to come into my bedchamber. Get out."

Mary turned away from him and continued to brush out her hair. She could see him in the hazy reflection of her mirror and he was advancing rather than retreating. He'd changed into a long dark blue robe, belted at the waist. His feet were bare and his black hair was damp and swept back from his face. Even in the mirror he looked beautiful. How could she and Simon have ever thought him plain?

"I said, get out."

"I'm afraid I can't do that. I promised Simon I would see if you were all right."

"And you can see that I am. Now leave."

He sank down into the chair beside her bed and studied her averted profile.

"Don't you want to know how he is?"

"After you brutally assaulted him?"

His eyebrows rose. "That's patently untrue and you know it. Some men crave being dominated in bed. Simon is obviously one of them."

She slammed her brush down on the surface, making her crystal perfume bottles tremble. "You *used* him."

"Yes."

"You even admit it!"

He shrugged, which widened the *V* of his robe to display more of his chest. "I had to do something, and this seemed to be an opportunity for mutual satisfaction. Simon got what he wanted, and so did I."

"You are callous."

"I'm simply trying to find out the facts, my lady."

"What possible interest do you have in whether Simon and I are related?"

"Don't be naïve. If you lie about such a fundamental thing, why would anyone believe anything else you have to say?"

"That's ridiculous!"

"It's the way of the world. If George Mainwaring has *his* way, you and your brother will be on trial for incest and intent to deceive the Crown to obtain an inheritance with an incestuous bastard."

"He's far too miserly to ever finance such an endeavor."

"He will—if my employer agrees to pay half the costs."

Mary's heart thumped so hard she thought he'd hear it. "And will he?"

"It depends on my report, doesn't it? Which is why I feel I have a right to inquire as to your relationship with Simon Picoult."

"And if I tell you the truth?"

His blue gaze was sharp, but also amused, which irritated her immensely. "I'd really appreciate it. I suspect tying you up wouldn't have the same results as it did with Simon."

She gritted her teeth. "I'd like to tie you up, Mr. Smith, and drop you in the nearest canal."

He stretched out his bare feet and crossed his ankles like a man with all the time in the world. "You are more than welcome to do so, my lady. I've always enjoyed being restrained. But I'd rather not end up dead."

"As if I'd give you a choice."

His sudden smile was as unexpected as it was beautiful. Damn the man for making her want to respond to him, for making her want to trust him. . . .

"You probably don't believe me, my lady, but I admire your courage and your desire to protect your brother immensely. You remind me of my sister, Violet, and there is no higher compliment I can give you than that."

"Did she sleep with you too?"

"We did once share the same bed, but there was a man in the middle of us who demanded all our attention."

"Is there nothing obscene you haven't tried in your spare moments, Mr. Smith?"

He contemplated her for a moment, his brows creased in thought. "I've never copulated with an animal. I've never wanted to."

She had to bite down on her lip to stop herself from either smiling or asking him why.

"Now, tell me how you and Simon came to be brother and sister."

There was a hint of command in his voice that made her bristle.

"If you don't tell me, George Mainwaring will spin his tale to my employer instead. Which truth would you rather he had?"

"All right!" Mary retorted. "I met Simon when I was eleven and he was thirteen. My mother was . . . widowed. We had to leave our house, and find somewhere else to stay."

She'd never forgotten the horror and humiliation of that day. Of the loud angry voices, the threat of violence, her mother weeping and being left sitting in the rain out on the pavement with all their possessions strewn around them. She'd been the one to make her mother move on, to walk away from their old home with as much dignity as they could muster.

"You rented rooms in the same house?"

"Simon's mother owned the house, and she rented the room to us. My mother was very frail and spent most of her time in bed."

"She couldn't work?"

"She—did her best. Simon took me under his wing, and helped me make enough money for us to get by." She raised her gaze to his face. "He also protected me from other men."

"You were eleven."

"I was very pretty and there are men who prefer younger flesh."

"And Simon protected you."

"Yes, until I was old enough to make my own choices and become financially independent." He nodded, but didn't comment, which surprised her, and enabled her to continue with more confidence. "When I was fourteen, I was introduced to the Earl of Storr."

"Ah, did he ask you to come and live with him?"

"He did."

"And you refused to go alone?"

"I insisted that Simon come with me." She forced a smile. "It seemed safer that way. It was the earl who suggested we pretend to be siblings. He thought it would make it easier for us in the village."

"But in fact, it's made things more complicated. Half the village and all of the gentry suspect you of carrying your own brother's child."

"But now you know that isn't true, and can tell your employer so."

"I know that you aren't carrying your *brother's* child, but are you carrying Simon's?"

She raised her chin. "I am not carrying his child. I will swear it on the family Bible if you insist."

His smile was skeptical. "Why should I believe that?"

"Because it is the truth!"

"He does fuck you, though."

"Occasionally."

"As did the earl?"

"He was my husband."

"Eventually. Did he marry you to protect the estate from George Mainwaring?"

"His reasons were his own. I simply did as he asked me."

"Why?"

To her surprise he looked genuinely interested. "Because he gave me and Simon a home."

"Even though that home came with conditions?"

She looked down at her hands. "We were willing to pay the price."

"*You* were willing." His faint smile died. "At fourteen, no one should have to make that choice."

"Are you feeling sorry for me?"

"Who wouldn't?"

She rose and glided over to him, rolling her hips like a wanton. "Have I satisfied your curiosity now, Mr. Smith? Are you going to hurry back to Simon and fuck him again?"

"He needs to sleep. He'll be too sore." He looked up at her, his head resting on the back of the chair. "I'd much rather fuck you."

"Why, when you have found my brother so willing and so complacent?"

"Because I prefer women?"

"One would never guess it." She placed her hands on the wings of his chair, caging him in and giving him the perfect view of her breasts. "Although even as a woman I found the sight of you mastering Simon quite stimulating."

He reached out and cupped her breast. "I like fucking, my lady, in all its glorious, messy, filthy ways. I like making people cry out and scream and come for me. I enjoy it even more when they reciprocate."

"And what about love, Mr. Smith?"

He raised his eyebrows. "What does that have to do with fucking?"

"Doesn't it change how you 'fuck'?"

"I don't know. I've never been in love. It seems a remarkably uncomfortable experience that almost never turns out well." He squeezed her breast. "Do you love Simon, then?"

"If I loved him, would I be here with you now?"

"Possibly. I think you are like me and perfectly capable of splitting off fucking from loving."

"I love him as a brother. I'm not in love with him."

"Ah, that makes perfect sense." He undid the ribbons at the front of her robe. "Why do you still have that damn corset on?"

"Because I am vain enough not to want to be seen in my present condition by the man I am trying to seduce."

She gasped as he pinched her nipples. "I thought I was seducing you?"

She reached for the sash of his robe and undid it, spreading the heavy satin wide to reveal the perfection of his body and the thick shaft of his cock.

He cupped his balls. "Do you want this?"

She walked over to her bed and climbed up on it. "I want you behind me and I don't want you to be gentle."

"Are you sure?"

She settled on her knees and looked back at him over her shoulder. He'd shed his robe and was naked. His thumb glided over the wetness gathering at the crown of his cock.

"Yes."

"With your corset on."

"*Yes.*"

He moved behind her and pulled up her shift, one hand resting on the lacing of her corset. "If you weren't with child, we could play a very interesting game where I keep tightening

your laces while I fuck you until you come close to uncon-
sciousness. I understand it heightens one's climax remarkably."

"Perhaps another time."

She sighed as he pressed the head of his cock against her
folds and slid deep. Bracing herself on one hand, she stroked
her already swollen bud. His arm curved around her hips,
holding her steady for the increasing power of his short thrusts.

"I want your arse, too. May I have it?"

"Simon's was not enough for you?" She managed to gasp
out the words even as her first climax hit.

"I want yours. I'm a greedy man." He bit down on her
shoulder, and she shuddered into another spasm of pleasure.
"I'll take anything I can get." He pressed deep and held himself
there. "I want you both at the same time. I want to see you full
of our cocks."

He chuckled as she shivered and spasmed around his shaft.
"You want that, too, don't you? Think of all the permutations
we could try together."

"Oh *God* . . ."

He pulled out and she cried out at the loss of him but he
took her hand and pressed it against her wide-open entrance.
"Use your fingers while I fuck your arse."

"Oil," she gasped.

"I have it."

She shivered as the cold oil dripped onto her warm skin and
his finger penetrated her arse. "Not that, I want your cock
there, now."

"I'm too big." He bit her ear. "Let me—"

"No, do it, take me, make me feel every inch of you possessing me there."

"Mary . . ."

"Please."

She arched her back and felt the far thicker presence of his oiled cock at her entrance. He probed the tight ring of her arse hole and she gradually gave way, allowing him to press and press again and work his way inside her. He felt huge, like a man's fist.

She groaned as he retreated then pushed in a little more; each inch felt like a mile, each small gain sending her forward onto her embedded fingers. He rocked again, another inch, and then another, widening her beyond her dreams, his cock impaling her again and again, a huge presence that she craved and feared at the same time.

His fingers joined hers in her cunt. She moaned as he stroked his cock through her tightly stretched walls connecting the two spaces, making her come so hard she had to close her eyes. When she opened them again he was fully inside her, a thick, hot presence that made her want to moan out loud.

"That's good," she managed to whisper.

"My cock in your arse? It's damned good, and a tight fit."

She couldn't help but squirm down on him making his breath hitch. "I've always wondered whether a woman could take two men inside her."

"Or three."

"What do you mean?"

"Arse, cunt, and mouth." He bit down on her throat. "I'd love to see you like that."

"Mmm." She touched her clit and shivered. "But what about two men in one space?"

He went very still. "I've seen it done. In truth, I've participated. You'd like that?"

"Was it with a woman or a man?"

"Both."

"Oh." Inside her, his cock jerked and seemed to fill out even more. "I think I'd like to try it at least once."

"Dammit, Mary, I—" He started to come, and she smiled

and gave in to the pleasure herself, glad that for once she'd been the one to push him into climaxing. It was unusual to find herself in the role of supplicant, and yet she'd almost enjoyed it. She'd begun to think of men as interchangeable pawns that she could dominate at will, but Jack wouldn't allow that at all. It was unsettling and arousing at the same time.

When he'd finally finished, he rolled them both over until she was pressed against his chest and he was on his back. His eyes were closed and his breathing started to even out. Mary nudged him.

"You have to go. I can't have the servants finding you here in the morning."

He opened his eyes, the vivid blue startling against the white of her linen. "Give me a moment."

She elbowed him again. "No, because you'll fall asleep. All men are the same." To aid his departure, she moved away from him and found his robe. "Here you are."

He slid off the bed and tied the sash of the robe. "You do realize this falls into the category of just fucking, don't you?"

Her warm glow of satisfaction cooled. "You can hardly imagine I'm falling in love with you?"

"Of course not. I'm more worried that you think you might influence my opinions by pretending to be everything a man could want in his bed."

"*Pretending* to be?"

"There's no need to take offense." He didn't look up as he tied a neat bow. "You are an excellent bed partner, but you know that already."

Mary moved over to him and poked him hard in the chest. "I'm not as devious as you. Sometimes sex is just sex, not a plan to persuade someone else to do their will. Perhaps I should be asking myself why you *allowed* me to make love to you like that?"

"Perhaps you should. Good night, my lady."

She let him leave without answering him. She was too afraid to. At least she hadn't blurted out the whole truth like her stupid brother. Had she made a terrible mistake by admitting him into her bed again, and sharing her desires with him? She had a sense that she had. What a pity she'd only remembered how manipulative he could be when it was too late. . . .

9

Jack packed a small valise with the essentials he would need for an overnight stay and contemplated the journey he was about to make to find Lord Keyes. Sunlight streamed in through his bedroom window and the sky for once was clear. He knew it wouldn't last and was glad he'd brought a heavy cloak to protect himself from the inevitable rain.

It was easier to think about Keyes than the night that had just passed. True, he'd had a series of extraordinary sexual encounters that made his cock stir just thinking about them. To his considerable disquiet, it was becoming harder and harder to simply *enjoy* his ill-thought-out deception and disassociate himself from the Picoults. He not only lusted after them both, but he *liked* them.

He placed a pair of folded cravats in his case. If he'd been in their shoes, and he was very aware that Mary Lennox had left out a lot of the grim details of her early life, he would've done the same thing—*had* done the same thing. Taken every advantage that was offered, and fought to find a place in the world for himself and his sister, real or not.

"Damnation!" Jack muttered as he stuffed a pair of wool stockings into the side pocket of the valise. Violet wouldn't approve of his actions at all. She'd always said his lighthearted attitude to his fellow man would get him into trouble one day. But she hadn't been left with their father, who'd taught Jack that nothing was forever and that there was always a new horizon, a new card trick to learn, a scheme to become rich. . . . It was no wonder he'd learned that life was a game of chance, and he viewed the world with a cynical eye.

By getting away from Pinchbeck Hall, and his fascination with the ever-resourceful Mary, he could at least sort out his thoughts and decide exactly what he wanted to do about the thorny matter of his inheritance. If the expected child was indeed the son of the last earl, then he deserved to accede to the title. Jack stared down at his possessions. How often had his clothes been the only things he'd owned? Just because he yearned for more, it didn't mean that he had to do it at someone else's expense.

He closed the valise and picked it up, relieved to see that unlike his father, he had some morals. On his trip with Simon he could try and find out more details of the Picoults' arrival at Pinchbeck Hall. He smiled. He could also share a bed with a very alluring man.

Simon was waiting for him in the hallway. As he came down the stairs, Jack remembered his first sight of him. Who would've imagined that the grim-faced man who'd practically hauled him into the Dowager Countess's presence would turn out to be such an engaging bed partner? Still waters truly did run deep, especially in Simon Picoult's case. All the same, he wondered what his reception would be after his unconscionable behavior during the previous night.

Simon turned around and Jack went still.

"Good morning, Mr. Picoult."

"Mr. Smith. May I ask for a moment of your time?" A muscle twitched in Simon's jaw, and he jerked his head toward the open door of the steward's room.

"Certainly, Mr. Picoult."

As soon as the door shut behind him, Jack was hauled up against the wall, Simon's hand around his throat.

"You *used* me."

Jack didn't bother to fight back. "I know."

"You took advantage of me when I was too far gone to do anything but agree with you and beg you to continue."

"I *know*." Jack met his lover's furious, wary gaze. "And I deserve to be shot for doing so."

Simon's grip tightened and Jack started to cough.

"What's worse is, I'm sure you planned the whole damned thing."

"I did," he managed to gasp.

With one last contemptuous shove, Simon let go, and Jack collapsed back against the wall. "You aren't even going to try and defend yourself?"

"How can I? I did what I needed to get the information I required. Believe me, it was a last resort. I didn't think I'd get it any other way."

"And the act itself meant nothing to you."

"That's not true. I enjoyed every second." Jack licked his lips. "Are you going to claim you hated it?"

Simon sighed. "I can't."

"And if our positions had been reversed, would you not have tried to do the same thing?"

"Exploit your sexual weaknesses?" Simon looked away from Jack. "I suppose I might do that."

"Then will you forgive me?" Jack came away from the wall. "I promise I will never use you like that again." He sighed. "I mean it, Simon. I'll never even touch you again if that is what you want."

Simon shook his head. "That's the trouble, Jack. I *want* you to touch me, but I don't want my nature used against me. Can you understand that?"

"Yes." Jack held out his hand. "Friends?"

"Hardly that, but I'll forgive you." Simon shook his hand. "Now, are you ready to leave for Lindsey St. Joan?"

With a huge sense of relief, Jack followed Simon toward the back of the house and the stables beyond. "Indeed I am. Have you taken leave of your sister?"

"I have. She said to send you her best wishes for a successful journey."

"Considering the circumstances, that was remarkably kind of her."

Simon's gaze slid sideways to meet Jack's. "She was a little tired this morning and decided to stay in bed."

"I'm not surprised. In her condition she deserves all the rest she can get."

Simon held the door open for Jack to pass through into the kitchen gardens. "I don't think it was the babe that tired her out."

"Well, you did ask me to make sure she was feeling all right."

"And was she?"

"I'm sure she told you exactly how she was feeling when you spoke to her this morning."

They'd reached the stable yard, and Simon called out to one of the grooms to bring the horses round. Once their possessions were strapped onto the saddles and they were safely mounted, Jack led the way out under an archway toward the main driveway to the house. Simon caught up with him and they rode together.

"She was extremely angry with me for revealing the truth."

"What a surprise."

"She was even angrier with you for putting me in that position. Despite what I just told you, I told her I didn't blame you for using me. If I hadn't, she would've been after you with one

of my pistols. And, devil take it, I enjoyed every second of it."
He looked down at the saddle and grimaced. "I'm probably too
sore to be riding today."

"Do you wish to turn back?"

"No, I rather like it." Simon's smile was wry. "I can't help it."

"If you are sure."

"Oh, I'm sure."

Jack clicked at his horse and tightened the reins. "Then let's
increase our pace a little or we will never get there."

A resigned groan was his only answer. He turned to smile at
his companion. "If you keep up, I'll make sure you are well
looked after tonight at the inn. I'm reputed to be very good
with my hands and I have a lot to atone for." He kicked his
horse and was away, leaving Simon trailing in his wake.

Very early the next morning, Jack and Simon stood at the
rusting, locked gates of Alford Park, which was reputed to be
the original home of the Keyes family. From the road there was
no sign of the actual house. The driveway was choked with
weeds, and the trees, which hadn't been trimmed in years, met
in the center, making a dark green, impenetrable tunnel.

"Are you sure someone still lives here?" Simon asked.

"So they said at the inn last night." Jack studied the flint and
stone wall that bordered the estate. "Are you willing to break a
few rules of hospitality?"

"I assume you want me to go over the wall with you?"

"Yes, but if it offends your principles, you can stay here and
keep watch."

Simon was already advancing toward the six-foot-high wall.
"I have no principles."

"Neither do I." Jack joined him in searching for a handhold
in the rough-set stone.

"But you are so respectable."

"Not at all."

"But you depend on your employer for your living."

Cursing his unruly tongue, Jack kept climbing. "I doubt he's going to hear about this, and if he does, he'd probably find the idea of his dull employee behaving so recklessly quite amusing. I believe you have corrupted me, Mr. Picoult."

"I damn well hope so."

They reached the top of the wall at the same moment and gazed down at the long grass on the other side.

"Let's hope the Keyes family doesn't use mantraps. We'll never spot them in this."

"I don't hear any dogs either. Maybe it is our lucky day."

"Or maybe this place really is deserted." Jack jumped and landed safely on his feet. Simon did the same. Apart from the noise from some disturbed birds, nothing stirred to indicate their presence had been detected.

Jack checked the pistol in his pocket was loaded and then started to move forward. "Let's follow the line of the drive, but keep off it."

"Agreed."

Taking the more direct line meant that the shape of the main house came toward them more quickly than he'd expected. It was a low stone building that looked more like a ruined castle than a dwelling. On the edge of the copse of trees, Jack paused to wait for Simon to catch up.

"I think this is the side of the house," he whispered. "Do you see any signs of life?"

Simon slowly inhaled. "I smell wood smoke from the chimneys and fresh manure. How about you?"

"The same, which means we aren't alone. Let's move a little closer."

Keeping to the line of trees and overgrown bushes that skirted what had once been the more formal gardens of the estate, Jack headed toward a single-story building, which had the unmistakable aroma of a stable. The neigh of a horse and the shuffling of feet made him pause.

"At least one horse then. I wonder if it is Keyes's?"

"Which Keyes?"

That was twice in less than a day that he'd forgotten to stay in character as the stolid and dull Mr. Smith.

"Any Keyes. Aren't they supposed to live here?" He edged forward until he could see into the cobbled stable yard. "There's a rather nice hack in there and two or three work horses."

The soft *click* of a pistol being armed was all the notice he got that they were no longer alone.

"Put your hands up."

He and Simon turned slowly around to find a young woman aiming a serviceable pistol at them.

"What are you doing here?"

Jack smiled. "I do beg your pardon, ma'am. The gates were locked, and no one answered my knock at the front door. I was beginning to think the place deserted."

"What do you want?"

The woman didn't lower the pistol an inch. She was dressed in an old-fashioned high-neck gown and her hair was bundled into an untidy coronet on the top of her head. Jack thought her to be about thirty and judging from her suspicious expression, he doubted she would be swayed by even his charms.

"I should introduce myself. I'm Mr. Jack Smith, the personal secretary of the Honorable John Lennox."

"So?"

"My employer's solicitors asked me to pay a call on this estate to ascertain whether a Miss Malinda Keyes still lived here."

"Why do they want to know?"

"I believe there is a matter of a small bequest for the lady from another client's will."

"Do you have any proof of this?"

Jack pretended to look hurt. "My dear lady, of course I do. If you would just let me lower my hands and—"

"You." The woman gesticulated at Simon. "Take out what he needs from his coat pocket."

Jack met Simon's gaze. "The letter is in my right-hand pocket and my card is in my waistcoat pocket. I don't think we need anything else at present." He didn't want Simon retrieving his pistol and making a difficult situation even worse.

Simon did as Jack asked him and, at the woman's command, dropped both the letter and Jack's engraved card at her feet.

"Now you may leave."

"But, ma'am," Jack remonstrated. "I need to see Miss Malinda in order to make sure that the right lady receives the bequest."

"You've seen her."

"You are Miss Malinda Keyes?"

"Leave now, or I'll set the dogs on you." She didn't bother to reply to his question and just motioned at them both with her pistol.

"If that is your wish." Jack bowed and slowly lowered his hands. "A pleasure, Miss Malinda, and our apologies for disturbing you."

Simon started to back away toward the drive and Jack followed. The woman kept the pistol sighted on Jack until they had both disappeared from sight around a bend in the drive.

"Not a very hospitable or grateful family, then, the Keyes?"

"Obviously not." Jack let out his breath and then glanced behind him. "Oh devil take it, she's let out the dogs. We're going to have to make a run for the wall." They barely made it, the large pack of hounds snapping at their heels as they climbed and jumping up in a frenzy of barking and yelping that made it difficult to think let alone speak.

With a groan, Jack jumped off the wall and made for his horse, which, thankfully, was still tied up where he'd left it.

Simon joined him and they turned to retrace their journey back to the inn.

"What will you do now?" Simon asked.

"Stop at the inn long enough to write a letter to Mr. McEwan and relay the events of our attempt to contact the Keyes family, and then go home."

"To London?"

Jack forced a smile. "I meant to your home, obviously. I'll probably wait until I hear back from my employer or from Mr. McEwan before I decide what to do next. That is, if you and your sister will be so kind as to continue to offer me a bed."

"Oh, I'm fairly sure that will suit us both nicely."

Jack glanced up at the leaden skies. "Perhaps we should eat at the inn as well."

"Or stay the night again."

"Don't you want to get back to your sister as quickly as possible?"

"I'm sure she'd rather we took our time and didn't catch a chill. Those clouds do look rather threatening."

"We can make a decision after we've eaten." The roof of the inn came in sight and Jack increased his pace. "Now let's get back. I have a letter to write."

Half an hour later, they were sitting in a cozy private parlor enjoying an excellent repast while he finished regaling Mr. McEwan in his letter with his attempt to meet the Keyes family. Knowing the information would be passed on to Adam at the Sinners Club, Jack went into a lot of detail as to the locale and appearance of the house, and the uncooperative behavior of the woman who'd claimed to be Miss Malinda Keyes. He hoped it would be enough. If Adam wanted him to venture further into the distinctly hostile territory, he'd have to answer the letter and directly tell Jack to do so. Considering what awaited them, he might prefer to send men who knew what they were doing.

"Are you done, then?"

"With the letter, yes. With my dinner, not quite." He signed his letter and blotted the paper before folding it shut and sealing it with candle wax and his signet ring. "I got the impression from Mr. McEwan that Miss Malinda Keyes was an elderly lady."

"Unlike the lady we just met." Simon drank some ale. "Mayhap it is a family name, and has been passed down to a new generation."

"I suppose that's a possibility." Jack wrote the direction on the front and put the letter aside. "The good thing is, it's not our problem. Mr. McEwan will have to work out the wrongs and rights of that one." He wiped his mouth with his napkin. "I'll go and give this letter to the innkeeper to go on the Mail, and inquire if our room is still available."

Simon picked up the letter, read the direction, and tossed it back to Jack. "That's a wonderful idea."

"I thought you'd like it."

Jack found himself whistling as he sought out the landlord. He'd done his best for Adam and the mysterious Earl of Westbrook. He'd found the Keyes house and the fact that the current residents seemed extremely reluctant to admit visitors, which did seem rather suspicious. The rest was out of his hands.

Jack found the innkeeper in the taproom and waited patiently while he poured a few pints for the regulars before handing over the letter and being assured the room was available for one more night. A crack of thunder followed by a flash of lightning made him feel even better about delaying his journey back to Pinchbeck Hall, the house he might never get to call home, but one he would always remember with great fondness.

Rain splattered against the windows as he went back to the parlor to give Simon the good news. It wouldn't be just the house he'd miss either. The Picoults were his sensual and intellectual matches in many ways. It was a pity he'd had to meet them under such false circumstances. If Mary gave birth to a boy, he'd never see them again. If he was honest with himself, it would be too hard to see another achieve what he'd begun to think of as his. If she gave birth to a girl, he doubted she would choose to stay in the area and he'd lose her anyway. A Dowager Countess would hardly want to meet him as the new Earl of Storr. . . .

Damnation.

Jack pushed open the door of the parlor and went in. Simon looked up from his plate.

"What's wrong? Are there no rooms?"

Jack remembered to smile. "Our room is ready whenever we wish to occupy it. After our harrowing day, perhaps we should both take a nap before dinner?"

Simon crossed over to the desk and blew out the candle. "I do believe we should." He tossed something to Jack. "Don't forget your signet ring."

"Thank you, I used it to seal the letter." Jack replaced the ring on his finger and opened the door. "After you, Mr. Picoult."

Hours later, Jack was awakened by the sound of a noisy group of revelers leaving the inn. Their shouting set the dogs to barking and the innkeeper's wife to scolding. It took several minutes for the hubbub to subside.

Simon, who was draped over Jack's chest, stirred and opened one eye. "She's making more noise than the rest of them put together."

"I know. It's no wonder everyone is scared of her."

"Women can be quite formidable, you know."

"I know, your sister, Mary, certainly is."

"Even when I first met her, she was a force to be reckoned with."

"She told me she came to live with you and your mother."

"That's right. Her mother was very frail. After she was evicted from her house, she and Mary ended up with us."

"And you protected her."

"I did my best." Simon sighed. "As I said, she was determined not to be a burden on anyone and, despite her upbringing, resolved to do what she had do to survive."

"Unless a girl goes into service or trade, there's not much for a young woman to do employment-wise, is there?"

"She did the best she could. I made damn sure she was never harmed or used in any way she didn't want."

"While she prostituted herself."

Simon came up on one elbow. "You make that sound like an accusation. What do you think I was doing? Offering her out to my friends and receiving the money?"

"It seems possible."

"Damn you." Simon shoved Jack away from him. "Where do you think I learned these skills, Mr. Smith? From Mary?"

Jack remained still and stared up at Simon's furious expression. "You worked together?"

"Aye. It seemed the safest way."

"You protected each other." Jack reached forward and stroked Simon's rigid shoulder. "That's remarkable."

"Or sordid, depending on your point of view."

"I find nothing disreputable in it. You did the best you could to ensure your survival with the hand life dealt you."

Simon let out his breath. "I don't have to tell you to keep this to yourself, do I? It seems Mary is right, and I am remarkably indiscreet in bed."

Jack pulled Simon back down on top of him. "Don't worry, I'll keep it to myself as long as you continue to be as indiscreet as you like in *my* bed."

Simon kissed him and Jack allowed himself to be persuaded

to forget his concerns for a while in the joy of having his cock and balls well sucked.

It was only later, when he still couldn't get back to sleep, that he allowed his mind to sift through the new information Simon had given him so freely. His lover had confirmed Jack's suspicions as to the nature of the initial liaison between the late earl and Mary Picoult. Had the earl always liked young girls? Jack pushed that unpleasant thought to the back of his mind. If, as he suspected, Mary and her mother had fallen on hard times and ended up in Simon's mother's brothel, it was possible that the house might still be in existence.

It was time to write another letter and ask his new acquaintance, Mr. Christian Delornay, who ran the House of Pleasure, if he knew of anyone called Picoult who owned a brothel in London. The name was unusual enough to be remembered, and also of French origin like the original owner of the pleasure house, Madame Helene. If Christian couldn't help him, he'd wager Helene could.

On that positive note and tired out by the exertions of the day, Jack allowed himself to fall asleep.

10

"You are not welcome here, Mr. Mainwaring."

Mary drew herself up to her full height and glared at the unexpected visitor who had been awaiting her in the drawing room. When she entered, he was busy picking up the ornaments on the mantelpiece as if assessing their value.

"I know that, Mary. I didn't come to see you. I came to see Mr. Smith, the new earl's secretary."

"He's not here at the moment."

"Good Lord, don't tell me he isn't languishing at your feet and that you haven't managed to wind him 'round your little finger, lass?" His gaze dropped to her rounded belly. "Maybe he doesn't find you attractive while you're breeding."

"Mr. Smith is an honorable man. His attentions toward me have been those of a gentleman."

George laughed. "That's because he doesn't know he's dealing with a hussy yet, does he? I did try to warn him that you'd go after anything with a prick."

"I'm the Dowager Countess of Storr, Mr. Mainwaring. That is a fact."

"I'm not so sure about that." He picked up another piece of porcelain and examined it. "You can give Mr. Smith a message from me. Tell him I'm willing to pay my half of the costs to get you and your misbegotten bastard out of this house once and for all."

"I'm not leaving Pinchbeck Hall."

"You might have no choice." George winked at her. "You'll soon be on your knees, begging me to ask you to be my mistress again."

"That will *never* happen! I'd rather rot in the street!"

His face darkened. "Why, you little bitch—"

Behind Mary, the door opened and Mrs. Lowden and one of the footmen came in.

"Do you need any assistance, my lady?" the housekeeper asked.

George's hand dropped to his side. "Oh, don't worry about bringing me refreshments, Mary, love. Just give Mr. Smith my message, won't you?" The figurine fell from his hand and smashed into pieces on the marble fireplace. "Oh dear, it slipped through my fingers."

"It's of no importance," Mary said. "I never liked that piece. I believe it was a gift from your wife."

George turned purple and he took a step back toward Mary. She held her ground, but Mrs. Lowden moved in front of her.

"If you don't want tea, Mr. Mainwaring, James will see you out. Good day to you."

He left accompanied by the footman. Mary sank down into the nearest chair, her knees shaking.

"Thank you, Mrs. Lowden."

"The butler was out, and that great lummox James opened the door and let Mr. Mainwaring in. I'm glad he told me, though. I knew he'd make trouble."

Mary shuddered. "I thought he meant to strike me."

Mrs. Lowden patted her shoulder. "So did I, lass. I might

not agree with what you did, making that old man marry you, but I don't like Mr. George Mainwaring one bit."

"Thank goodness for that. He makes my skin crawl."

"He has a very free hand with my staff, a *very* free hand, if you know what I mean. The maids don't appreciate being fondled, and neither do I."

"He tried to touch you?" Mary raised her head.

"Not recently, lass, but when I was a parlor maid here, he pinched my backside more than once. He stopped doing it when he followed me out into the servants' corridor and I slapped his face."

"I had to do the same thing. But it was only after Simon threatened to castrate him that he finally stopped pawing me." Mary took a deep breath and stood up. "Thank you again, Mrs. Lowden."

"You're welcome, lass. When is Mr. Simon back?"

"Tonight, I hope."

"Well then, my lady, I'll have a word with James and the rest of the newer staff and make sure they know not to let that Mr. George Mainwaring in again." She nodded at the broken piece of porcelain. "I'll send one of the maids to clear that mess up."

"Thank you."

Mary walked over to the mantelpiece and fell to her knees beside the smashed figure of the shepherdess. It was damaged beyond repair. She could remember it sitting on her mother's dressing table. Its pair—a shepherd—had sat right beside it. Her mother had told her they were valuable and had come from France with her grandparents. The shepherd had been sold off to pay her father's debts, but her mother had smuggled the other piece out in her luggage, determined to keep at least one beautiful thing from the hands of the rent collector's thugs.

And now it was broken too. . . .

Unaccustomed tears rose in her throat and she fought them back. With so much at stake, now was not the time to be weak.

She still had to fight for her future, and for the family she had left. But how was she to survive? Ever since John Smith arrived, she'd felt less sure of herself. Vestiges of her gentle mother's teachings returned to haunt her, to accuse her of being a liar and a thief. But how else was she supposed to survive? She wasn't ashamed of a single thing that she had ever done—up until now....

A knock at the door heralded the entrance of one of the maids, who came over to sweep up the debris. Mary rose from her knees and went to sit in her chair. Despite everything, she'd made her choices, and perhaps letting this last reminder of her mother go was the sign she needed to move on and carry out her plan. Whatever happened, she and Simon would never be beholden to anyone for anything again.

The next morning Mary rose after a night of little sleep and found Jack awaiting her in the breakfast parlor. It appeared that he had already eaten and was finishing a cup of coffee. He rose when she came in and walked around the table to pull out her chair.

"Good morning, my lady. We arrived back rather late last night, and decided not to disturb your rest."

"How thoughtful of you." She sat down and poured some tea from the pot the footman placed at her elbow. "Did your trip go well?"

"We found the Keyes dwelling, but the occupants were rather unwilling to talk to us."

"How odd."

He shrugged. "We did our best. It is difficult to have a conversation when you are being held at gunpoint."

She put down the teapot. "They tried to *shoot* you?"

"The lady of the house did, and then she set the dogs on us. Luckily, we escaped without injury."

"So your work here is done."

He regarded her steadily across the table, his blue eyes half-hidden behind his spectacles. "Almost. I would appreciate your hospitality for a day or so more until I hear back from the Lennox solicitors and my employer."

"You are welcome to stay as long as you like."

"That is very kind of you." The butler came in bearing a silver tray. "Ah, here is the post now."

"I believe they are all for you." Mary handed the letters to Jack and he thanked her. The butler and the footman began removing some of the breakfast plates, leaving them alone.

"May I make use of the study to attend to my correspondence?"

"Of course you may."

He stood and bowed. "Simon was here earlier, and is already out visiting the home farm. He sent his love if I should see you." He paused. "I heard from Mrs. Lowden that George Mainwaring had been bothering you."

"He came by with a message for you." She met his gaze. "He wanted you to tell your employer that he was willing to pay half the costs to institute a lawsuit against me."

"He mentioned that when I visited him." Jack frowned. "I wonder why he felt it necessary to come here and tell you."

"He was bursting with the desire to tell me something. He probably wanted to frighten me, and make me suspicious of your motives."

"And has he done that?"

"Frightened me?" She made a dismissive gesture. "Of course not."

"And what of your suspicions of me?"

She opened her eyes wide. "Just because we've shared a bed doesn't mean we trust each other, does it?"

For a second something that looked like regret or guilt flickered in his blue eyes. "No, of course it doesn't."

"My opinion of you hasn't changed, Mr. Smith."

He bowed. "I understand that, my lady, even as I regret it."

"Why the regret?"

"Because it would've been far easier if you'd been what I initially thought you were—a fraud and a charlatan."

She swallowed hard. "But to many people, I am those things, sir."

"No, you are a woman who has done what she can to safeguard her future. My own mother would've done no less."

She covered her face. "For God's sake, don't compare me to your mother. I don't deserve—"

He moved swiftly across to her and kissed her gently on the forehead. "Whatever happens, my lady, I swear I will never leave you to the mercy of George Mainwaring. If your child proves to be a girl, I will make certain my employer provides for you in a manner fitting your current station in life."

"Brave words from a man who relies on his salary to survive."

His smile was crooked. "I know you don't trust me in all things, but trust me in this."

She could only nod, and be thankful when he moved away and left the room. The desire to throw herself on his mercy and tell him everything had almost overwhelmed her. The thought of what such a confession would mean almost stopped her heart. Did she want him to recoil from her in disgust? And it wasn't just her story to tell. There were others involved. She had no choice but to shoulder her burden, and hope for some way out of her increasingly complicated dilemma.

Jack cursed slowly and silently as he made his way to the earl's study. How could he comfort Mary Lennox when he was masquerading as his own secretary? He wanted to tell her the truth, but for the first time in his life was too afraid to do so. She'd hate him and for some reason he didn't want that. Other than Madame Helene Delornay-Ross, she was the most remarkably resilient woman he'd ever met. Her desire to protect those she loved reminded him of his sister, Violet, who had even offered herself as bait for a killer from love of him. Mary had been forced to sell her body simply to survive, and having finally managed to marry respectably, was now being threatened by a bully.

And by him.

That fact couldn't be ignored. If he hadn't turned up, would George Mainwaring ever have found the balls to start a lawsuit? He doubted it. Jack crossed to the desk, sat down, and put his head in his hands. So much for his lark, so much for amusing himself by rushing into Lincolnshire and finding his ancestral home. He was an idiot who was too old to meddle in other people's lives, especially those of people he'd come to like and admire. . . .

Did he want to end up like his father, alone and unloved? A man who preferred the lure of deception to reality and the love of family? Because his father, John, might have insisted he lived his life fecklessly because he was spying for his country, but he'd never done much of that. Jack had been the information-gatherer from an early age, the one to put his drunken father to bed, to make his excuses to the bill collectors, to *charm* his way out of situations that made his skin crawl to even think about them again.

He groaned. And what was he doing now? Trying to charm his way out of this mess he'd single-handedly and unthinkingly created. Maybe he was more like his father than he'd ever realized. . . .

He raised his head and stared at the portrait of the last earl that hung on the wall opposite the desk. No, he wouldn't be that person. He'd be honorable and uphold Mary Lennox's claim to the title regardless of what she thought of him later. For once in his life, he'd give up what he wanted for someone who deserved it more. He took a deep, steadying breath and faced his correspondence.

All three letters were ostensibly from the Lennox solicitors. He opened one at random, and discovered a rather agitated letter from Mr. McEwan asking a thousand questions about the legality of the marriage of the late earl and the current countess's pregnancy.

Jack had already stolen down one night, taken the original documents from the hiding place where Simon had concealed them, and left the copies offered to him in their place. He'd also replaced the key in the top drawer and, having heard no more about it, assumed nothing had been missed. In order for the Lennox solicitors to protect Mary, they would need to see the originals of the marriage lines and the deceased earl's will.

The second letter was concealed behind a solicitor's bill, and although unsigned, obviously came from Adam Fisher, who had excellent methods of communication with the far-flung county of Lincoln. These methods were described in detail in the letter to Jack for further use, and involved a new stable boy at the inn who would be more than willing to send anything Jack needed to Adam within as few hours as possible.

He contemplated sending the will and the other documents ahead of him, but was reluctant to entrust them to strangers. The last letter was another one from Adam, but styled as if it came from Jack. It was quite strange to read orders from himself. In the letter, his "employer" expressed surprise and dismay at the discovery of the Picoults at Pinchbeck Hall and asked Jack to return as soon as possible to give him a full report on the matter.

Jack hid a smile at his apparently peremptory manner. That was one of the reasons why he'd never employed a secretary. He found it extremely difficult to give other people orders. He'd never taken them well himself either. Again, beneath the first sheet was a second that promised Jack that Adam would look in to the matter of Mary and Simon Picoult as a matter of urgency.

He extracted the sheets that needed to be burned, and left the other correspondence on the desk. It wasn't worth hiding. If Simon or Mary wished to see what he was up to, they'd find nothing incriminating at all and might perhaps feel more secure.

Should he leave right away? Jack crouched down and fed the sheets of paper to the fire. He'd have to go soon, but only after he'd received a reply from Adam about Simon's mother and her house of ill repute. Devil take it, he didn't *want* to go. He liked Pinchbeck Hall. It felt like home. He'd even begun to remember his father telling him about it when he was small, before the man had become a drunkard, and an inconvenience to the British government more likely to betray them than to aid them.

Jack had almost got himself killed trying to make his family name respectable again. Playing the fool had become the easier thing to do, to make them think he didn't care, that he was as useless as his father. But that hadn't worked either. When his sister was in danger, Jack had discovered his backbone and found himself willing to kill without mercy. He'd also taken a long hard look at himself and decided it was time to settle down. His interactions with the Picoults had certainly made him wish he'd changed his ways far sooner.

Poking the fire, he made certain the incriminating letters from Adam had turned to ash and returned to the desk. He'd write to Mr. McEwan and await the last two replies, then leave Pinchbeck Hall to face the consequences of his stupidity.

Mary cornered Simon as he ascended the stairs and insisted on accompanying him to his room.

"What's wrong, love?" The sideways glance he gave her was a mixture of irritation and amusement.

"George Mainwaring came here."

"What?" He stopped walking and swung around, a scowl on his face. "What the devil did he want?"

"To tell me that because I refused to become his mistress, he was going to take me to court and dispute both my marriage and any child of mine's claim to the title."

"Damn him. What does he expect to gain? With Jack's employer being the next male heir to the title, he won't inherit it anyway."

"I think he'd just rather anyone but me had a claim to it." Mary shivered. "He frightens me, Simon."

He wrapped an arm around her. "I'll never let him hurt you, you know that."

"Jack said the same thing, although heaven knows how he thinks he'll manage that from London." She tried to smile. "I believe even if I have a girl, he intends to petition his employer on my behalf for a decent allowance for us both."

"That's good of him. Why are you so downhearted?"

"Because I hate all the lying."

Simon leaned against the door and studied her. "To Jack or to society?"

Mary chose not to answer him and instead closed his curtains and checked the fire.

"You like Jack, don't you?" Simon asked.

"He is not what I expected at all."

"He certainly isn't." Simon chuckled. "His sexual appetite is as voracious as yours."

"And yours."

"Not really. I'm only just rediscovering that bedding someone can be fun—that *fucking* can be fun."

"Then perhaps we both have a lot to thank Jack for." She smoothed his bedcover and walked back over to the door.

"So you do like him."

"Despite myself." She smiled. "I still don't think he is being entirely honest with us, but I sense that he is trying to do his best. He received some correspondence today from the Lennox solicitors. I wonder how they reacted to the news of Jasper's marriage?"

"I suspect they weren't pleased." Simon moved aside and opened the door for her. "Do you want me to try and read the letters?"

"If you can. I'd rather be prepared for the worst."

"I'm sure Jack won't mind."

"You're going to ask him?"

"Why not? The worst he can say is no, and if he has something to hide we can go back to distrusting him again, can't we?"

"And pack our bags."

"You don't think it will come to that, do you?" Simon frowned. "Despite everything, this place has come to mean a great deal to me. I thought you said you'd never leave."

"But I didn't know about Jack's employer then, did I? I thought everything was going to fall into George Mainwaring's hands." She sighed. "Sometimes I wish I'd just left things alone."

He kissed her nose. "I won't say I told you so, but I believe I might have mentioned it a few times."

"I did it for both of us, you know that. If you no longer support me I'll—"

He put a finger to her lips. "You know I'd walk through hell for you. I love you and whatever you choose to do I will support you."

She nodded and he stepped away. "I wonder if Jack will be leaving tomorrow?"

"I suppose it depends on the news he received in his correspondence. We can ask him about it at dinner."

"*You* can ask him, love. I'm going out."

"You don't mean to leave me alone with him, do you?"

"Why not?"

"Because . . ." She stared helplessly at her brother. "Oh, I'm sure I'll be fine. I have no idea what I'm worrying about."

"Neither do I. Jack may be more astute than we give him credit for, but I'd still wager on you."

"Thank you." She gave him her most dazzling smile. "Now I really must go and change."

11

Mary stole into the study and looked around. There was no sign of Jack. She assumed he'd gone upstairs to change for dinner. She crossed over to the desk and saw his correspondence laid out on the blotter. After another quick glance at the door, she read quickly through each piece of correspondence. One was a bill from the Lennox solicitors, which she immediately put aside. The longest letter came from Mr. McEwan, who was obviously concerned about what had been happening at Pinchbeck Hall without his knowledge. His list of questions was even more extensive than Jack's had been when he'd arrived.

She put the letter back in the exact same spot she'd found it. Was Jack right? Should she put her faith in the solicitors and hope that they'd uphold her marriage and the future of the earldom? But whose side were they on? If the honorable John Lennox, Jack's employer, was paying them, wouldn't they be biased toward him?

The final letter gave her a sense of Jack's employer and seemed far more levelheaded than the solicitors, although rather peremptory in tone. Hadn't Jack mentioned that his master was also employed by the government in political matters? Perhaps the title of Earl of Storr wasn't one he cared about too greatly. If she remembered the family history correctly, the earls' fourth son had run away from home, married unwisely, and never been spoken of again. . . .

"Good evening, my lady."

Mary steeled herself not to jump at Jack's sudden appearance. "I assume you didn't mind if I read your letters. You *did* leave them open on the desk."

He bowed. "I left them there deliberately. I hoped they might set your mind at rest. As you can see, neither my employer nor the Lennox solicitors are condemning you out of hand. In fact, they might both be willing to support you."

"Is that because Jasper's younger brother was not universally liked?"

"I understand that John Lennox, the elder, was something of a black sheep. Even my employer admits that." He took the seat in front of the desk and sat at his ease in his dark coat and well-fitted trousers.

"It's a shame no one thought to disinherit him."

"And let George Mainwaring advance his claim to the title?"

Mary shuddered. "I hadn't thought of that. I've never met a man who was so obsessed with his family tree. He hates the fact that Jasper married me and 'diluted the bloodline.' "

"Some might say the old earl added new life to the family. Too much inbreeding results in a lack of brains and a higher possibility of congenital deformities. Look at the Hapsburgs, look at George Mainwaring himself."

Mary couldn't help but smile as she rose to her feet. "It must be time for us to dine. Simon sends his regrets."

Jack placed her hand on his sleeve and headed for the door. "Where is he off to this evening?"

"To a meeting of the local farmers." She grimaced. "He *says* it is fascinating to hear about herds of cattle, milk yield, and how many bushels of barley one can grow on an acre, but I can't quite imagine it myself."

Jack chuckled. "Your brother is obviously a countryman at heart."

"He does seem to have taken to it rather well, considering—"

Jack ignored her hesitation. "Considering he was born in London."

"Did he tell you that?" She sat down at the table and spread her napkin on her lap. As it was such an informal supper, all the dishes were laid out on the table for them to help themselves, leaving them free of the staff.

"Not exactly."

She frowned at him. "Did you beat it out of him?"

"No, I promised never to do that to him again. I just made a reasonable guess based on what he told me about his upbringing."

Mary put down her soup spoon. "What exactly did he tell you?"

"There's no need to worry. I don't intend to share the details with anyone."

"What details?"

"That you grew up together in a brothel."

Silence threatened, and then she laughed as if she didn't have a care in the world. "I must remind my dear brother not to be so indiscreet in bed."

"As I said, I don't believe this information is relevant to your claims on the earldom."

"Some would think it very relevant—your employer, for example." She forced herself to meet his gaze, hating the sympathy in it. "Who would want the mother of an earl to be revealed as a whore?"

"That is something I wanted to ask you about. Is it possible that George Mainwaring knows?"

"About where Simon and I came from? I don't think so. The only person in Jasper's confidence was the vicar, and that was only near the end when he was afraid of dying without confessing his sins."

"I doubt the vicar is the sort of man to share such sacred confessions with his congregation, or with George Mainwaring." He frowned. "Then what does George think he knows that might sway the court in his favor?"

"I have no idea, but he is very knowledgeable about the family tree. Perhaps he discovered some earlier aberration that means his branch should really have inherited the lot."

"That wouldn't surprise me in the least. The thing is, the authorities are very reluctant to mess with ancient history. Once a precedent for a title is set, it is extremely hard to take it away from someone."

"Which George must know?"

"One would think so. If he simply got rid of you, then he'd still have to deal with John Lennox. Do you think he's the murdering kind?"

"I think he'd consider it."

"Indeed." Jack's faint smile disappeared to reveal the acute intelligence in his eyes and the hardness of his jawline. "Perhaps you should take more care of your personal safety."

"Simon will guard me."

"But he isn't always here."

"Then I'll be careful."

"Can you warn the staff?"

Mary rose to her feet and took to pacing the carpet. "Really, Mr. Smith, I don't think the situation is so dire that I need to involve the entire household."

"You were the one who said George was dangerous." He met her gaze without flinching. "I happen to agree with you."

She widened her eyes at him. "Perhaps you should stay and take care of me, Mr. Smith."

To her disappointment he didn't take the opportunity to respond to her flattery. "I almost wish I could. Unfortunately I'll have to go back to London quite soon. My employer is anxious to speak to me."

"I noticed that in his letter. Is he always so abrupt?"

"He's a busy man, my lady."

"Perhaps you need a different job."

His smile was wry. "I couldn't agree with you more. I wish I'd never taken this ridiculous assignment on."

"Because you thought you were dealing with a pair of tricksters and ended up rather liking us?"

He took her hand and kissed it. "Exactly."

"We didn't mean to put you in a difficult position."

"Oh, don't worry, I did that all by myself. When is the baby due?"

She blinked at the abrupt change of subject. "I'm not quite sure."

"You must have some idea. The previous earl died several months ago."

She placed a hand on her rounded stomach. "It should be fairly soon. Mrs. Lowden reckons in the next four to six weeks."

"I would appreciate it if you or Simon could inform the Lennox solicitors as to the sex of the child when it is born."

"Naturally." She contemplated his rather stern profile. "Do you not intend to return for the birth to verify that I'm telling the truth?"

"I doubt that will be necessary, my lady." He took a deep breath. "In truth, I suspect that whatever the outcome of that happy event, we will not meet again."

"Oh."

She was aware of an unexpected sense of disappointment. Shouldn't she be pleased that a man as clever as Mr. Smith wouldn't be near her when the child arrived? It would make her life much simpler.

"I have enjoyed meeting you and Simon immensely."

She sank down in the nearest chair and contemplated her joined hands.

"If it were not for my position—"

"Mr. Smith, it's quite all right. I do understand. You have been more than willing to listen to our side of the story, and for that I am very grateful. At least your employer will gain a balanced view of the issues."

He turned abruptly and came to kneel at her feet, taking her hands in his.

"Know this. I will never willingly harm you or your brother. I will do everything in my power to make sure that neither George Mainwaring nor my employer will deprive you or your child of your rights."

"That is very good of you."

He held her gaze and then brought her fingers to his lips and kissed them. "I mean it." He rose slowly to his feet. "Now I will wish you good night. If the letters I'm expecting arrive tomorrow, I should imagine I'll be on my way the day after."

"And you don't want to spend your last few hours with me?" She forced herself to sound flirtatious and amused.

He stopped, but he didn't turn around, presenting her with his broad back. "Don't do that. Don't pretend."

"How do you know I'm pretending?"

"Because like knows like, and in your position, I'd be offering exactly the same currency."

"And what would that be?"

He slowly turned to face her. "My body for a few hours of pleasure."

"And if it were more than that? More than just carnal lust. If I wanted—*you*?"

"You have no idea who or what I am, or what I've done."

"Because you refuse to be honest with me."

He shrugged. "I regret that more than I can say."

"Do you truly wish us harm?"

"No, as I just told you, I will do all I can to protect you."

"But you can't be honest with me about who you are and what you've done."

"No." Regret shadowed his blue gaze.

She forced a smile. "Don't despair, Mr. Smith. As you said, we're obviously not destined to meet again, so why does it matter?"

"Because that's *why* we can't meet again. It's my own damn fault." He bowed. "Good night, my lady."

He quietly closed the door behind him, leaving Mary with a sense that something vital had been missed—that some connection that should've been made between them had been lost forever. She wrapped her arms around her waist and fought unexpected tears. If Mr. Smith had lied as well, did it somehow make it better that she hadn't quite told him the truth either? Did the two wrongs balance each other out? And what had he meant about his deception preventing him from ever seeing her again?

Jack retired to his room and locked both the door and the internal door to the dressing room that led to Simon's bedchamber. He spent an aimless few minutes sorting through his clothes and stuffing them into his valise, leaving out only what he'd need for the morning. His last day at Pinchbeck Hall . . .

After another few hours staring at the fire, he'd begun to hate his own company and even contemplate seeking out Mary and telling her the truth. Driven by some strange compulsion, he lit a candle and let himself back out into the corridor. He vaguely remembered her telling him that there were some formal apartments in the opposite wing that had once been used for visits from local grandees or the occasional member of the royal family.

Holding the candle aloft, he traversed the silent hallways and the gallery and passed into the unlit west wing. The smell of damp and decay immediately assaulted him. If he ever came into his inheritance, he would make everything new again, make the house the showpiece it had obviously once been.

He opened a door at random, and found himself in a room with gold drapery, a high four-poster bed crowned with a coronet and a rather fine Turkish carpet. He kept moving, opening up each new set of double doors of what he assumed were the state apartments until he was brought back out through a small antechamber onto the corridor again. Another door beckoned, and he opened it, the woodwork creaking from lack of use. He paused, but there was no sign of pursuit, or any interest from the already quiet house.

It was a small room, which, he suspected had once been a lady's personal sitting room. The chairs drawn up to the cold grate were comfortable rather than grand. A collection of novels and embroidery had been left lying around as if their owner had got up for a moment and would return momentarily. So strong was the sensation that Jack shivered. He held the candle up and turned his attention to the many pictures and portraits on the wall. From what he could gather, the room might have belonged to his grandmother.

A portrait of a black-haired woman surrounded by four children drew his gaze. The youngest child was the only one as dark-haired as his mother, and leaned against her knee, his blue eyes gazing worshipfully upward. Jack's hand tightened on the candlestick. Why had his father left? Why hadn't he appreciated what Jack had never had? A mother to love him, and the security of a family behind him? Exhausted by her husband's antics, Jack's mother had left with Violet as soon as she could, and made a home for herself with Jack's maternal grandmother. He didn't blame her.

Damnation, yes, he did.

He stepped back from the picture, his throat tight. How could she have left him behind? He and Violet were practically identical. Had she seen in him the same characteristics as his father? Had she not wanted to watch another man she loved become a charming, dissolute failure? He'd never know. She'd died before he'd had a chance to ask her anything at all.

Love had caused all this. He wasn't a deep thinker but even he could see why he'd avoided the emotion ever since. After a deep, steadying breath, he walked out of the room, taking with him the scent of old perfume and an unexpected hint of bitterness and betrayal. This house had changed him. The *people* in it had changed him, both the living and the dead.

As he walked back along the top of the main staircase, one of the grooms came running up the stairs.

"Mr. Smith, I was just coming to find you." He held up two letters. "These were just delivered and need your immediate attention."

"Jenkins, isn't it?" Jack held out his hand. "Thank you. Is Mr. Picoult back yet?"

"No, sir."

"Will you ask the groom who brought these to wait and see if I need to answer them?"

"Yes, sir."

Jack continued on his way and relocked his door before sitting down on his bed to examine the contents of the letters. They were brief. Adam didn't want him to do anything about the Keyes situation, and advised him to come back to London as soon as possible. He also added that he had some information from Christian Delornay that might interest Jack and to call in at the Sinners Club.

Jack contemplated the letters and then stuffed his remaining clothes in his valise. It seemed his journey into Lincolnshire was destined to end more quickly than he'd anticipated. . . . He carefully burned his correspondence, wrote a polite note to thank Mary and Simon for their hospitality, and did what he'd always done when a situation became intolerable.

He ran away.

For the first time in his life, he hated himself for doing it.

"Simon!"

Mary finally found him in the estate office at the farthest end of the house. For once the early morning sunlight was streaming through the long front windows, illuminating the parquet floor and casting her shadow ahead of her.

"What is it, love?"

"He's gone."

He looked up from the accounts. "Mr. Smith?"

"Yes." She held up the letter. "He says that he was asked to return to London posthaste."

"Sounds rather peculiar. Did you two have an argument or something?"

"No, he—" She paused, remembering the odd conversation they'd shared the evening before, the look on his face when he'd sworn to protect her and her child. It was as though he'd shown her a different side of his personality entirely. "He was very kind to me."

Simon pulled back his chair and came around to take her in his arms. "Don't worry, love. I'll check with the staff as to whether he really did receive a message, or if he just decided to leave. I'll also make sure the silver isn't missing." He kissed the top of her head. "I'm surprised he didn't stay to say good-bye."

She registered the faint hurt in his voice and hated Jack Smith for putting it back there. It was the first time Simon had risked a physical relationship since the earl had died. Jack deserved to be shot.

"I'm sorry, love." Mary kissed him back. "I told you he wasn't to be trusted." She put her hand over Simon's. "Maybe we really should check the silver. I'll ask Mrs. Lowden and the butler if there were any late letters last night, while you go and check with the stables."

* * *

Half an hour later, she was seated in the earl's study, her mind in a whirl. Simon didn't bother to knock as he came through the door smelling of straw and horse manure.

"Simon, neither the butler nor Mrs. Lowden saw any messages coming in."

He halted beside her. "There's no need to look so grim, my dear. I spoke to Jenkins, and apparently a groom did arrive directly from London demanding Mr. Smith. He carried two letters. Mr. Smith left with him."

"Oh."

Simon frowned. "You almost sound disappointed that he had a good excuse for leaving in a hurry."

Mary groaned and rubbed her hands over her face. "I don't want to like him, Simon. It would be much easier to justify my actions if he and his employer were obnoxious scoundrels."

"Poor Jack." He held out his hand to her. "Come and eat something. Mrs. Tyler gave me an armful of London papers full of gossip for you to peruse. You know that always cheers you up."

She took his hand. "Are you sure you're feeling all right about this?"

"About Jack?" He patted her cheek. "Why wouldn't I be? He helped me remember how it feels to be attracted to someone without any rules or duty or . . . you know."

"But did you care for him?"

Simon laughed. "Do you mean, am I in love with him? No. He told me right from the start that he prefers women."

"That's good then."

"I think it is. I have no regrets whatsoever. How about you?"

She punched him on the arm. "Why would you think I feel any differently from you? He was an interesting and inventive bed partner, and I enjoyed him."

"And that's all?"

"Why would there be anything else?" She raised her chin.

He studied her for far too long. "I'm not sure. It's just that this time I sense something different about you."

"I'm just a superb actress." She disentangled herself from his embrace and marched toward the door. "Don't be ridiculous."

How to explain to her closest friend and sometime lover that the connection she'd made with Jack Smith had shaken her to the core? He matched her in so many ways that it was unsettling, and she didn't want to think about him ever again. She'd just have to hope that her heart soon learned to agree with her.

12

London

"You are more than welcome to stay here, Jack."

Jack smiled at his stepmother across the breakfast table. "That is very kind of you, love. I was rather hoping to have a home of my own by now. As I explained to you last night, things have gotten rather complicated."

"So you said." Sylvia poured him more tea. "It has all the makings of a Drury Lane melodrama. I can't help sympathizing with the Picoults, though." She shivered. "I know how it feels to be left widowed and alone."

"Whatever happens, I won't let them suffer."

"I know that, Jack. You are one of the kindest men I've ever met. Look how well you took care of me and Violet."

"I did my best."

"Under very trying circumstances. Your father would've been proud of you."

"I doubt it. Nothing I did was ever quite good enough for him." Jack used his napkin and rose to his feet. "I have several appointments this morning, so I'll probably be back quite late. Do you have any commissions for me?"

"None at all." She smiled up at him. "Unless asking you to have dinner with me tonight is considered a commission?"

"No, *that* will be a pleasure." He bowed.

He'd never understood how his aging father had managed to marry yet another lovable woman like his stepmother. Sylvia had nothing but good to say about Jack's father, and stubbornly refused to believe he was anything but the perfect husband. Jack had given up trying to persuade her otherwise. It was both cruel and unnecessary to destroy her memories. It was also possible that in his later years, Jack's father had mellowed and truly appreciated the love of his new young wife.

"Ha!"

"Did you say something, sir?" The butler gave him an inquiring look as he opened the front door for Jack.

"No, Batlock, I was just clearing my throat. Can you find me a hackney cab?"

"Certainly, sir."

Jack thanked the butler, put on his hat and gloves, and stepped out into the drizzle. He climbed into the hackney cab and directed the driver to the Sinners Club. He might as well face Adam and get that over with. Then he intended to see the Lennox solicitors, and perhaps Christian Delornay if Adam didn't have the information Jack required. As the cab made its way through the crowded, noisy streets, he pictured Pinchbeck Hall set amongst the quiet of the fens and wished himself back there.

"Here you are, sir. I don't think I'll get any closer than this!" The cabby's voice rang out, disturbing his thoughts.

"This will be fine."

Jack avoided a few puddles, and made his way up the steps of the club. The footman inside merely nodded as Jack strode through the hall and down toward Adam's office.

"Ah, Jack. I thought you might be in this morning." Adam

sat behind his desk, one of the thick ledgers belonging to the club open in front of him.

"Your note made it seem like the best course of action." Jack removed his hat and coat and sat down. "I assumed you might want more details about what happened at the Keyes house."

Adam retrieved a sheet from under the ledger and perused it. "No, I think you were fairly comprehensive in your letter."

"Do you think Keyes is there, then?"

"If he is, there isn't much we can do about it."

"Why not?"

"He's obviously not being held for political reasons."

"But I thought the Sinners Club was set up to help when the government couldn't or wouldn't? Have you spoken to Lord Westbrook about this?"

"I have, and he is of the same opinion as I am. It was time for Keyes to go home and sort out some family issues. In fact, it was long overdue."

"So you know more about this than you are letting on."

Adam smiled. "I'm afraid so."

"And you believe that despite the woman with the pistol, Keyes is in safe hands?"

"None better, wouldn't you think? No foreign government or agent will be able to get to him either."

"I suppose that's true—if he's there."

"Oh, I think he is."

There was a hint of amusement in Adam's voice that made Jack narrow his eyes. "One might think that you were enjoying this."

"One might." Adam shifted the book to one side. "Now on to other matters. I'm sure you'll be seeing Mr. McEwan, but I wanted to address the matter you asked me about before you saw him."

"The Picoults."

"Indeed." Adam sat back in his chair and studied Jack.

"That must have been something of an unexpected surprise for you."

"It certainly was."

"Why didn't you throw them out?"

"Because I wasn't myself."

"But even as your own secretary, you had the power to order them to leave."

"I found I couldn't do that."

"Is the widow that attractive?"

Jack sat up straight. "The Dowager Countess is one of the most beautiful women I've ever seen."

"Oh dear."

"But that wasn't why I let her stay. She's expecting a child. If she delivers a son, that child should inherit the title."

"Come now, Jack, she obviously schemed to marry an elderly, sick man in his dotage to protect herself and her brother from eviction. Who's to say that the child is even his?"

"I find I cannot blame her for wanting security for herself and her family. Wouldn't you do the same thing?"

"Good Lord, she must be exceptional to have gotten around you. What did she do? Seduce you?"

"That is none of your business." Jack flexed his fingers in an effort not to leap across Adam's desk and plant him a facer. "I am convinced the Picoults are not to blame for this debacle."

Adam sighed. "Then you won't be pleased to hear what I've found out about them."

Mary turned over a page of the society newspaper she was reading. Sometimes she missed London, with all its noise and crowds and entertainment. When she was younger, she'd assumed that like her mother, she'd be having a Season. She'd dreamed of attending Almack's, and making her come-out to the queen. . . . Reading about those who were fortunate enough to still inhabit that world was somewhat bittersweet. Occasionally, she recognized the names of her contemporaries from school and wondered if they even remembered her, or whether her family's downfall had made her invisible.

She picked up the next newspaper and saw it was dated three weeks previously. Not that she minded. Any news was welcome in the quietness of Pinchbeck Hall, where no one ever visited them anymore. It was very kind of the vicar's wife to pass the papers on to her and Simon. She skimmed dutifully through the political news and turned with relief to the society columns, which detailed the goings-on of the *ton*, both actual and invented. The more scandalous the story, the less real information that was given, which left Mary happily trying to fill in the details for herself.

She read about births and deaths, about betrothal announcements and funerals with equal attention.

> Lady Gina hears that the Honorable Richard Ross, heir to Lord Philip Knowles, the Earl of Swanford, has married in a private ceremony. His bride is Miss Violet Lennox, daughter of the Honorable John Lennox of the County of Lincolnshire. She recently returned from being schooled in France. Miss Lennox is the twin sibling of Mr. Jack Lennox, who is rumored to be the next Earl of Storr and has been setting the hearts of the ladies of the *ton* afire this season.

Mary read through the announcement again, and then for a third time. A terrible premonition roared through her and she fought a wave of sickness.

"Simon, did Jack ever tell you the name of his sister?"

"His sister?" Simon sat opposite her by the fire doing the farm accounts. "Some kind of flower name? I don't quite remember."

"I think he said it was Violet."

"Why do you ask?"

She put the paper down on her knee, and smoothed it out beneath her trembling fingers. "Because, according to the newspaper, the Honorable Jack Lennox's twin sister, Violet, got married last month."

"*What?*"

"Do you think it possible that John Lennox and Jack Smith both have twin sisters called Violet?" She waited until Simon came across to join her, and pointed out the offending passage in the newsprint. "I *knew* he was lying to us!"

"But—why would Jack pretend to be his own secretary?"

"To catch us off guard? To make us his fools?" Mary threw the paper to the floor. "I'd like to roast him very slowly over a large fire!"

"I don't believe it."

Mary stood up to pace the carpet. "What other explanation can there be?"

Simon sank down into Mary's abandoned seat. "I don't know." He hesitated. "Do you think it was all a game to him?"

The expression on his face made her want to weep, but she couldn't console him, couldn't console herself.

"We have to think. What will he do now? Did he go to London to get support from the authorities to throw us out?"

"Mary, he swore that he wouldn't do that."

"While he was *lying* to us and pretending to be his own secretary. How can we believe a word that came out of his mouth?"

What was worse, *she'd* believed him. Was she a complete fool? When had she decided to let her guard down and allow herself to be seduced by a trickster? It wasn't as though she were a flat. She should have spotted him for what he was the moment they met.

"What do you want to do, love? Should we leave?"

"Leave?" Mary scowled at Simon. "He will have to drag me out by my hair!"

A knock on the door interrupted their discussion and heralded the arrival of Mrs. Lowden, as it was the butler's night off. She hated being dragged away from the kitchen fire, and wore her favorite martyred expression.

"The vicar's here, my lady. I have no idea why he's bothering us at this hour."

"Please show him in." Mrs. Lowden departed to fetch the vicar from the hall. "I wonder what he wants?"

Mr. Tyler came in and smiled at them both. "Good evening, my lady, and Simon. I apologize for bothering you, but I have something for Mr. Smith." He took a package out of his capacious pocket. "I wonder if I might deliver it to him?"

"Mr. 'Smith' isn't here," Mary said tightly.

The vicar's gaze flew to her face. "Is everything all right, my dear?"

"No, it isn't."

"Is there anything I can help you with?"

Mary picked up the paper and held it out to him. "Did your wife happen to mention a society wedding that took place recently?"

"I don't believe she did."

"It was in the newspapers she lent me." She pointed out the paragraph, and waited until he'd put on his spectacles and read it through.

"Ah."

"Mr. Smith insinuated that his employer was old and married."

Mr. Tyler sighed. "Mr. Smith said a lot of things that I didn't believe."

"You *know*, don't you?" Mary asked. "You know that Jack Smith and John Lennox, the would-be Earl of Storr, are the same man."

"I don't think it matters if I tell you now." He took the seat beside her and held her hand. "I knew his father, John, very well. We occasionally corresponded so I was aware he had a son. Jack looks very much like him."

"The wastrel who ran away from home, and was never spoken of again? That sounds *just* like him."

"I don't think he's quite as wild as his father."

"He's worse! Why on earth did he deceive us? What was the point?"

"I think the young man should explain that to you himself."

"If he ever comes back here. And if he does, I'll shoot him on sight!"

"He might well be back, my dear."

She pulled her hand out of his grasp, and placed it over her stomach. "Do you think he'll try and deprive my child of his inheritance?"

"If your child is a girl, he has a perfect right to ask you to move out, you know that."

"He told me that his employer would support me whatever happened, but I'm beginning to doubt that is true. How can I trust a man who can't even admit who he *is*?"

"I think you should believe he means to support you."

Mary smiled, but didn't reply. The vicar was a good man and truly believed every soul was redeemable. He'd believed in her and Simon, and had risked his reputation to help them. Why shouldn't he trust Jack? She didn't want to think about that too much—didn't want to think of him as another misunderstood soul.

"I can't believe you are defending him, Mr. Tyler. That he confided in you and you didn't tell us until it was too late."

"Many people confide in me, Mary, including you. I try to help when I can."

The gentle reproof made her feel like a child again and her cheeks heated. "You didn't tell him anything about us, did you?"

"Of course not." He searched her face. "But are you *certain* you want to continue with this? I didn't realize how many people would become involved in such a minor matter as a private wedding ceremony."

"Are you saying you won't support us any longer?" Mary faced him despite the terror coiling itself around her heart.

"I'll support you until the Good Lord tells me not to. If I am asked as to the particulars of the marriage, I can't lie to the authorities, Mary. But that child of yours deserves his inheritance and you have both suffered enough."

"Thank you, Mr. Tyler." Mary let out her breath and stamped down on her rising guilt. "I cannot tell you how much that means to me, and to Simon."

"Yes, thank you, sir." Simon went to shake the vicar's hand.

"If Jack does come back, do you want me to give him the package you brought?"

The vicar glanced over at the table where he'd laid the wrapped parcel. "Perhaps I could send it on to him? Do you have his direction in London?"

Mary picked up the parcel before the vicar could reach it. "You could send it to the Lennox family solicitors. I have the details of their place of business in the study."

She left Simon in the drawing room, and took the vicar along to the old earl's study. Jack's correspondence with the solicitor still sat on the desk where he'd left it—obviously quite deliberately to make her think he was trustworthy. Anger coalesced in her stomach, making it hard to breathe. She waited until the vicar lit a candle and then sat down at the desk. The key was in the lock and she used it to open the drawer and take out a fresh sheet of paper. Her hand shook as she carefully copied the directions from the top of Mr. McEwan's letter onto the paper.

"Thank you, my dear." The vicar took the note and folded it in half before putting it back in his pocket with the parcel.

"What are you sending him?" Mary asked.

"I found some of his father's letters. I thought he might appreciate reading them."

"That was very kind of you."

"I know you are thinking the worst of him now, but I'm sure things will become clearer when he returns."

"I'm sure you are right."

She went to stand, and the vicar held out his hand. "Don't bestir yourself. I can see myself out. I just wanted to have a quick word with Simon. Is he still in the drawing room?"

"Why don't you go and see? I'll just put these letters away."

"Good night, my lady."

She nodded, and he departed, leaving her staring at the solicitor's clear handwriting. She picked up the other letter, which was in a different hand, and supposedly from the honorable John Lennox himself. Who had written it? Who else was involved in this charade?

For the first time since her mother died, she'd trusted someone. He'd proved to be as false as the diamonds her father had given her mother and just as worthless.

"The dishonorable John Lennox more like!" she said into the silence. She closed the inkwell, and cleaned off her pen before glancing down at the key in the drawer.

She grabbed the key, shot to her feet, and ran for the door. To her immense relief, the vicar had left and Simon was sitting by the fire, his expression pensive. He looked up as she came in and forced a smile.

"All you all right, love? Fancy the vicar knowing all about Jack."

He was trying to sound amused, but she knew him too well to be fooled. Unfortunately, she didn't have time to comfort him. She held up the key.

"Did you leave this in the desk?"

He frowned and patted his waistcoat pocket. "I don't think so."

"Then who did?"

He stared at her. "The last time I remember seeing it was when Jack asked me for some paper to write on and I took out the key to unlock the drawers."

Mary turned right around and went back to the study. By the time Simon reached her, she was busy unlocking all the drawers of the desk.

"What are you doing?"

She found the ribbon-tied bundle of the earl's will and other documents and dumped them on the top of the desk.

"Mary, calm yourself. They are all still here. Did you think he'd stolen them?"

She ignored his question, untied the ribbon and scanned through the documents before raising her head.

"He *has* stolen them." She held up the will. "This is the copy we gave him. He must've taken the originals."

"When?"

"When he took the key."

Simon groaned. "I think I remember what happened. I must've left the key in the drawer after he distracted me."

"And how did he do that?"

He blushed. "Guess."

"I don't blame you." Mary sighed. "We've both been fools, haven't we?" She put the documents back in the packet. "But I'm not going to let him get away with this."

"Mary, you have that look on your face I've learned to dread. What on earth do you plan to do?"

She raised her chin. "We're going to follow him to London and make him wish he'd never been born!"

13

"The Picoult family is quite interesting. Did you know that Mary and Simon are not actually brother and sister?" Adam asked.

"I discovered that while I was at Pinchbeck Hall. I understand that Mrs. Picoult took Mary and her mother into her house when they were homeless." Jack crossed his booted feet at the ankle and tried to look relaxed.

"That's correct. I still have men working on discovering Mary's identity. She definitely did not come from the same social class as Simon and his mother. I hope you don't mind, but I concentrated my efforts per your original request on tracking down the Picoults."

"And you found the mother?"

"I did. She is still alive and runs a brothel in Whitechapel."

Inwardly, Jack shuddered at the thought of Mary growing up in a bawdy house in that particular region of London. It was amazing that she had turned out so seemingly unscathed.

"Did you speak to her?"

Adam sat back in his chair and regarded Jack. "I thought you might prefer to do that yourself."

"Thank you for your admirable discretion. I would."

"I also spoke to Christian Delornay, and he was well aware of the Picoult establishment. He wanted to talk to you himself, but he's currently in the countryside with his wife and stepchildren."

Jack frowned. "I didn't think he liked leaving the pleasure house in anybody's hands but his own."

"He doesn't, but Elizabeth insisted. She wants to own a house outside of London, and Christian is more than willing to accommodate her every desire. I believe she is expecting his child."

"When will he return?"

"In a few days."

"Good. I'll contact him after I've spoken to Mrs. Picoult." Jack rose to his feet. "Thank you for all your help."

"You are welcome." Adam handed him the directions. "Thank you for yours."

Jack shrugged. "I didn't do much. It seems that you knew where Keyes was all along."

"I suspected where he was. You merely confirmed it."

"And almost got shot for my pains."

Adam grinned. "I'm sure she wouldn't have gone through with it."

"You didn't see her face." Jack shuddered. "If Keyes has offended Miss Malinda, she's probably got him locked up in a dungeon somewhere."

"Oh, I hope so."

"I thought you liked the man."

"I do, but he's become very hard, and I'd started to worry about him. This little holiday with his family might be just the thing he needs."

"Is there anything else I can help you with, Adam?"

Adam leaned back in his seat to look Jack in the eye. "There is one thing. Seeing as Keyes is absent, and I have to go away on official business, I was wondering if you'd like to take up residence here for a few weeks and keep an eye on the old place."

"On the Sinners Club? Didn't you say that the Earl of Westbrook and his wife have offices here?"

"They do, but they don't live here or involve themselves in the day-to-day management of the place anymore. After ten years, they decided to step back and enjoy their lives."

"I can understand that." Jack studied Adam's deceptively benign expression. "I do need somewhere to live while I wait to see if the Countess of Storr produces a boy or a girl. This would suit me very nicely."

"Good. There are three apartments on the top floor—one is vacant, the other belongs to Keyes and the third is mine. You are more than welcome to make yourself comfortable in the unoccupied one. It is fully furnished and the staff here will treat you very well."

"I'm sure they will."

"Would you like to see the rooms?"

"If you have time to show me them."

Adam led Jack up two flights of stairs to the level just below the servants' quarters, and unlocked the first of three doors that led off the circular landing.

"Here you are."

There was a large, cozy sitting area, a bedroom beyond that, and two other doors that were closed. Adam opened the first of them. "Here is your study. The door at the far end leads down to the servants' stairs and gives the staff access to your rooms."

"And what's in here?"

"Oh, I think you'll like this. We've had all the most modern conveniences added to this floor."

"Good Lord, my own bathtub and convenience!" Jack marveled at the large bath and the water closet. "I can soak in there for hours."

Adam leaned across him and turned the tap. "There is also running water."

"How modern!" Jack smiled. "I do believe I'll take the place. Now tell me the truth. What will I *really* have to do to repay such a generous offer?"

Adam gave him the key. "Be on hand for any emergencies amongst the membership."

"That sounds remarkably easy."

Adam held open the door that led out of the apartment. "With our membership you never quite know what will come up. Now come down to the kitchens and meet the staff."

Jack consulted the directions Adam had written down for him, and searched in vain for any indication of a street name on the grimy walls confronting him at the crossroads. His boots were covered in mud and his coat was already splashed with filth from a passing horse and cart. He spied a small gaggle of urchins eyeing him speculatively and held up a penny.

"Who wants this?"

A fight broke out amongst the boys. Jack waited until one of them shoved the others aside and approached him. Jack guessed he was at least ten, but he looked half that age due to lack of good food.

"What 'cha want, mister?"

"Directions to Leland Street."

"Leland?" The boy scratched his head and something dropped out and crawled away. "Never 'eard of it."

"The Picoult place?"

" 'E means the brothel, Jude," a smaller boy piped up. Jack produced another penny and tossed it to the lad.

"Oh, that place!" Jude turned and pointed back the way he'd come. "It's the third house on the left with the black door and brass knocker." He leered at Jack. "You want some dick to suck then, Molly?"

"Thank you." Jack dropped the penny into Jude's waiting hand and smacked another thieving hand away from delving into his pocket. Keeping a careful eye on the boys, he retraced his steps and banged on the knocker of the peeling black door.

"You don't need to knock, sir, you just go on in." The smaller, helpful lad spoke again, and got his ear cuffed by Jude for his impudence.

"Thank you." This time Jack threw the boy a sixpence and dived through the door, leaving an unholy mass of heaving bodies on the street outside. He stood with his back against the door, breathing hard, and held it firm against the banging. He hoped the small one survived. He suspected he would.

"May I help you?"

His gaze flew to the young woman who had emerged from the gloom at the back of the house. She didn't look like either a whore or a servant.

"Ma'am." Jack swept her a magnificent bow. "I am looking for Mrs. Picoult. Is she here?"

"She's sleeping. What do you want?"

"Just to speak to her."

"Why?"

"When will she be up?"

"When it pleases her." The woman took a step closer. "This is a brothel, everyone sleeps during the day if they can."

"But not you."

"Someone has to be up and making sure everything is ready for the night."

"Then Mrs. Picoult is lucky to have you." He tried again. "Do you have any idea when I should return?"

"Not before six."

He bowed. "Thank you." The noise outside seemed to have subsided. "Will you tell your mistress that Mr. John Smith wanted to speak to her?"

She nodded briskly. "I will." She hesitated. "Are you sure I can't help you? I can see if someone is awake and willing to take you upstairs."

"That's very kind of you, but I'm not here for carnal purposes." In truth, even if he were, he wouldn't touch any whore in this district without the fear of what he might catch.

"There's no shame in it, sir. Each to their own. Or is it that you like to watch, then?"

"I like to do everything, but not today."

He cautiously opened the front door, allowing light into the darkened space. She cocked her head to one side. Her hair was reddish in color and in dire need of a good wash.

"I'll tell her you will come back, then."

"Yes, please do that."

He escaped through the door and slammed it shut. The ragged band of boys was nowhere in sight. All he had to do was find his way back to Mile End Road, obtain a hackney, and tell Sylvia about his change in lodgings. It was frustrating that he had to wait on answers. He did have some time before the heir presumptive was born, so he wasn't despairing quite yet.

After he washed off the dirt of this neighborhood, he'd set out again for the Lennox solicitors and deliver the original copies of the will, the marriage lines, and the vicar's letter he'd taken from the earl's desk. He didn't feel guilty about borrowing the papers. If Mary were worried about George Mainwaring, Mr. McEwan would be her staunchest ally in the battle to come.

He kept his guard up and his hand on the hilt of his dagger as he walked through the filthy streets. He'd lived in such places when his father was down on his luck, and learned how to pick a few pockets himself when times were tough. No one approached him in daylight, but he knew it would be a different story in the dark. That thought was enough to make him hasten his steps.

It would be interesting living at the Sinners. He'd heard that the second floor of the house was dedicated to the pleasures of life but had never had a chance to participate in any licentious behavior. Perhaps that was about to change. Even if his heart wasn't in it, sexual excess might help him forget about what he'd done. It had always brought him relief in the past.

An image of Mary and Simon flashed in his mind and he was immediately hard. Damnation, he *needed* to forget them. Once he'd fucked another anonymous body, he'd remember who he was, and why he didn't deserve anything better. He was too much like his father and thus incapable of love and fidelity. His parents' misalliance and his mother's abandonment had taught him that. He had no desire to destroy a woman as his father had, dragging her down until she had nothing left to give him.

Not that Mary was like his mother. . . .

He shoved that thought away and held out his arm to hail a hackney.

"You can't stay here." Simon caught hold of Mary's elbow and kept her inside the hackney cab. "It isn't fitting."

"Don't be silly. I grew up here just like you did."

"But you're a titled widow now. You can't stay in a *brothel!*"

The hackney driver cleared his throat and spat. "Are you getting out or not? I'll charge you extra if you stay in there chatting."

"We're coming out." Mary pulled away from Simon's grasp and stepped out into the street. The foul stench of Leland Street immediately surrounded her. She felt as if she'd come home. "Thank you."

She knocked boldly on the door of the brothel, and when there was no reply, she pushed the door open and went in, leaving Simon to deal with the hackney cab. A faint light at the back of the house drew her and she walked down the long corridor and into the kitchen.

The fragrant smell of baking bread overrode the usual smells of the brothel and Mary smiled.

"Ginny?"

The red-haired woman turned away from the stove and almost dropped the loaf pan in her hands.

"Oh my word! Whatever are you doing here? Is Simon with you?"

"He's just paying off the hackney." Mary allowed herself to be enfolded in Ginny's warm, floury embrace. "Is your mother here?"

"She should be down at any moment. She'll be right surprised to see you both." Ginny paused. "Has something happened? Have you both been kicked out?"

Before Mary could answer, the kitchen door slammed and Simon entered bearing their luggage, his expression still grim. She sensed he was about to continue their argument, but luckily Ginny had other ideas.

"Simon!"

He dropped the bags and held out his arms. "Ginny, lass! You've grown!"

Mary couldn't help but smile as she watched the brother and sister hug each other. Simon had obviously missed his real sister more than he'd let on. She sat down at the kitchen table and rested her chin on her hand. She had a terrible headache. After the endless journey on the Mail coach it was nice simply not to be in motion.

"You need to eat."

She blinked as Ginny thrust a plate of buttered bread and a

mug of ale at her. The warm bread did smell delicious. She picked at the crust while Simon sat opposite her and drank a whole tankard of the weak brew down in one.

The kitchen door opened again, and she forced herself to sit upright.

"Well, what have we here?" Mrs. Picoult's familiar dry voice made her look up. "I was told to expect a visitor this evening, but I wasn't anticipating two such familiar ones."

Simon rose to his feet and went to his mother to kiss her cheek. She had red hair like her children, and wore a black dress with a very low-cut bodice. To Mary, she'd never looked like a woman who ran a brothel, but more like the headmistress of a boarding school or a nunnery, which, considering her clients, made rather good business sense.

"We won't be staying long, Mum. I told Mary we have enough coin to put up at a decent hotel, but she insisted on coming here first."

"Did she now?" Mary stiffened as Simon's mother, Audrey, took a seat at the head of the table. "I would've thought you'd want to avoid all references to your past."

She raised her eyes to meet Mrs. Picoult's cynical gray gaze. "I'm not ashamed of what I've done, or where I've lived. In truth, I owe my life to you."

"You paid me back, love, many times over when you two caught that earl."

"He married her, Mum, last year, not long before he died," Simon interjected. "She's the Dowager Countess of Storr now."

"So I heard. So, what are you both doing here, then?"

Mary drew in a deep breath. "Some charlatan is trying to deprive us of our home."

"And who might that be?"

"The earl's nephew, John Lennox. He believes he's the heir to the title, and is prepared to do anything, even masquerade as his own secretary, to achieve his aim."

"Oh dear." Mrs. Picoult sat back. "And is it possible that he is right?"

"If I and my unborn child didn't exist, he would be the heir presumptive."

"You're with child?" Mrs. Picoult's gaze flicked over Mary. "And it's the earl's? Knowing him, I find that difficult to believe. What if it's a girl?"

"Then John Lennox will inherit everything. If he doesn't contest Jasper's new will I'll be left with a pension, and Simon will have *nothing*."

"That hardly seems fair, but when has the law ever favored anyone but the rich? They have a vested interest in keeping the power, the land, and the money to themselves."

"Not if I can help it." Mary drank her ale and finished her bread. "John Smith will *never* get the better of me."

Ginny came to refill Mary's mug. "John Smith, you say? That's the name of the man who wanted to see you, Mum."

"Jack came here?" Mary glared at Simon. "What a *remarkable* coincidence. He must be trying to discredit us even further by exposing our pasts."

"Why would he do that?"

"Because he's as bad as George! He doesn't want anyone or anything to stand between him and claiming that damned title."

Simon didn't look convinced, which somehow enraged her even more. "Just because you liked him doesn't mean that he isn't out to destroy us. The best thieves are always the most charming ones."

"That's true." Mrs. Picoult brought the pot to the table, spooned in a few tea leaves, and added some boiling water from the kettle sitting on the stove. "I gather that this Jack Smith might also be John Lennox?"

"Yes."

"He's coming back after six, Mum," Ginny added. "Will you see him?"

"Oh, I'll definitely see him." Mrs. Picoult turned to Mary. "Now, what exactly do you want me to say?"

Jack glanced up at the façade of the Picoult brothel. Cracks of light showed through some of the windows, but for the most part, the house was shuttered close. He knocked on the door and then tried to open it. This time it was locked. He knocked again, and eventually an elderly man who bore the battered looks of an ex-boxer opened it and glowered menacingly at him.

"What do you want?"

Jack presented his card. "I'm here to see Mrs. Picoult. I believe she's expecting me."

The man took the card and didn't attempt to read it. "I'll go and see."

He shut the door in Jack's face. After what seemed like a long interval, he reappeared and held the door open wide. "You can come in."

"Thank you." Jack stepped into the hallway, which was now illuminated by candlelight. Somewhere in the house he could hear the murmur of voices, laughter, and the regular *thump thump* of someone fornicating.

"Mrs. Picoult's in her study. Third door on the left."

He followed Jack down the hall as if he suspected he'd try and deviate from his instructions, and then leaned past him to push the door open.

"Visitor for you, ma'am."

"Thank you, Marshall."

Jack stepped into the room, which was smaller than he had anticipated and dominated by a large desk. A fire burned in the grate. Tall windows covered by crimson velvet curtains gave the space a luxurious appearance it probably didn't merit in the harsher light of day.

"Mr. Smith?"

His attention was drawn back to the woman who sat behind the desk. Her red hair was tied back from her face in a tight bun, and her skin was sallow. Her unwelcoming expression reminded him forcibly of every schoolmaster he'd ever encountered in his misspent youth. She looked nothing like the owner of any cheap brothel he'd ever encountered before, and he'd been in a few.

"Mrs. Picoult." He bowed. "I appreciate you seeing me."

She gestured at the solitary chair placed in front of the desk. "How can I help you, Mr. Smith?"

"I represent the Honorable John Lennox. My employer is seeking information about Simon and Mary Picoult, whom I believe may have lived in this house."

"I have a son called Simon. He no longer lives here. He found employment in Lincolnshire."

Her tone was not encouraging.

"And your daughter?"

"In the kitchen. Do you want to see her?"

Jack almost leapt out of his chair. "Lady Storr is here?"

"Lady who? My daughter's name is Virginia, Mr. Smith. You met her when you called earlier today."

"And what about Mary Picoult?"

She met his gaze head-on. "I don't know anyone with that name, sir."

"I accept that she might not be a daughter of yours, but I believe she lived here for several years and left with your son. Have I been misinformed?"

She folded her hands and studied them. "It seems as if you have, Mr. Smith. May I ask what interest your employer has in these people?"

Jack shrugged. "I have no idea, Mrs. Picoult. I exist merely to serve his every whim." He paused, but saw no sign of any softening on the stony face of his adversary. "May I be frank? I encountered Simon and Mary at Pinchbeck Hall, and then had to bring the information of the earl's late marriage back to my employer. He was obviously perturbed that his claim to the earldom had been usurped."

"So, he asked you to dig up some dirt on his rivals by visiting the brothel where they grew up?" Mrs. Picoult's expression turned withering. "Does he hope to deprive the countess of her child even if it is a boy? To declare her an unfit mother?"

"I doubt that, Mrs. Picoult, he is merely—"

She spoke over him. "Why else would he send you sniffing around like a rat to do his work?"

Jack barely held on to his temper. "You grossly misjudge my employer. His interest is in helping the countess, not harming her."

"So you say."

"He's a good man, Mrs. Picoult."

"Then he should come and visit me himself. I'd respect him more if he lowered himself to do that rather than sending you!"

For a second Jack was so furious that he contemplated revealing his true identity and then hastily discarded the idea. "You do not intend to help me at all, do you?"

"Why would I?"

"Because I wish no harm to your son, or to Mary."

Mrs. Picoult stood up. "Which has no bearing on the discussion at all, does it? You aren't the one who wishes them harm or can affect anything. You are merely the hired help. Good night, Mr. Smith, and please don't bother to call again."

Jack stared at her. "Where was Mary's mother buried?"

Her face went blank.

"I know that she came here with Mary, and died soon afterward."

"Who told you that?"

"Your son." Jack rose to his feet. "Please tell me."

Mrs. Picoult crossed to the door and held it open. Marshall was already lurking outside. "Where are paupers usually buried, Mr. Smith? In unmarked pits, that's where. You'll learn no secrets from the dead. Now please leave, or I'll get Marshall to throw you out."

Jack headed for the door. "I only hope your lack of help in this matter doesn't prevent your son and Mary from getting what is due to them. Good night, Mrs. Picoult. If you need to contact me, leave me a message at Thirty-two Cumberland Square, Mayfair."

"The Sinners Club?"

"Indeed."

"You have interesting friends, Mr. Smith."

He bowed and walked out. When he regained his temper, he'd ask Adam to set a watch on the house just in case she had any contact with Simon, or any other person of interest in the case. He doubted anything would come of it, but it always paid to be cautious. As he traversed the dark streets, he had the distinct impression he was being followed. If Mrs. Picoult wanted to see where he lived, he had no issue with that. The Sinners Club was the perfect venue to keep her out, yet it also confirmed he'd given her his real place of abode.

Damn the woman for being so unforthcoming. His steps slowed as he reached a more respectable thoroughfare. But wouldn't he have done the same in her position? Protected his family? He couldn't really fault her for that, and she did have a point. Asking about Mary's true parentage had only led her to suspect that the aspiring "wicked" earl wanted to steal her child—something that hadn't even occurred to Jack.

Had it occurred to George Mainwaring?

Jack stopped again. Was it possible that Mrs. Picoult had somehow met with George and was conspiring against her own son? If money was involved, anything could happen. If he'd been offered enough, his own father would've sold him without a qualm. So much for family loyalty. Jack set off again. He'd set a watch on Mrs. Picoult and if there were the slightest hint that she was involved with George Mainwaring, he'd contact Mary and warn her. Mrs. Picoult's comments about his courage stung. She hadn't believed he wanted to help. But he did. For the first time in his life he was genuinely worried for someone who wasn't part of his family. It was an unsettling sensation and one he didn't want to examine too closely at all.

"Well, what did you think of him?"

Mrs. Picoult sat down at the kitchen table and accepted the mug of tea Simon slid across to her. They'd all gathered around the kitchen table waiting for her while she talked to Jack.

"He's a charming rogue."

Mary nodded, her hands clasped tightly together on the scrubbed wooden table in front of her. "As I said. Did you send someone after him?"

"I did, although he told me quite openly that he was living at the Sinners Club. It never hurts to check."

"What's the Sinners Club?" Simon asked. "Considering his sexual tastes, it sounds remarkably appropriate for Jack."

"I've never been there, but I've been told by some of my clients that it has a rather exclusive membership comprised of men and women who have served their country in some unrecognized way."

"As spies and exploiters?" Mary said. "That would suit Jack too."

"It might also explain where he learned his remarkable sexual skills," Simon added.

"It's not a brothel, or like the Delornay pleasure house. It's supposed to be a proper gentlemen's club. But I've heard that there are rooms where more unconventional behavior occurs too."

Mary raised her gaze from her hands. "I wonder how one would get invited to such a place?"

Mrs. Picoult studied her. "I'm sure it could be arranged. What are you going to do?"

She smiled for the first time since she'd reached London. "I'm going to teach Jack Lennox a lesson he will never forget."

14

Leaning heavily on Simon's arm, Mary took a swift glance around the busy foyer of Grillons Hotel through her black lace veil. She recognized no one, but she was already the center of attention. A member of the staff rushed forward to greet them. Well aware of the number of eyes on her, Mary slowly raised her veil to reveal her beautiful face, causing an excited hum of whispers to cascade through the lobby like a rushing stream.

"Lady Storr, what a pleasure it is to meet you."

"Oh, thank you so much, Mr. Featherstone." She dabbed at her eyes with a small black handkerchief. "It is such a relief for me to be received with such *kindness*."

"Of course, my lady. I will do anything in my power to ensure that your stay here at Grillons is as perfect as I can make it."

"You are *so* thoughtful."

In his eagerness to settle the Dowager Countess safely in her suite, poor Mr. Featherstone almost tripped over his own feet. Mary went upstairs, her entourage behind her bearing her luggage, her lap dog, her jewelry case, her own monogrammed sheets, and everything else a pampered widow might need.

It took quite a while to persuade the besotted Mr. Featherstone to leave, but eventually Simon accomplished it and shut the door behind the man with a final flourish.

"If your aim was to make yourself the talk of the hotel, I believe you have accomplished it."

"I hope so." Mary patted the seat beside her. "I want you to call on Mr. McEwan's office and tell him to meet me here in the hotel."

"Where you will stake your claim on the title for your future child?"

She took his hand. "Why do you sound so skeptical?"

He sighed. "Is it really worth it, Mary? I could skim off a considerable amount from the estate books without the next earl ever knowing. We could live quite happily on that for years, and travel to the Continent, and forget all about this damned country."

"And let Jack Lennox get away with lying and stealing from us?"

"Why do you care about what he's done? If our positions were reversed, you would've done exactly the same. In fact you *are* doing the same! Your whole *position* is based on a lie."

She pulled away from him. "But don't you see? He's no better than I am. That makes it even more vital that I beat him."

"That's not quite true, is it? Behind his masquerade is an unavoidable truth. He *is* the rightful heir to the title."

"Don't try and make me feel guilty. For all we know, he might be masquerading as John Lennox's son." She spun around to face him. "I'm not doing this for myself!"

His face softened. "Please don't say you're doing it for me, love."

"Why not?"

"Because you don't owe me a thing."

"How can you say that? You protected me, you *saved* me, I—"

He stood and pulled her into his arms. "I did the best I could, and so did you. Neither of us owes the other anything."

She dashed a tear away. "How can you say that?"

"Because it's true. I don't want to look back. I want to move forward. Can't you do the same?"

"Not yet." She met his gaze. "I promise I'll think about that once I've dealt with Jack Lennox."

"Does it occur to you that your anger is out of proportion to what he did? Why can't you simply admire him for out-witting you?"

"Because he lied to me, and I'd started to—" She clamped her lips together and glared at him.

"You'd started to like him. I can see why. I thought the two of you were mirror images of each other. It was fascinating."

"I do not like him!"

He smiled in a particularly infuriating male way and kissed the top of her head. "I'll go and call on Mr. McEwan, then. What do you intend to do when I've accomplished that?"

"We're going to take the *ton* by storm."

"How will that punish Jack?"

"Don't worry, that won't be the only thing we'll do. Your mother has given me plans of the Sinners Club and a way to meet with our adversary on our terms there as well."

Jack sat at his ease beside one of the many fires in the Sinners Club reading the paper and toasting his toes. The club was quite busy, and he'd been idly listening to several strands of conversation as he read. He looked up as a shadow fell across his newspaper.

"Jack."

"Adam, are you leaving?"

"In about an hour. I wanted to show you around the second floor before I left." Adam was dressed for traveling, a heavy cloak over his arm.

"The second floor?" Jack put his paper away and stood. "I'm all yours."

Adam left his baggage in the hallway and led the way up the staircase. "I gather Lord Westbrook was inspired by Madame Helene from the pleasure house. They knew each other in France long before she started up her business here. I believe he was one of her first financial backers."

"There's a brothel here?"

"Not exactly." Adam stood back to allow Jack to enter the large salon before him. "We hold certain *events* here for our members every week. There are also a number of available bed-chambers for those who want to stay the night. We don't ask for details, or have any restrictions as to how many a bed will hold, or what sexes the members are. It's another way of offering our clients a safe place to be themselves."

"So I could bring a whole tribe of men and women up here with me and no one would bat an eye?"

"As long as you were in your own chamber."

"And what if I wanted everyone to have the opportunity to join in?"

"That's what our weekly events are for."

Jack viewed the salon, which had gold silk wallpaper and elegant crystal chandeliers. "It doesn't look very busy, or much like a brothel. I think I'm disappointed."

"On Friday night it will look rather different. There's a troup of dancers from the Indian continent coming to perform for us."

"Men or women?"

"Both, I believe." Adam continued, "They are considered quite scandalous."

"By whom?"

"Everyone." He mock-sighed. "I'm just sorry I shan't be here to see them."

"I'll tell you all about it when you get back."

Adam turned toward him. "Perhaps if you pick up any new tricks you can show them to me personally."

Jack studied Adam's unremarkable face before reaching out to trace the line of his jaw. "In your bed?"

"That would probably be best."

"You don't favor fornicating in public?"

A faint smile was Jack's reward. "I don't."

"I never suspected you would be shy, and I never realized you liked men."

"I like sex. The person's gender isn't important."

"A man after my own heart. I strongly believe that we should experience every kind of copulation available to us." He needed to move on from the Picoults, and fucking Adam would be a most satisfactory way of accomplishing that.

"I heard that about you." Adam looked right into Jack's eyes. "That's why I finally had the courage to approach you. I don't want anything but sex."

Jack's smile faltered. Was that what he'd become? A known whore who had no feelings and could be used simply for sex?

"Are you all right?" Adam touched his arm. "I hope I haven't offended you."

"No, not at all." Wasn't that the best way to conduct his life? To enjoy a good fuck and move on? To not allow anyone to get close to him and see beneath his charming facile shell? When he loved people, he hurt them and they abandoned him. "I look forward to furthering our acquaintance."

"Good."

Adam turned his head a fraction and nipped Jack's thumb before licking it into his mouth. Despite himself, Jack's cock twitched and lengthened. He pushed his thumb deep into Adam's mouth until the other man started sucking it.

"I wish that was my shaft," Jack murmured. He imagined Simon and Adam both on their knees in front of him taking turns to suck him off. Mary would enjoy watching that, he was sure of it. Damnation, where had that thought come from?

He slowly withdrew his thumb from Adam's mouth.

"You probably have to leave."

"Unfortunately I do." Adam stepped back and gave Jack a glorious view of his thick cock trying to escape his tight buckskin breeches. "I do hope you are here when I return."

"Oh, I will be." He reached out and ran his finger down Adam's shaft. "How could I miss revealing this?"

"God." Adam shuddered and pushed into Jack's waiting hand. "Now I have to get on a horse and ride all day thinking about what I'm missing."

"It will help pass the time."

"True, but I'll be blue-balled by the time I get there."

"I could help with you with that." Jack tightened his grip. "I'll be quick, I swear it." He fell to his knees and started unbuttoning Adam's breeches as he spoke. The other man made no further protests as Jack expertly rearranged his clothing and drew his cock deep into his mouth in one smooth motion. He sucked hard, using all his skill. Adam's hand fisted in his hair driving him on, fucking his mouth with every thrust of his hips.

Jack used his teeth, and slid his hand down to cup Adam's balls, exploring the smooth skin of his taint and the tight pucker of his arse.

"God, yes, I—"

With a final shove, Adam started to climax, and Jack willingly swallowed every jet of come until he was done. With a smile, he rearranged Adam's clothing and stood up, wiping his hand over his mouth.

"I think that should do it."

"I think it should." Adam looked slightly dazed. "I really must go now." He turned, and left Jack standing alone in the middle of the empty salon.

Jack's smile faded, and he sat down on the nearest seat and contemplated the silence. His cock was throbbing like a rotten tooth, and yet he didn't feel like attending to it, or have his normal sense of pleasurable relief after a sexual encounter. He felt . . .

empty. Yes, that was it. He'd been unable to banish the thought of Mary Lennox watching him while he sucked Adam's cock. He'd wanted to do it for her, not for Adam. Had wanted her to reward him by letting him fuck her.

What in damnation was wrong with him?

He covered his face with his hands. If he couldn't lose himself in the physical act of fornication, how was he going to continue? Without Violet beside him, whom could he even ask for help? He slowly raised his head, and contemplated the unlit fire in the grate. Mary would understand how it felt to be used. He suspected Simon would too. Perhaps he had more in common with them than he'd ever imagined.

Mary contemplated her reflection in the mirror of her bedchamber. She couldn't have re-created the charming-widow-with-child effect more perfectly. She looked vulnerable, but quite beautiful. Every man who met her at the dinner party would be desperate to help her—especially after she'd spun her tale of woe. . . .

She clasped a ruby necklace around her throat. How long would it take for word of her presence to get back to Jack? Not long, she hoped. And then they would see who was the winner in their private battle of wit and wills. Would he take issue with her publicly, and declare her a fake and a whore? She didn't think that was his style, but desperate men had been known to act out of character. When Jasper wanted something, he'd been prepared to do anything to achieve it. George was apparently the same.

A knock on the door heralded the arrival of Simon, clad in his new evening clothes. He looked remarkably handsome and rather anxious. Mary held up her hand.

"Please don't try and dissuade me again."

He sighed. "I've given up. You are quite stubborn beneath those golden curls and sweet smile."

"It's all an illusion, you know that." One she'd become so familiar with that she doubted she'd recognize her true self anymore. What had happened to that vulnerable young girl? She was better off hidden away where she couldn't be hurt and used again. But sometimes maintaining the artifice was hard. . . .

"I just want what we deserve." She held Simon's gaze. "Jasper promised."

"When did he ever mean what he said?"

"He married me, didn't he?"

"Only because he hates George. If he'd known about Jack, I'll wager he wouldn't have done a thing."

"Don't say that." She shivered.

"It's true. Don't forget that in many ways, I knew him better than you did. You only saw the kinder side of him because he doted on you like a daughter."

"I'm sorry."

He shrugged. "It's in the past." He held out his hand. "If you're determined on this course, the least I can do is support you through it."

"Haven't you always?" She smiled at him as she took his hand. "This isn't your fight. If you want to go back to Pinchbeck Hall, or stay with your mother, I'm quite capable of carrying this off by myself."

"I know you are, love. But I'm staying." He kissed her fingers. "When have I ever let you down?"

"Are you sure?"

"Now you are being foolish. To watch you and Jack square off will be one of the most fascinating things I've ever witnessed in my life. Nothing would keep me away!"

Later that evening, in an effort to avoid the majority of the members of the Sinners Club, Jack decided to seek refuge in Adam's office. He'd received no further word from Mrs. Picoult, or any hint of Christian's return. Sitting around was not something he enjoyed. It gave him too much time to think. Despite his efforts to educate himself on the current state of politics, even the newspapers failed to excite him.

He looked up as someone knocked on the door. "Come in?"

The butler bowed. "Mr. McEwan to see you, sir."

"Send him in." He'd given the solicitor his new direction but was rather surprised the man had bestirred himself to come and visit.

Long before Mr. McEwan appeared, Jack heard him wheezing down the corridor, and the tap of his walking stick. He stood up.

"Good evening, sir."

"Mr. Lennox." Mr. McEwan sat down so heavily that the chair creaked alarmingly.

"How may I assist you?"

The solicitor fumbled for his handkerchief and mopped his brow. "I had an unexpected visitor this afternoon—a Mr. Simon Picoult."

"You did?" Jack kept his smile in place even as his senses tightened. "And what did he want?"

"To escort me to visit the Dowager Countess of Storr at Grillons Hotel. She is a very charming woman indeed." He hesitated. "Not what I expected at all."

The clever little minx. "She is a remarkable woman. What did she want from you?"

"Just to state her case, and ask for my help."

"Which you intend to offer her, I'm sure."

Mr. McEwan spread his hands wide on his knees. "After reading the late earl's will, I was able to reassure her that even if she does have a daughter, she will be well provided for. She was also rather concerned about the matter of guardianship if she had a son."

"In what way?"

He chuckled. "She had the rather fanciful notion that if you were appointed as one of her son's guardians, you would do your utmost to usurp the boy's position. I believe she even mentioned something about King Richard III and the poor princes in the tower."

"She would," Jack muttered.

"I beg your pardon? Of course I reassured her that you would be unable to do anything without the other trustees' approval, but I'm not sure whether I allayed her fears. She is such a fragile, delicate little thing that I found myself quite unable to be too firm with her."

Jack fought back an urge to laugh. "I'm glad you were able to reassure her as to her future position even if I am to figure as the villain of the piece. You believe her claim to be married to the late earl is valid, then?"

"It seems to be. The letter from the vicar also helped."

"Then I wonder what George Mainwaring thinks he knows that will discredit the countess?"

"He wrote to me yesterday."

"George did?"

"Luckily, after reading the documents you brought back, I was able to reply immediately and hopefully convince him that he doesn't have the necessary grounds to instigate a lawsuit—even if he doubts the moral turpitude of the Dowager Countess."

"Let's hope he heeds your advice and doesn't come haring down to London as well. I have a horrible suspicion that he'll appear breathing fire at any moment."

Mr. McEwan shook his head. "Inheritance issues do tend to bring out the worst in my clients." He started to lever himself out of the chair. "I thought you should know the Dowager Countess was in Town. She still thinks you're Jack Smith, doesn't she?"

"Unfortunately." Jack grimaced. "Is she planning on returning to Pinchbeck Hall to await the birth of her child?"

"She said she'd decided to confer with a new birthing physician here in London and would take further instruction from him." Mr. McEwan frowned. "Considering when the earl died, and how ill he apparently was, I would've expected her to have given birth a while ago. But women know best in these matters. I find it better not to interfere."

Jack came around the desk to shake his solicitor's hand and escort him to his carriage. As he returned to Adam's office he considered Mr. McEwan's last words. Exactly how long was Mary's pregnancy going to last? And why in God's name, having got the solicitor's unwavering support, wasn't she on her way back to Lincolnshire? Was she fearful that her pregnancy had gone on for too long, or was there something else?

He decided to go back upstairs to his own apartment, where he could at least think more clearly. By openly approaching Mr. McEwan, she must have known he would find out she was in London. Was it a challenge? He found himself smiling despite everything. If she wanted to get his attention, he'd be damned sure to give it to her.

15
_____

"Now, where would she go?" Jack asked himself as he contemplated the bright afternoon sunshine. Advised by the butler, he'd walked around to the mews at the back of the house in search of the appropriate transportation. "She'll want to be seen, and remembered, by as many members of the *ton* as necessary."

He put on his hat and gloves. "It has to be Hyde Park."

"Did you want something, sir?"

He smiled at the young stable hand. "Does Mr. Fisher own a carriage and horses?"

"He does, sir. Do you want to borrow them? He said it was all right. He has a nice pair of matching grays and a new phaeton."

"That will do very well."

He waited while the groom and the boy got the horses harnessed to the carriage and contemplated exactly how he was going to handle an encounter with Mary Lennox. He rather wanted to wait and see how she handled him. A knot of excitement unfurled in his gut, and he suddenly felt more alive. Was she anticipating their first meeting as much as he was? If she'd discovered who he really was, she'd be furious with him. He'd much rather have the opportunity to tell her himself and beg forgiveness. Her descent on London so quickly after his desertion unsettled him.

"They're ready for you, sir."

"Thank you."

Jack gave the boy a coin and took a moment to meet the horses and make friends with them. One day, when he was settled, he wanted to have his own stable and never have to borrow or rent from anyone else again. He was tired of his roving existence, which was probably why he'd allowed himself to become infatuated with the idea of Pinchbeck Hall. But there were other houses and other counties where he was certain he could exist quite happily. Perhaps when Richard and Violet were settled, he could find a place near them.

He gathered the reins and his whip and waited as the groom stepped away from the horse's head and got up behind him before setting off toward the gates. He'd always loved driving a team. Adam's horses were perfectly behaved despite the usual mayhem of the city traffic. He turned on to the street that led to Hyde Park and merged into a stream of fashionable carriages bearing the leaders and beauties of the *ton*.

There was so much traffic in the park that he was able to drive slowly and look about him at his leisure. He'd made some acquaintances in London, and was more than willing to pull up his horses and chat to the gentlemen and flirt with the ladies. It wasn't long before he caught a glimpse of Simon's red hair and the widow herself in glorious black surrounded by a large crowd of solicitous gentlemen. He paused for a moment to appreciate her. If she hadn't been his adversary, he would've admired her even more.

He drew up his horses and waited to see if she would acknowledge him in any way. She seemed oblivious to his presence, her soulful gaze on the gentleman in front of her who was holding her hand, and about to press a kiss on it. Simon's gaze finally tangled with Jack's and he swiftly looked away. A certain hardness around his mouth indicated he'd seen Jack and chosen to ignore him.

With a sigh, Jack signaled to his groom to hold his horses, and stepped down from the carriage. As the crowd around the dowager was so thick, it took him a while to work his way through to the front. Mary's gaze fell on him and she inclined her head.

"Mr. Smith?"

"Not quite, my lady." Jack bowed but not before he'd seen the hastily concealed fury in her eyes. "I *do* have a confession to make."

"Surely not in such a public venue, sir." She glanced up at Simon. "Isn't it time for us to be going? I believe we have a prior engagement."

Jack held his ground. "May I beg for a private audience, then? I understand you are putting up at Grillons."

She looked down her perfect nose at him. "I hardly think that is necessary, sir. I don't think we have anything to say to each other."

"I beg to differ."

Her fingers tightened on Simon's arm. Jack got the impression that he either moved out of the way or he would be mown down. He spoke as quickly and as quietly as he could. "Don't I deserve a fair hearing? I gave you and your brother one."

"While you deceived us." She looked away from him. "All right. You may meet us this evening for dinner at our hotel at six."

He bowed. "Thank you for that, at least." He turned his attention to Simon. "Are you well?"

"What is it to you?"

Jack cursed under his breath as Simon deliberately pushed past him with Mary on his arm and was soon swallowed up by the strolling crowds. He'd hurt Simon and enraged Mary. He couldn't decide which made him feel worse. But at least he'd been offered a reprieve and an opportunity to explain himself. Although how could he explain his stupidity? Looking back on his foolish idea to masquerade as his secretary made him want to howl. It wasn't the first time that he'd crashed around like a young unbroken colt without thought for anyone, but it was the first time he'd cared enough to try and fix matters.

On his way back to the Sinners, he called in at the House of Pleasure, but Christian still hadn't returned. He was, however, expected within the next two days, which at least gave Jack hope. While his groom inquired at the kitchen door about Christian, Jack checked his watch. He still had three hours to fill before he could present himself at Grillons. . . .

"Do you want to go anywhere else, sir?"

He gathered up the reins, aware that he'd been staring at nothing for far too long.

"No, I think we can go back now."

"Right you are, sir."

When he got in, Maddon, the butler, caught his eye and glided forward.

"Mr. Lennox? There have been some messages for you. I've left them on Mr. Adam's desk."

"Thank you." Jack changed direction and went into the study. He picked up the first letter, which was from Adam, and opened it.

> *My dear Jack, I forgot to tell you that I have asked my friend, Mr. Nicodemus Theale, to report to you while I am away. (He is the man I asked to look into the family history of Mary Picoult.) He is completely trustworthy and I have no hesitation in recommending him.*
> *Yours, A. F.*

Jack put the letter aside and turned to the handwritten note, which stated that a clerk from Mr. McEwan's office had called to tell him that a Mr. George Mainwaring was in town and was seeking a meeting with the solicitor.

"Devil take it!" Jack balled up the paper and threw it in the direction of the fire. "I knew he wouldn't be able to resist meddling!"

At least he could warn Mary and Simon to be on their guard. But what did George think he would gain by trying to bully the solicitor? What did he think he knew that everyone else was unaware of? Jack had no clue. He rang the bell and waited until the butler returned.

"Could you find out where a Mr. George Mainwaring from the county of Lincoln is staying here in London?"

Maddon inclined his head. "I'm sure that can be discovered for you, sir."

"Thank you."

Perhaps he could meet with George and head him off, or even better, find out what he believed he knew. He wasn't sure how he would achieve that, but there had to be something the man wanted. Everyone had their price.

He wrote a quick note to Mr. McEwan, and then went back up to his apartment to enjoy the luxury of a hot bath in the privacy of his own suite. He was surprisingly nervous about the dinner ahead. He'd never been one to stay around to apologize or attempt to explain his actions. His father had taught him that. It was a creed that had stood him well—until now. He stretched his legs and fought off the suggestion of a headache. Perhaps he was finally growing up and willing to own up to his mistakes. Violet would be so proud. . . .

He presented himself at Grillons promptly at six, and waited in the lobby to be escorted up to the Dowager Countess's suite. He'd dressed in a new dark blue coat and white waistcoat and wore dark trousers. While he lingered, he couldn't help but overhear several discussions centered on Mary Lennox's plight and beauty. Gossip seemed to think she deserved the title more than he did. For once he almost agreed.

Eventually, he was allowed up the stairs and knocked on the door to Mary's suite. It was opened by Simon, whose uncompromising expression reminded Jack forcibly of their first-ever encounter at Pinchbeck Hall.

"Good evening, Mr. Picoult."

"Jack."

Simon allowed him to come into the room, where he found Mary sitting on the couch. She looked as beautiful as ever, but far more distant. Gathering his courage and his supposedly famous wits about him with surprising difficulty, Jack approached his adversary.

"My lady."

She stared directly into his eyes. "Mr. Smith."

He went down on one knee in front of her. "As I said, I have a confession to make. That isn't my real name. For years I thought it was, but eventually my father told me who I really was."

"And what was that? A liar, a cheat, and an opportunist?"

He let the insults flow over him. He certainly deserved them. "The son of the fourth son of the Earl of Storr."

"How convenient for you."

"It was something of a surprise, seeing as my father never had a penny to his name, and lived off his wits."

"You obviously take after him."

"If I wanted to survive, I really had no choice." He forced himself to meet her gaze again. "If I'd had any idea that the old earl had married, I would never have come to Pinchbeck Hall in disguise."

"So you say."

Despite her hostility, he persevered. "I was asked to find out what happened to a friend of mine, Lord Keyes. I only decided to visit Pinchbeck Hall because I was in the area."

She shrugged, dislodging her shawl and displaying her magnificent bosom. "Why are you telling me this?"

"I'm trying to explain how I came to meet you as my secretary and not myself."

"Even if what you say is the truth, it doesn't explain why you stole from us."

"I took the documents to Mr. McEwan. I believe he is the best person to advocate for you. I still believe that. You've met the man. He told me he will do anything in his power to make sure you receive what is owed to you."

"You still had no right to steal them."

"I tried asking, but you didn't trust me enough."

"And in that I was proved right, wasn't I?"

Jack sighed. "I put the documents into the right hands. Whether you agree or disagree as to my motives for doing so, you can hardly suggest I did it to benefit my own claim."

She waved an impatient hand at him. "Please get up, Mr. Lennox. I have no idea why you do anything, or the slightest interest in finding out. If I have a son, that child will inherit the title. I will do everything in my power to keep you away from making any financial decisions for my son or having any influence on him whatsoever."

"Why?"

She glared at him. "Because I don't trust you, and you are not respectable!"

"And you are?"

She looked over at Simon. "I told you he would use my past to discredit me and take control of my son and the earldom! Why else has he been snooping around at your mother's?"

Jack set his teeth. "Because George Mainwaring insists that he knows something that will discredit your claims. In truth, he is on his way to London to speak to Mr. McEwan about it right now." He met Mary's furious gaze head-on. "Now perhaps you could stop seeing me as your enemy, and concentrate on the man who really means you harm and always has!"

"You are both my enemies! You are the one who encouraged him to take me to court!"

Jack looked heavenward for more patience, which was rapidly deserting him. Mary Lennox was the only woman apart from Violet and his maternal grandmother who had the ability to make him lose his temper. "I came to apologize for deceiving you about my identity, and to warn you about George. If that is all you are willing to allow me to say, perhaps I should take my leave?" He bowed. "If you need me, I'm sure you know where I am."

He turned and left, dinner forgotten. Not that he would've been able to eat anything with his stomach all knotted up. At least he'd said his piece, apologized, and warned them. What else had he expected? An opportunity to throw himself at their feet and be welcomed back? They had each other. What need did they have for him? Apologizing to someone and expecting nothing in return was surprisingly hard.

"Jack."

He turned to find Simon exiting the hotel behind him.

"She's upset. She isn't thinking clearly."

Jack nodded at the doorman's offer to find him a hackney cab. "She has a right to be upset."

Simon hesitated beside him. "May I come and speak to you?"

"Without Mary? Will she approve?"

Simon sighed. "Don't be as difficult as she is being. Sometimes you two are so much alike I want to bang your heads together."

The hackney pulled up, and Jack got in. He looked back at Simon. "All right. You may come with me."

"Thank you."

He held out his hand. Simon took it, and he pulled him into the dark interior of the cab.

"I promise I won't take up much of your time."

* * *

Jack led Simon into Adam's office at the rear of the Sinners. He knelt to light the fire and turned to find Simon regarding the room with great interest.

"This is your office?"

"I don't have one. I have rooms upstairs. This belongs to an acquaintance of mine."

"It doesn't look like a brothel."

"Neither did your mother's."

Simon sat down beside the fire. "She has always enjoyed the element of surprise. It puts her clients off-balance and gives her an advantage."

"This place isn't actually a brothel at all. My friend manages his business interests from here."

"So why is it called the Sinners Club?"

Needing something to do, Jack poured them both a brandy and gave one to his companion. "I have no idea. You'd have to ask him. I'm just staying here until he gets back."

"I find that hard to believe."

Jack downed his brandy in one swig. "Of course. Being a liar, why would I ever speak a word that was true?"

Obviously he needed to work at not expecting any gratitude or understanding for apologizing. He sounded petulant and bitter.

"That's not what I meant." Simon looked down at his drink. "My mother said this place is for people who serve the government in unconventional ways."

"Your mother is very well informed for a brothel keeper in Whitechapel."

"She has an interesting clientele."

Jack retrieved the decanter of brandy and poured himself another full glass. "So what do you want?"

"You?"

Jack blinked at him. "What?"

Simon's smile was self-deprecating. "I've missed you."

"Your supposed sister is hell-bent on destroying me, and you *want* me? Does she know this?"

"I should imagine she does." He shrugged. "You're angrier than I've ever seen you before. I'd like to offer myself up to you for punishment."

"You're obviously deranged."

"When Mary calms down, she'll realize that George is indeed the biggest threat to her child. I'm certain she'll be calling on you to mend her fences, and maybe even apologize in her turn." His smile was wry. "Although the apology, I can't guarantee." He stood and approached Jack. "That's why I left her alone, you see. She needs time to consider her options."

Simon took the decanter out of Jack's unresisting hands and placed it back on the sideboard. He dropped down onto his knees and stared down at the floor.

"Please. Use me."

Even as he started to utter a denial, Jack's cock stirred and Simon leaned forward to lick the obvious swell. Jack's hand ached to cup Simon's head and press his face against his shaft.

"Not here."

"Where, then?"

"Upstairs in my rooms. And I'll be damned if I'll hurt you."

Simon rose. "Then just fuck me hard instead."

Jack led the way up to his apartment and unlocked the door. The maids had been in, made his bed, and tidied up his scattered possessions. A fire burned in the grate, warming the space.

"It needs more furniture." Jack shut the door and leaned back against it. "But as it is only temporary, it will do."

Simon looked back at him. "Don't you have a house of your own?"

"How could I? I've lived on the Continent for most of my

life. I didn't even know who my father's family were until I was an adult and I was the executor of his will."

"And then you had hopes of inheriting Pinchbeck Hall."

Jack shrugged. "It's just a house. I'm sure I'll find somewhere else to live." He forced a smile. "Perhaps this isn't a very good idea after all, Simon. I'm—"

His companion leaned in and kissed him hard on the mouth. "Please. Take me to bed and fuck me. Even if you don't let me come, I'll do anything you want."

God, Jack wanted to, wanted to bury himself deep in the other man and fuck him until he forgot everything but his own selfish needs. Simon kissed him again, his whole body now pressed against Jack's, their cocks aligned and creating a throbbing heat between them.

"Jack, please," Simon breathed against his lips. "Take me to bed." He grabbed for Jack's hand, and drew him toward the bedroom door and the invitation of the turned-down covers. As Jack watched, he stripped off his clothes, revealing his muscled arms and then the thick column of his wet shaft. When he was naked, he went down on his knees again.

Jack rubbed a hand over his throbbing erection. "Simon—"

"I know you don't feel the same for me as you do for Mary. But that's all right. I don't want to fall in love with you, or for us to be together as a couple." He licked his lips and hurried on. "I just want, I *need,* to be dominated sometimes. I crave it, and last time you . . ." He shuddered. "You made me feel alive."

"And Mary was furious."

Simon's quick smile surprised him. "Only because she is so protective of me. She's never quite understood that I love the things that most whores hate." He looked up at Jack. "And she wanted you herself, of course."

"Not anymore, especially if I fuck you now when we are at odds."

"She knew where I was going, and she knew what I wanted.

She didn't stop me. She wouldn't. Please, Jack." Simon wrapped a hand around his own cock. "Look how hard I am for you. Fuck me, and order me not to come. Make me wait."

Jack closed his eyes and leaned back against the door frame. Before he could protest, Simon's hands were on his breeches easing the buttons free and releasing his cock. He sucked it deep into his mouth until Jack groaned, his hands fisted at his sides as he tried not to touch or encourage the other man. But his body had other ideas, his hips thrust forward fucking Simon's willing mouth without rational thought. It was rough and hard, and so good he couldn't stop himself from enjoying it.

He shoved a hand into Simon's auburn hair and yanked his head back, almost yelping as the other man's teeth scraped his shaft.

"On the bed. On your knees."

Simon climbed onto the high bed and went down on hands and knees, his arse facing Jack, his face hidden. Jack slapped his buttock hard.

"Spread yourself wider. Show me where you want my cock."

"Here, sir."

Jack swirled his fingertip in his own pre-cum and rimmed the pucker of Simon's exposed arse hole before easing the tip of his finger inside.

"Yes, there, sir, *please*."

"When I'm ready." He pushed his finger in to the first knuckle and moved it back and forth. "You're tight. I need oil."

"No, sir, I can take you just as you are."

"It would be too rough. I'd hurt you." He shoved his finger deep making Simon's back arch. "I'd have to work my way so slowly inside you—you'd cry out and beg me to stop."

"I won't say a word. I swear."

"And what if you did?"

"You could gag me."

Jack's cock thickened even more. "I wouldn't do that. How would I know if you cried out again? I would, however, stop fucking you and punish you."

He withdrew his finger and Simon moaned. Grabbing Simon's ankles, Jack moved him nearer to the edge of the bed and stepped in, his cock held in his hand, the soaking wet crown sliding against his lover's taint and arse hole making his skin shine with pre-cum. He was wet enough to press inward, but it was still going to be rough. He inhaled slowly and pressed again, watched in fascination as he started to slide in through the tight ring, which widened and retreated just enough to allow his thick length passage.

Simon groaned. Jack reached around to pinch his nipple hard.

"Be quiet."

He braced his feet and angled his hips, setting up a slow rhythm of penetration that was both excruciating to maintain and yet highly arousing as his shaft was gripped so hard. Beneath him, Simon shivered, but made no sound. Jack stared down at his cock.

"Are you full?"

"No."

"Good, because I'm only halfway in." Jack wrapped a hand around Simon's hip until he could touch the wet tip of the other man's cock. He sank his finger into the thick wetness until he found the slit at the crown. "Don't come or I'll pull out. When I'm buried deep inside you, I'm going to fuck you so hard you'll scream."

He eased forward again and flicked his fingernail back and forth over Simon's slit until he bucked against Jack's hand. Each frantic twist of Simon's hips pushed Jack deeper until he was panting and straining against the need to come himself.

He bit Simon's ear. "When I send you back to Mary, my come will be inside you so deep that you'll smell of me for days. You'll be so sore that you won't be able to sit down without thinking about me behind you doing this."

His only answer was another jerk of Simon's hips that meant Jack was finally balls deep in the man, and unable to go any further. He took a deep breath and let go, thrusting hard until he could no longer see anything but the pleasure like a red haze over his gaze. He pumped even harder, ignoring the other man's desperate gasps as he was pushed into the mattress by the force of Jack's thrusts.

Jack climaxed, the sensation so exquisite that he had to close his eyes and just let it consume him. When he slowly pulled out, Simon winced. Jack pushed him over onto his back. His cock was still hard.

"Make yourself come while I watch," Jack said.

He settled on the side of the bed as Simon used both hands to jerk his shaft to a quick and obviously satisfying conclusion. His chest was heaving as if he'd run a mile and his eyes heavy-lidded with satisfaction. Jack leaned forward and scooped up some come on his finger and rubbed it against Simon's lips.

"You don't get to wash. You go back to Mary like this, so she'll know what you did with me." He sat back. "Maybe if you're lucky, she'll punish you too."

"Yes, sir."

"Are you sore?"

"Yes, thank you."

Jack got off the bed and did up his breeches. "It's not a sensation I've ever enjoyed."

"You've taken a man like that?"

"Once or twice." Jack headed for the door. "I'm going to have a bath. I suggest you leave as soon as you are dressed."

Simon sat up. "Did I not please you?"

"You pleased me." Jack sighed. "And I deserve to be shot for letting you."

"I told you it was what I wanted."

"But I didn't have to agree, did I? That's always been my problem. I have a total inability to say no to the more salacious elements of sex."

"I'm glad about that."

"Well, I don't think I am anymore. Good night, Simon."

Jack bowed and escaped to the bathroom, locking the door behind him. Escaped was the right word. He wanted to get back in that bed, take Simon in his arms, and sleep the night away. But he couldn't do that because, like everyone else, Simon understood that Jack was only useful for a quick fuck. He didn't even require payment like a whore. He meant nothing.

Jack tore off his clothes and managed to get the mysteriously produced hot water for the bath working without either scalding himself or blowing up the steam tank. He added cold water from the bucket by the side of the bath and got into the tub. After scrubbing himself nearly raw, he laid the soap on the floor beside the bath. Leaning his head back against the edge, he listened for sounds of his companion leaving, but heard none. If Simon were still there when Jack finished his bath, what would he do? Probably fuck him again.

Jack groaned, the sound echoing around the empty space. He was quite pathetic. Why had he given in to Simon's demands?

Mary raised her head as Simon crept into her bedchamber and hurried to sit up. She wrinkled her nose as he sat on the bed beside her.

"You smell of him."

"You knew I'd try and get him into bed regardless, didn't you? Otherwise you would never have let me go after him."

"I didn't think he'd fall for such an obvious ploy."

"He almost didn't. I had to literally push him up against the wall and take his cock out before he would consent to fuck me. I'm beginning to suspect that our Jack has standards after all."

He sighed. "If I hadn't enjoyed myself so much I would've been feeling terribly guilty. He isn't what you think, Mary. I do believe he is genuinely on our side."

She snorted, ignoring the guilt Simon's confession stirred in her heart. "If he took advantage of you, he's still out for himself."

"I'm not sure about that." Simon hesitated. "You know how it is when you are servicing so many clients that you become inured to anything?"

"What does that have to do with Jack Lennox?"

"It's almost as though he gave in to me because he thought that was all I wanted from him—as if I was paying *him* to use *me*. It was a peculiar sensation."

"And one that has no bearing on our current situation. Now, tell me what you discovered about the Sinners Club, and most especially the layout of Jack's rooms."

16

———————

Jack woke up with the sensation that something wasn't right. Sun streamed through his bedroom window and he was definitely alone. What had he been dreaming about to make him so uneasy? Was it the advent of George Mainwaring, or his general concerns about the way his life was going?

He groaned and sat up. What a time for his newly acquired conscience to assert itself—just when he needed every ounce of his charm and trickery to find a path through the current maze. What was it about Mary and Simon that made him *think* so much? He got out of bed and proceeded to shave and get dressed. A twinge from his cock reminded him of Simon. How was the other man feeling this morning? Sore, no doubt, and also facing the wrath of his "sister."

His hand stilled as his tied his cravat. He'd been dreaming about Mary Tudor. A Mary whose dreams of bearing a child had come to nothing, her pregnancy going on for so long that no one had dared to tell her, a queen, that her womb would never produce a living child. Was that what he secretly wanted for Mary Lennox? A nonexistent child?

Disgusted with himself, Jack strode downstairs and into the small breakfast room at the back of the house. An unknown woman sat eating at the table. Jack halted at the door and just remembered to bow.

"Good morning, ma'am."

She looked up at him, a piece of toast in her hand. He judged her to be in her late thirties or early forties. She wasn't a beauty by any standards, but her expression was full of such charm and intelligence that Jack immediately felt at ease.

"Good morning. You must be Jack Lennox. It is very kind of you to stay here while Adam is away."

He filled his plate from the silver dishes on the sideboard and took the seat opposite her. "I'm the one mostly benefiting from the arrangement. At the moment, I have no home."

She sighed and put down her cup. "I know. This whole business over the Storr title must be most upsetting for you."

"Hardly upsetting, ma'am. It's not as if I had years to assume the title would be mine. I only found out about it last year."

"But you still wanted it, didn't you?" She nodded. "I can understand why. With a father like yours, you were never allowed to put down roots. Everyone needs a home, even one like mine, which is in constant danger of falling into the sea."

"Excuse my curiosity, ma'am but who exactly are you?"

"I'm the Countess of Westbrook."

Jack went to rise, but she waved him back into his seat. "Please don't stand on ceremony with me. I consider this my home and you part of my family."

"You certainly seem to know a lot about me." He studied her for a long moment. "Did you know my father, then?"

"I met him once, I think, when he needed money."

"That sounds like my father. Did you give it to him?"

"I believe we did. He had you with him, you see, and I

couldn't bear to watch you running around in rags and without proper schooling."

"Did he say the money was for my benefit?" Jack laughed without humor. "I never saw any of it. I got my schooling wherever I could find it, and stole my clothes."

"As I said, you of all men deserve some security in your life." She sipped her tea. "As do the poor Picoults."

"You really do know everything about me, don't you?"

She smiled. "I ran this place for several years before Adam took over. I am rather good at finding things out."

"I'll wager you are. But you don't need to worry about the Picoults. I'm not going to stop Mary's child from inheriting the title."

"That is very noble of you." She hesitated. "And if you don't mind me saying, rather unexpected. You are known for your uncanny ability to get what you want."

"And this time I've met my match. Mary Lennox is determined to succeed. I admire her courage enormously, and I'm not going to do anything to stop her."

"Because you like her?"

Jack sighed. "As I'm sure you already know, she is very beautiful and I've shared her bed."

"Which usually means nothing to a man like you, who can have any woman he wants."

Jack looked down at his unfinished breakfast. "As I said, I admire her."

"She's rather like you, isn't she?" The countess rested her chin on her hand and studied Jack.

"That's what Simon said, although I don't quite see it myself." He ate a forkful of cold eggs and chewed determinedly. "She is more like my sister, Violet. More steady."

"Perhaps that's why you like her so much."

"I—" Jack glared at his companion. "Is there a point to this particular interrogation?"

"There is always a point. Perhaps you should reexamine what you think you know, and everything will become clear."

"It *is* clear. Mary married the old earl, and she is having his child. If that child is a boy, he will inherit the title. Everyone else, including George Mainwaring and me, will have our expectations dashed. If it is a girl, I will inherit and make damn sure Mary, her child, and her brother will never want for anything." He raised his eyebrows. "Unless you have something you wish to add?"

She blinked at him. "Only that I'd heard George is in London."

"So Mr. McEwan said." He exhaled loudly. "What does George think he knows that no one else does?"

"That's a very interesting question." She dabbed at her lips with her napkin and rose to her feet. "Don't get up. I just have to speak to Maddon about the entertainment arrangements for Friday night."

"Are you suggesting I need to talk to Mary again?"

"Who do you think is more likely to tell you the truth? Mary or George?"

"Neither of them," Jack grumbled. "How in God's name can I get Mary to trust me?"

A bell jangled in the distance, and the countess walked around the table to drop a kiss on the top of Jack's head.

"I'm sure you'll work it out very soon. I wish you much happiness."

"In what?"

Her smile was mischievous. "Your future, of course." She looked at the door. "Here is Maddon. I suspect you have a visitor."

Maddon bowed. "You are correct, my lady." He turned to Jack. "I've put the Dowager Countess of Storr in Mr. Adam's study, sir. She assured me that you would want to see her. If I'm mistaken, I can of course inform her that you are out."

Jack stared at Lady Westbrook. "Are you a witch as well as an intelligence gatherer?"

She shrugged. "Or I pay my sources very well indeed." She blew him a kiss. "Good luck, Jack. It was a pleasure to finally meet you again."

She walked away with Maddon, leaving Jack standing by his chair. He took a moment to compose himself and assimilate the new information from the countess before heading to Adam's study. Mary stood by the window in a black bonnet with high feathers and a smart brocaded pelisse. She raised her lace veil and presented him with her classic profile. To Jack's eyes, she'd never looked lovelier, or less approachable.

"Good morning, my lady."

She turned toward him. "I owe you an apology."

"For what?"

"For treating you like my enemy when you've always tried to help me."

"That's not what you said last night."

She grimaced. "I was angry with you for stealing the documents."

"Would you like to sit down?"

"No, I—" She took three hasty steps away from him, and whirled around again. "Good Lord, I am making such a mull of this. I'm not used to explaining myself to anyone, or apologizing."

"You sound remarkably like me."

"So Simon says." She hesitated. "Can you forgive me?"

"For wanting to protect your future?" Even as he said the words, he didn't believe she was being sincere. "If I was in your position, I'd ally myself with the least dangerous of my enemies and use him to fight off the greater threat."

She went still. "Is that truly what you think of me?"

He shrugged. "It's what I'd do, and as everyone keeps telling me, we *are* alike. Doesn't it make everything easier? You don't need to pretend that you like me, or want my forgiveness. I'm perfectly willing to stop George hurting either one of us. Once we've disposed of him, you can go back to being suspicious of my motives as well."

"That's rather mercenary."

He forced a laugh. "It's the truth, though, isn't it?"

She glided closer, her gaze fixed on his. "You don't trust me, do you?"

"If you tell me exactly why George thinks he can take you to court and win, I might be more inclined to do so."

"But I don't *know*."

"How convenient."

"I really don't." She sighed. "I've racked my brains to think what it might be."

"Then I suppose we'll have to wait to hear what he tells Mr. McEwan."

"Aren't you going to attempt to force the information out of George?"

"I'm not that much of a fool. Have you tried asking him?"

She shuddered. "I try not to get within ten feet of the man."

"It's a shame you can't put aside your scruples and take him to bed like you did me. I'd wager he'd be more forthcoming then." She blushed, which he found quite amusing. "Did you think I wouldn't realize? I'm not a fool, Mary."

"I know that now." She stepped close to him, and placed her hand against his chest. "In truth, I enjoyed bedding you more than I expected."

"How pleasant for you."

Her faint smile died. "Jack, what's wrong?"

He removed her hand. "As I said, you don't need to try and seduce me now. Simon managed it last night. Isn't that enough?"

"I wasn't—"

"Perhaps you weren't, but it is as natural as breathing to you, isn't it?"

"Because I'm a whore?"

"Because you've learned to get what you want using any gift you possess. I understand because I'm the same. How do you think I survived my father's neglect when I was young? I fucked anything. I *excelled* at it. With such talents, it seemed a shame to waste them as I grew to adulthood."

Her eyes darkened and she reached for him again. "Jack—"

He caught her chin in his fingers in a hard grip. "Do you want me to show you? Is that the only way you will feel secure, if you have me on my back?"

She didn't pull away, and he kissed her, his tongue possessing her mouth until she kissed him back and leaned into him, the swell of her belly against his flat stomach and cock. He dragged his mouth away and she moaned his name.

"Do you want me, Mary? Right here, where anyone might see us? When you're likely to give birth at any second?"

"Do you despise me for that? That I still want you?"

"I've noticed most females can't bear a male near them when they're about to pup."

"I'm not a dog!" She swallowed hard. "In fact I've been told that sometimes making love with a man can send a woman into labor."

"Is that what your new doctor advised? Find a cooperative man to service your needs?" He gently set her away from him. "Don't assume I'm willing anymore. I'm as tired of being used as you probably are."

She wiped a hand across her trembling lips. "Then I'll leave."

"Perhaps that would be best." He retreated behind his desk. "I will support you, my lady, but not by offering you my stud services."

She raised her chin. "Then we are in agreement."

She swept out. Jack covered his head with his hands and

groaned. He was a fool. She gave him so much more than passing physical pleasure. He'd never known anybody like her before in his life. She challenged him on so many levels, made him lose his temper, made him laugh, made him want to simply be with her to see what she would come up with next.

And he'd sent her away. God, he hated becoming emotional about anything. It would be far more productive to think about other aspects of the situation. He slowly raised his head and rang the bell. While he waited, he wrote a hasty note and blew on the ink.

Maddon appeared at the door. "Yes, sir?"

"I need some information from the staff at Grillons Hotel."

"Private information, sir?"

"Yes, I want the Picoult suite watched, and all movements reported back to me. I also want someone you trust implicitly to speak to the chambermaid who is attending Lady Storr." He handed over the note with a small bag of gold. "And I need this information as quickly as possible."

Mary cast off her bonnet, and tossed it onto the nearest chair.

"You were right."

"About what?" Simon looked up from his newspaper.

"About Jack. He was *different*."

"Maybe it's because we're finally seeing *him* instead of Jack Smith."

"I don't think it's that simple. He seems to have lost his joy."

"His *joy?* What on earth does that mean?"

She sat opposite him. "Before, it felt like a dangerous but exciting game between us. Now it's turned deathly serious and he's no longer willing to be amused or charmed by us."

"Didn't he accept your apology?"

"He did, but he made no secret of the fact that he still doesn't trust me, and that he isn't willing to be used anymore."

"I told you so."

She bit her lip. "It was quite dreadful."

"Why? You haven't told him the truth, and you have used him. If he can accept that and is still willing to help you, then what's wrong? You've got exactly what you wanted."

"But it *hurt*." She sank down onto the nearest chair. "And I hate myself for it. I felt as if I'd destroyed something vital in him, taken something precious and ruined it. . . ." She raised her head. "I wanted to tell him everything."

Simon came across and took her hands in his. "It's all right, love."

"No, it isn't because he's right. I am a liar and a cheat, and I can't tell him because I can't bear to see the look of disgust on his face."

"Oh dear, you really do care about him, don't you?"

She swiped at the tears rolling down her cheeks. "It serves me right, doesn't it? The only man I've ever wanted is the one I have to deceive."

Much later that evening, Jack took the packet from Maddon and settled back to read the enclosed notes. He couldn't fault the speed and efficiency of the man. It appeared that the chambermaid had been willing not only to talk at length, but also to speculate wildly on the doings of the countess and her brother, and every guest they'd brought up to the suite.

It took some time to get used to the chambermaid's preference for going off at tangents and circling around issues, but eventually he managed it. Visitors to the suite were few, one notable absence being any appearance of the supposed physician Mary had intended to consult—a man who would definitely have come to the countess rather than the other way around. The maid speculated about that, and about the countess's pregnancy being less advanced than she should've been considering how long gossip said her husband had been dead.

"So the countess doesn't allow her maid to bathe her, and it is Mr. Picoult who laces her into her corset every morning?" Jack murmured. "Has she been sewn into her undergarments for the winter?"

He lowered the pages and stared blindly at the fire. There was a far simpler explanation. One that made a mockery of every single thing Mary Lennox had ever told him.

There was no child.

Damn her.

Jack realized he'd crumpled the letter up in his fist. He painstakingly smoothed it out and made himself finish reading. There was little else of importance, but he'd certainly gained a new perspective on the matter, just as Lady Westbrook had hinted.

He wanted to strangle Mary with his bare hands.

He wanted—

He closed his eyes. This was why he didn't get involved with anyone. Why hadn't she trusted him? It hurt too much, and this time he'd known that going in, known that she was too much like him, too dangerous. . . .

And now he had the ability to destroy her.

Part of him wanted that. Shouldn't she suffer for hurting him, for letting him down in some unfathomable way that he didn't even want to think about because it was too damn painful? He drew in a deep, slow breath. He had to think. Using his intelligence had always allowed him to distance himself both from the unsettling horrors of war and the emotions of others.

It was, after all, the only thing he had left.

Mary Lennox's past held the key to this puzzle. It was useless asking George for help, so he'd have to rely on other sources. If he knew what George knew, he was suddenly in a position of power.

He rang the bell for Maddon, who never seemed to sleep.

"Do you have the direction of a Mr. Nicodemus Theale?"

"I believe I do, sir."

"Would you be so good as to send an urgent message, and ask him to visit me here at his earliest opportunity?"

"Certainly, sir."

He'd also ask Mr. McEwan to finally grant George the interview he'd been seeking so desperately, and make sure he was there to overhear every word. Whatever happened, it appeared that he would inherit the title of Earl of Storr whether the Picoults liked it or not. Mary and Simon would be his pensioners, and he would determine their fate. He was ashamed to say he found some bitter satisfaction in that.

Grabbing the brandy decanter from the sideboard, Jack made his way up to bed. On Friday, the Indian dance troupe was performing at the Sinners. He'd make damn sure that he was awake for that. It seemed the perfect opportunity to forget everything except what he was good at. Anonymous sex with strangers.

He drank straight out of the decanter and toasted his reflection in the mirror. He looked dangerous and wild, quite like his old self. But would that illusion be enough to allow him to survive?

Mary pulled on her oldest gown and grabbed a dark cloak and a shawl. It was no use; she had to speak to Jack. Had to explain what she'd done, and why, before someone else did it for her. Perhaps Jasper had confided in George at the end. They had been alone together for a little while. As the original idea had been Jasper's, why would he then betray her and Simon? It made no sense.

She sneaked out of the suite without waking Simon, and used the backstairs to bring her out at the rear of the hotel. A cold wind blew through the narrow passageway that led down to the mews and the lesser-used cobbled alleyways that ran behind the majestic London squares. She had an excellent sense of direction and was able to plot a more exact course to the Sinners Club than by following the main streets.

The stairs leading down to the basement and kitchen of the house were dark, but faint light shone through the barred lower windows. Mary hesitated. Should she attempt to enter the place without being seen? Thanks to Simon and his mother, she knew the internal layout of the building from top to bottom. Where was Jack likely to be at this hour? She turned to look up at the topmost windows but none of them were lit.

As she took a step toward the stairs, a hand grasped her elbow in a firm grip.

"Will you come with me, please, miss?"

She tried to pull away, but the unknown man who held her simply tightened his hold.

"Who are you?"

"I'm employed to keep the premises safe and secure."

"Then unhand me! I have a perfect right to be here."

"We'll let the owner decide that." He turned her toward the front of the house, and Mary had no choice but to follow him. Security at the Sinners Club was obviously much better than it appeared. The butler who had admitted her earlier appeared in the hall and bowed.

"Do you wish to see Mr. Lennox, my lady? I will inquire if he is still receiving visitors."

"Thank you." Mary tried to look as if she always paid calls in the middle of the night without thought to her pregnant state or her consequence.

"May I suggest you wait for him in his office?"

She'd already heard the sound of voices and laughter behind some of the closed doors, and was more than willing to agree.

"That would be perfect."

He escorted her down the hallway and left her in the study. The remains of a fire in the grate drew her, and she knelt down to warm her cold hands and feet. Her notion of finding Jack suddenly seemed as ridiculous as her certainty about her original plan to successfully deceive him.

The door opened again and she looked up.

"Mr. Lennox says he will see you if you wish to come upstairs."

Mary nodded, and followed the butler up two flights of stairs to a landing, which contained three doors. He knocked on the first one, and opened it wide.

"Your visitor, Mr. Lennox."

Was there a note of censure, or anxiety in the butler's voice? Mary glanced up as she murmured her thanks and went past him. Perhaps he didn't approve of late-night visitors. He didn't follow her in, just closed the door quietly behind her.

"My lady."

Jack sat sprawled by the fire, an almost empty decanter of brandy in his hand. He'd shed his clothes and wore only a robe fastened with a tie at his waist. The dark blue silk only seemed to emphasize the glittering sapphire of his remarkable eyes.

"What do you want?"

His smile was brilliant as he carefully put down the decanter, his voice light.

She leaned against the door, her hands grasped together in the small of her back.

"I had to tell you something."

"At this hour? It must have been very important." He studied her, his gaze moving from her face, down to her bosom, and back again in an insulting way that made her stiffen. "Let me guess, you decided that you really did need to be fucked, and I was the obvious choice because God knows I'll fuck anything that moves."

"Are you drunk?"

He winked at her. "Don't worry, I'll still be able to perform to your satisfaction."

"I didn't come here for that."

"I don't think I believe you."

He slowly stood up and came toward her, the hardness of his expression so much at odds with his charming smile that she found herself wishing she could disappear through the solid oak door.

She raised her chin and met his gaze. "You asked me not to use you like that. I believe I agreed."

"And when have you ever meant anything that comes out of your lying little mouth?"

She held on to her composure with all her strength. "I assume you've been talking to George. What did he tell you? Am I not to be allowed the privilege of defending myself? I thought we were allies."

"I haven't seen George."

"Then what's wrong?"

He grinned at her. "Whatever could possibly be wrong? I'm merely a little drunk. Does it offend you?"

Dammit, he might be smiling, but there was nothing pleasant behind it. How could she look into his face and have no idea what he was thinking? How could she tell him what she needed to?

"I have a confession to make."

"Dear, dear, another one?"

"I lied to you about something very important."

He reached forward and carefully placed his hand on her belly. The words froze in her throat.

"I know. Is that why you came back to London? To ask Mrs. Picoult to find you an abandoned pauper brat from the gutter to pass off as the earl's heir?"

"No, I never intended to—"

He moved his hand and covered her mouth. "I don't want to hear any more of your lies. You did it because you are an ambitious, grasping woman who used every weapon in her arsenal to get what she wanted."

She tried to shake her head, but he didn't stop.

"And here's the most farcical part. If you'd only been honest with me, I would've understood. In your place I'd probably have done the same thing, but you couldn't trust me, could you?" He took his hand away and stepped back. "Now get out."

Her legs were trembling and it was difficult to breathe. "That's not why I did it, if you will only let me explain." Her breath hitched as he reached past her, and wrenched open the door.

"Get out. My solicitor will contact you when necessary."

Her temper flared. "Why won't you listen to me!"

"Why should I?" His blue gaze was unflinching. "I try to avoid making the same mistakes, and you and your brother were definitely a mistake. My father denied me my birthright, and you have tried to do exactly the same. I thought—" He stopped and stared down at the floor before looking up and smiling. "It doesn't matter now, does it?"

"What?" She tried desperately to reach him, but he'd retreated behind his charming icy façade. "That if circumstances had been different, we might have come to care for each other? That I've come to care for *you*?"

She saw it then, the desolation behind the flippancy and reached out her hand. "Jack, please . . ."

He shook his head, and shut the door in her face. She slammed her hand against the oak but it didn't move. For a moment, she rested her cheek against the wood and simply breathed. He didn't understand, and he didn't want to understand. She'd taken something from him that she'd lost herself—her place in society, her home, and her parents. Having experienced it, why hadn't she realized the enormity of that deception for Jack? She dashed away a tear. In her own desperate need to stay at Pinchbeck Hall, she'd deprived him of a home.

How would he ever find it in his heart to forgive her that?

17

"Mr. Nicodemus Theale to see you, sir."

Jack raised his aching head and nodded at Maddon. "Please show him in."

Maddon stepped aside to reveal a man of medium height with black curly hair and dark eyes, dressed in the modest garb of a city dweller. He was younger than Jack had anticipated and brimmed with quiet confidence.

"Mr. Theale. Please sit down."

"A pleasure, Mr. Lennox." His visitor sat and took out a notebook from his capacious pocket. "I assume you wish to know how I'm getting along with my investigation into Mary Lennox?"

"I'm not sure if I do."

Mr. Theale went still. "You don't wish me to continue?"

Jack stared at him. Did he? Part of him wanted nothing to do with Mary and her past. Common sense told him he should know everything possible about his enemy. If he were protected against her lies, she would lose the power to hurt him.

He sighed. "Please excuse my indecision. I would be very interested in hearing what you've discovered."

Mr. Theale opened his notebook. "She was not an easy woman to find, Mr. Lennox. I initially focused on identifying her mother, Catherine, first by scanning records of the deceased in the appropriate year. I found nothing."

"I was told she was buried in a paupers' mass grave."

"I have to assume that information is correct. After failing to discover her through those means, I turned my attention to financial matters, records of houses being bought and sold, fortunes won and lost, disasters on the exchange."

"What relevance would such things have to Mary and her mother?"

"They were thrown out on the street, Mr. Lennox, and forced to seek shelter in a brothel. That indicates a catastrophe of quite epic proportions."

Despite himself, Jack sat forward. "I suppose it does. Did you find anything?"

"Eventually, I did." He flipped over a page. "A Mrs. Catherine Miller and her daughter, Mary, were evicted from their house in Hans Town due to arrears in the rent."

"Did Mrs. Miller have a husband?"

"That still remains rather unclear. Her neighbors believed that she was a widow. She claimed to have been married to a captain in the Hussars who died in India."

"I assume there is no record of him?"

"There is not. I did however, find out that the rent was paid by another man."

"Her protector?"

"It would appear so. That man died suddenly that same year without providing for Mrs. Miller or her child. Eventually, when the rent stopped being paid, the house was repossessed by the family lawyers, the contents sold off, and Catherine and her child deposited on the streets."

Despite himself, Jack could only imagine how terrifying that had been for the two unprotected females. "Did Mrs. Miller not ask for help from her own family?"

"I believe they disowned her years ago. If she did contact them, they ignored her plight."

"Leading to her ending up in a brothel with her young daughter," Jack murmured. "I assume that the gentleman who paid the bills was married?"

Mr. Theale consulted his notes. "I don't know that yet."

"Titled?"

"I'm not sure. He used the name Desmond Norris. I'm currently trying to find out who exactly he is, and whether anyone in his family was aware of him keeping a mistress and having an illegitimate child."

"You believe Mary is his child?"

"He bought the house two years before her birth and significantly increased the monthly sum he paid to Catherine after she delivered the child."

"Which he wouldn't have done if he'd believed she'd cuckolded him."

"Yes." There was a great deal of sympathy on Mr. Theale's face. "It is astounding how many men never think to make a will to include their permanent mistresses or bastard children."

"I don't think they *want* to acknowledge such things, let alone put them in their wills for their family to see."

"I suppose that's true." Mr. Theale sighed. "I'll have the information about Mary's father in the next day or so. From what I understand from talking to the neighbors and former staff, Mary had no idea that her parents weren't married, and was a happy and contented child."

"Until she was thrown out on the street." Jack studied his tightly laced fingers. "How did they end up at the Picoults? Was it blind chance?"

"I believe Catherine Miller knew Mrs. Audrey Picoult when she was employed as a nursemaid for Mary. Mrs. Miller was disappointed when Audrey left, and attempted to keep in touch with her despite her lover's disapproval."

"Did Mrs. Miller intend to prostitute herself?"

"One must assume so, although I understand that she was already rather fragile. I believe Mary eventually stepped in to supplement their income."

"She must have been terrified."

"From all I've learned about Mary Lennox, sir, she is an extremely tenacious woman."

"She certainly is."

"Of course, you've met her, haven't you?"

"Many times. She is as beautiful as she is brave." He pushed the image of her face away. "Do you have any idea how she met Jasper, the Earl of Storr?"

"I believe the earl patronized Mrs. Picoult's brothel."

"I wonder why he didn't just set up a mistress?"

"I believe the earl's tastes were rather specific, sir."

Jack swallowed hard. "So he invited Mary and Simon Picoult to live with him at Pinchbeck Hall."

"That's correct. Mary was fourteen, and Simon two years older. Pinchbeck Hall has been their home since then."

No wonder she was reluctant to give it up. Despite the price she'd had to pay, it had at least got her out of the brothel and back into the more leisurely existence she had assumed would be hers for the rest of her life. He could understand that after more than ten years of putting up with the elderly earl, she'd felt as if she deserved some form of compensation. But why hadn't marriage been enough? Why had she tried to pretend she carried the next heir?

"Do you wish me to continue my search for the name of Mary's real father, Mr. Lennox?"

Jack forced his attention back to the patiently waiting Mr. Theale. "Yes, I'd like that information, please, and as soon as possible."

"Then I'll take my leave of you." Mr. Theale rose and bowed. "Good day, Mr. Lennox."

"Good day, and thank you, Mr. Theale."

Jack remained in his chair and thought through Mr. Theale's information. He'd been right that Mary wasn't born in a brothel. She'd been summarily dispossessed both of her identity and her social status by the demise of her mother's protector. It was interesting that he'd grown up thinking he had nothing and was a nobody, while she'd been dreaming of her Season. He had to admit that his change in prospects had been remarkably easier to deal with than hers must have been.

Damnation, if he wasn't careful he'd be feeling sorry for her again, and that would never do.

There was a knock on the door and Maddon looked in, his expression concerned. "I'm sorry to bother you again, sir, but there is a Mr. Delornay here to see you."

"That's quite all right. Please ask him to come in."

Jack stood and came around the desk to shake hands with Christian Delornay, who was his usual beautiful, blond self. Since his marriage, he had even been known to smile occasionally, and was doing so now at Jack.

"It is delightful to see you again. I apologize for being unavailable in your hour of need."

Jack waved the other man to a seat. "You are here now, and that is all that matters. I'm trying to find out about a family by the name of Picoult."

Christian sat and crossed one elegant leg over the other. "So I heard. May I ask why?"

"Does it matter?"

"It might."

Jack waited but Christian didn't say anything else. That wasn't a surprise; he wasn't known for his open and confidential nature.

"Can I rely on your silence in this matter?"

"I give you my word that nothing you say to me will be repeated—except to my wife, from whom I am not allowed to keep secrets."

Jack nodded. "I met Simon and Mary Picoult at Pinchbeck Hall in Lincolnshire. I was rather surprised to hear that the late Earl of Storr had married Mary and she was expecting his posthumous child."

"Storr is the title you expected to inherit?" Christian whistled. "Oh dear."

"When I attempted to discover more about them, I found that local opinion insisted Mary had been the earl's mistress for many years, and that she had forced the elderly sick man to marry her. The man who thought he had a chance of inheriting the title, George Mainwaring, was particularly violent in his hatred of Mary and eager to take her to court to challenge her marriage, and her right to any inheritance in the earl's new will."

"So, they are a pair of charming tricksters. Why didn't you simply pay them off and send them on their way?"

"Because when I investigated further I discovered the marriage appeared to be legal and Mary was increasing."

"What is the connection with the Picoult brothel?"

"Mary and her mother rented a room at the brothel after they were thrown out of their home. At first, Mary claimed that she and Simon were brother and sister, and gossip suggested the child was his, and not the earl's."

"And were they lovers?"

"Yes."

Christian sat back and studied Jack. "I still don't understand why you allowed this charade to continue for so long. You're not the kind of man who hesitates to act; in fact, you relish it."

"I liked them."

Christian raised his eyebrows. "What in God's name does

that have to do with anything? They were trying to steal your inheritance!"

"The earl married Mary. In my eyes that made her claim just as legitimate as mine. If her child had proven to be a boy, he should've inherited the title."

"Who'd have thought that you of all people had such a strong moral compass, Jack?" Christian marveled.

Jack glared at him. "Having been denied knowledge of my own inheritance for most of my life, do you really think I could deprive someone else of theirs?"

"Obviously not. But I still don't see how any information about the Picoult brothel can help you now—unless you've changed your mind and wish to discredit the pair after all?"

"I simply wish to know the truth. Why would the Earl of Storr choose to patronize a cheap brothel in Whitechapel?"

"Oh, Mrs. Picoult's isn't cheap." Christian's smile had disappeared. "Her particular services are much in demand."

"Because she provides young whores, the younger the better?"

"She does take them in young, but it is more than that. She caters to a particular type of client who craves unusual sex."

"You do all that in the pleasure house, so why didn't the earl come to you?"

"Because we only offer such services on a regular Tuesday night."

"Tuesday?" Jack frowned.

"Tuesday nights are when our clients gain the freedom to dress as they please and have the sex that they want with both men and women."

"And Mrs. Picoult offers that all the time?"

"As well as other role-playing activities. I believe she has a schoolroom there for those who wish to re-create their pasts in a more highly erotic way. Her clientele is almost exclusively male."

"Mary Lennox was fourteen when she first started working for that woman. She even prostituted her own son."

"I can't say I'm surprised. It is a mainly male environment. He was probably quite in demand. I understand that it can get quite rough there, although Mrs. Picoult isn't the kind of woman to allow things to get out of control. I wonder where the late earl's tastes lay?"

Jack went cold as he remembered what he'd done to Simon, and Mary's obvious concern. Had he been abused at the brothel? Had Jack forced him back into re-creating sexual situations he'd hated?

"From your stricken expression I have to assume that you are more involved with your opponents than you would like."

"Why didn't Mrs. Picoult tell me any of this when I asked her?"

"Why would she? The services she offers have to be kept quiet, you know that. Maybe she thought she was protecting her son and Mary Lennox." Christian stood up. "If the earl did buy Mary's exclusive services from the brothel, he probably did her a favor. She wouldn't have survived long and her spirit would've been broken in such a masculine place. I'm sure Mrs. Picoult promoted the match."

"She probably made a fortune out of it and, don't forget, she lost her son's earnings too."

"That's true. I'm surprised she let him go at all."

"I suspect Mary insisted on it." Jack rose, too, and shook Christian's hand. "Thank you for your help. I suppose I really will have to go back and speak to Mrs. Picoult again."

"Why?"

"To make sure I'm not missing anything."

"For the case you intend to bring against Mary?"

"I'm not going to do that."

"Then you are a better man than I am. If someone attempted

to deprive me of my birthright, I'd be damned if I'd stand aside and let them."

"They have nowhere else to go, and as the late earl's widow, Mary should receive her due from his will."

Christian shook his head. "There is more to this than you are letting on. Is Mary Lennox as beautiful as I've heard?"

"She is a diamond of the first water."

"So are you."

"We certainly make a pretty couple. But it isn't that. I—" He hesitated. "I like her."

"And her 'brother'?" At Jack's nod, Christian patted his shoulder. "Then I'll offer you my felicitations now. If you still like her despite everything she's tried to do to you then you are well and truly caught, my friend."

"Don't be ridiculous. I'll do my duty by her and Simon and that's it."

Christian's expression sobered. "If they survived Mrs. Picoult's, I have to agree that they deserve anything you are prepared to give them."

"Is it really that bad?"

"If you do decide to go back to see her, ask her to give you a tour." Christian shuddered. "She makes some of the activities on our top floor appear quite tame."

Mary sighed and stared out of the window at the rain-drenched street below.

"What's wrong?"

She turned to Simon, who was finishing his breakfast at the table.

"I tried to talk to Jack again last night."

His expression darkened. "*What?*"

"When you were asleep, now don't scold me. I think I just made things worse." She swallowed hard. "He already knew I wasn't pregnant."

"Who told him?"

"He claimed he'd worked it out himself."

"It's possible. He's a very intelligent man."

"I wondered if that was what George knew, but Jack said he hadn't even spoken to him yet."

"Was he angry?"

"He was absolutely furious!" She huddled deeper into her shawl. "I can't say I blame him."

"Neither can I, love."

"I never thought it would turn out like this! In the beginning there was just George to deceive, and I thought—"

"You thought it would be easy. Everyone makes a mistake once in a while." He hesitated. "Is it time for us to pack our bags and be off?"

"We can't do that until Mr. McEwan safeguards our interests."

"Is Jack going to uphold those bequests? If he is furious with you, perhaps he'll take us to court and tie up your allowance for years while we slowly starve to death."

"He said that he would communicate with us through his solicitors."

"Which only means that he doesn't want to speak to either of us face-to-face ever again." Simon sighed. "It's a damn shame."

"Oh, I think he'd speak to you. It's me he blames, and rightly so." She climbed off the window seat. "I can't bear to sit here worrying about what he will or will not do. Shall we go and see Mr. McEwan and ask how matters stand?"

Simon studied her critically. "You look more like your old self. Did you take off the padding?"

"Yes, I'm tired of pretending. We'll tell Mr. McEwan that the physician I saw convinced me it was a phantom pregnancy, and that after bleeding the bad humors out, I was fully recovered."

"I'm glad you're not pretending anymore."

She met his gaze. "So am I. Now let's go and see Mr. McEwan and find out if Jack truly does mean to abandon us."

"So you're back."

Jack bowed. "I am, but as I mentioned in my note, this time in my true identity as the Honorable John Lennox, heir to the Earl of Storr."

They were both seated in her tawdry crimson velvet office. Mrs. Picoult raised her eyebrows. "I didn't think you'd have the nerve."

"I have very little choice. Do you know a man named George Mainwaring?"

"Only by reputation. Simon and Mary have mentioned him in their correspondence over the years as a most unpleasant individual, but I haven't met the man."

"He isn't one of your clients here?"

"No."

"But the late Earl of Storr was?"

She nodded.

"I know that Mary came here with her mother, Catherine Miller, and that she isn't a Picoult by birth. I also know that her father was a gentleman who kept Catherine as his mistress, and supported his child until his sudden death."

"So you say."

"George Mainwaring seems to think he knows something more about Mary and Simon's relationship with the earl. If he does know something, he could damage Mary's chance of receiving anything in the late earl's will and keep her in court for years fighting over the title."

"Only if she doesn't have a son."

Jack sat back. "Mrs. Picoult, she has no chance of having a son. She isn't pregnant."

"What makes you say that?"

"She told me."

Silence greeted his answer. "So you will be the next earl."

"I believe so." Jack held her wary gaze. "I swear that I intend to give Mary exactly what she is entitled to from that will as befits a Dowager Countess of Storr."

"Why?"

He let his gaze stray around the room. "Because she survived this."

Mrs. Picoult smiled. "This isn't so bad."

"That's not what I've heard."

"It's better than whoring on the streets, which was where Mary and her mother would've ended up if I hadn't taken them in. Even though this is a house that specializes in pain, I make sure that none of the damage inflicted on my employees is permanent."

"How good of you."

"You seem to think I am a monster, Mr. Lennox. All of my employees work for me because they choose to. I force none of them to stay, and they are well paid for their efforts." She hesitated. "In my particular line of business there are always those who prefer pleasure to be painful, and that's what I cater to almost exclusively here. If my employees couldn't enjoy that too, they wouldn't stay."

His skepticism must have shown in his face as she rose to her feet. "Come with me." She handed him a black mask. "It will disguise you sufficiently for our tour."

She led him up a flight of stairs and into a large room at the front of the house that spanned the building. It was set up to resemble a classroom with rows of desks and chairs and a board at the front for writing on. Jack leaned against the back wall to survey the room. The current participants could hardly be described as children.

Four grown men sat at the front, diligently writing something on their slates while a voluptuous woman dressed in a tight black, high-necked gown patrolled the front of the room, a long birch cane swishing back and forth in her hand.

"Come on, who has the answer?"

One of the men raised his hand and the woman went over to him.

"You have it wrong." She pointed at the teacher's desk and the man hurried over, placed both hands on the edge and bent over presenting his arse. "Six strokes."

Jack watched in fascination as the woman expertly whipped the man's arse. When he was finally permitted to stand up, the thick bulge of his erection pushed against the placket of his breeches.

The teacher prodded the man's cock with the end of her cane.

"What is the meaning of this, Claude?"

His reply was inaudible. The teacher's was not.

"Unbutton your breeches!"

Claude fumbled to obey, releasing his cock with a groan.

"Do you think your teacher wants to see that? Do you imagine she wants to wrap her hand around you and suck you dry?"

Claude shook his head.

"You are a filthy little boy, aren't you?"

"Yes, miss."

"And what do we do to filthy little boys who show their cocks to their teachers?" The other men all raised their hands, but she ignored them. "We spank them, don't we? Pull down your breeches, sit on the desk and hold that *thing* away from your stomach."

Claude moaned something but did as he was told. The teacher positioned herself slightly to the side of him so that the rest of the men could see clearly, drew back her hand, and slapped Claude's cock hard.

Jack winced and fought an impulse to cup himself.

The other members of the class watched avidly as the teacher continued to slap Claude's cock. By the fourth stroke he was gasping and wriggling, by the sixth he was coming in thick jerking waves.

The teacher moved closer to inspect his now flaccid shaft and prodded it with her cane. "Who would like to help Claude?"

All the other men's hands shot up again. The teacher's smile was gracious. "As you've all been so good, perhaps you could form a line and take turns licking Claude clean until the task is complete." She frowned at Claude. "And you must remain quiet and not give into your animalistic urges again tonight, or I will have to punish you further."

Mrs. Picoult touched Jack's arm and nodded at the door. He was more than willing to follow her out onto the landing.

"As you see, my customers' requirements are very specific."

"Is everything here like that?"

"Most of it. We have rooms where a man can be tied up and fucked by anyone who cares to, rooms where men dress as women and are treated as such, rooms where—"

"So how did Mary survive in this male environment?"

"Some men still like to fuck both sexes, you know that. I understand that you are one of them."

"And what did the Earl of Storr like?"

Her smile was derisive. "He tried everything I had to offer him."

"Until he made his choice, and negotiated with you to get what he wanted."

She shrugged. "I am a businesswoman, Mr. Lennox. I knew that Simon and Mary would have a much better life at Pinchbeck Hall than they would here."

"How altruistic of you."

"Do you think I forced them?" Her smile was brief. "They were quite willing to go, I swear it, particularly Mary."

Jack looked around the darkened hallway. "To escape this? I can almost understand it. Is there anything else you are prepared to tell me, or have I exhausted your goodwill?"

"There is one more room you might wish to see. It is the one Mary and Simon occupied before they left."

"They shared a room?"

"Space is at a premium in a brothel, Mr. Lennox, and it kept them both safe."

"Until the Earl of Storr came along."

She headed up another set of stairs. "As we have already discussed, that is a matter of opinion."

They kept climbing until they reached the very top of the house, where the ceilings sloped inward and the rooms were usually set aside for servants. Jack had to duck his head to get through the doorway Mrs. Picoult opened. He found himself in a small chamber with one bed and a chest of drawers with a broken leg, which leaned against the wall. A thin patchwork quilt covered the straw mattress.

"Mary's mother used to rent the room next to this as well."

"Did she ever tell you who her protector was?"

"A Mr. Norris, I believe. I never met him." Mrs. Picoult gestured at the window. "Open the shutters if you need more light to see."

Jack automatically stepped forward, only turning at the last minute as Mrs. Picoult whisked herself out of the room and was replaced by her son.

"Jack."

"What do you want?"

"To speak to you? My mother let me know you were coming here tonight."

Jack smiled. "If you've come to plead Mary's case, don't bother. She tried to outwit me, and she almost succeeded. I can only applaud such ingenuity and cold-blooded disregard for the claims of others."

Simon winced. "Ouch, she did hurt you, didn't she?"

"It's no longer important. I've already assured her that I'm not a vindictive man. I'm quite prepared to deal with her through my solicitor."

"She's very upset, you know."

"Which is not my concern, and hardly surprising when her plans have been foiled." He walked up to Simon. "Will you get out of the way?"

"I don't think I can."

Jack's hand shot out and closed around Simon's throat. "Move."

"If you think violence is going to scare me away, Jack, you're wrong. There's something I want to explain to you."

"As I said, I don't care about that."

Simon held his gaze. "This isn't about Mary, it's about me." He licked his lips. "I grew up here, Jack. You might not believe it, but my mother tried to shield me from what went on in this house for years. I found out by peeping through the doors and was aroused by what I was seeing, men on their knees being whipped, being fucked by other men, being owned. . . ." He sighed. "I wanted that. I knew it was wrong, but I still wanted it. When my mother found out I'd been spying on her clients, she wasn't pleased with me. When she realized I craved such excesses myself, she offered me a job here."

"And you took it?"

"As I said, it was what I wanted." He swallowed hard. "That's when I met the Earl of Storr."

Jack walked away and leaned back against the windowsill. "You met him first? Am I to assume he fucked you both?"

Simon met his gaze steadily. "No, he fucked me in every filthy way he could think of. He liked Mary to watch and—hand him whatever he requested. Sometimes he would let her suck my cock, or let me fuck her, but that was quite rare. He preferred to use me himself."

Jack suddenly remembered all the erotic implements in Simon's room, and Mary's familiarity with them. "He gave you that book I found under your pillow."

"He was determined that we would attempt every single sexual position in that blasted book. The bastard almost killed me a couple of times by tying me up too tight, or for too long, or gagging me until I almost passed out." He shrugged. "Not that I'm complaining. For people like me, those things just make everything better."

"So, who did the earl really want when he bought you both?"

Simon shrugged. "Who knows? He continued to fuck me until he became too ill to wield a crop." He bit his lip. "In the last year or so, he became less careful, and used me too hard. When he finally stopped, I was quite relieved."

"And I came along and put you right back in that hell."

"No, you didn't, Jack, actually you made things all right again. I remembered what I loved." His smile this time was sweet. "Why do you think I'm telling you all this? I like you."

"It certainly does put a different perspective on things. Mary was obviously quite happy to use you to escape the brothel."

"No, it wasn't like that. I asked the earl if she could come with me. He was desperate enough to own me at that point to agree, and eventually to pretend it had been his idea all along. He was quite fond of Mary, really."

Jack's fingers dug into the wood of the window frame. "Did he ever—?"

"No, he never hurt her. I wouldn't have let him if he'd tried, but he never did."

Jack slowly exhaled. He couldn't think here, needed peace and silence to decipher what Simon had just told him. "Your mother's clients are a peculiar lot."

"Not really. They're just seeking what we all desire, sexual satisfaction. Don't tell me you've never been tied up, or enjoyed being told what to do?"

"I've certainly done that, but this? That schoolroom? That made my cock shrivel up."

Simon smiled. "I certainly wouldn't want that." He met Jack's gaze, his brown eyes steady.

"I wish I could dig up the sixth earl, and beat him to death with my bare hands."

"I wouldn't bother. He'd probably enjoy it."

"I don't know how you can laugh about such things." Jack drew in a deep breath. "What can I do to make things better for you?"

"As I said, you already did that. I've discovered I like sex again."

"Only when I tied you up and brutalized you."

"Please don't feel guilty about that."

"What if I offered you something different?"

"Here?" Simon's gesture encompassed the small, bleak bedroom. "I was at my happiest here with Mary."

"Would you let me make you happy here, too?"

"To give me another good memory of the place?"

"I thought you said you liked it here."

"I did, but I'm not sure I'd want to return to such excesses. I'd like to find one man who can own me to his heart's content."

"It won't be me, Simon."

"I know that." He held out his hand.

Jack stood and walked over to the other man. He cupped his cheek. "Are you sure? I'm certain Mary wouldn't approve at all."

"Mary is probably going to murder me for telling you about the Earl of Storr, so I don't have long to live anyway." He turned his head slightly until his lips brushed Jack's hand.

"Why didn't she tell me herself?"

"Because she is as proud and stubborn as you are? You'll have to ask her."

Jack brushed his lips over Simon's. "If she'll ever speak to me again."

"Of course she will. When she finds out about this, she'll probably come after you too."

Jack found himself smiling. "You are not encouraging me to proceed."

"Maybe this will help?" Simon kissed Jack's mouth, easing his tongue inside to tangle with Jack's. "I want you. Just you."

"I'm not going to hurt you."

"I know." Simon nuzzled Jack's lower lip. "Just fuck me."

Jack wrapped his arm around Simon's hips and drew him in until their cocks were rubbing against each other, silk pantaloons to buckskin breeches. He groaned at the sensation, and shoved his hand between their two bodies to fondle and play with both their straining covered cocks. He was determined to take his time, to try and show this beautiful man he was worthy of kindness and gentleness.

"Take off your coat." Simon murmured as he worked on the buttons. Jack reciprocated and soon they were both down to their shirts. He shoved an impatient hand inside Simon's breeches and unbuttoned the placket, pulling the shirt out and urging Simon to take it off. His own shirt and pantaloons were soon dealt with, and then they were naked, and Simon was leading him back toward the bed.

Jack sat down and Simon straddled him as they kissed, hands everywhere, teasing tight nipples, cupping balls and straining cocks until both of them were breathless. Jack was on his back, Simon over him, both of their cocks in his hand.

"Turn around," Jack urged him. "Take me in your mouth, and I'll do the same."

Simon reversed his position and Jack groaned as his cock was taken into Simon's clever mouth before swallowing Simon's shaft in his turn. He sucked hard, knowing the other man would love it, one hand sliding downward to play with his lover's tight balls and rim the pucker of his arse hole.

His cock vibrated as Simon hummed his approval and then Jack forgot everything but pleasing his lover, taking him as deep and as hard as he could until Simon climaxed and his come pumped down Jack's throat without spilling free from his mouth. Even as he swallowed, his own cock started to come in thick pulsing waves until he was almost crying out with the pleasure.

Eventually, he managed to roll Simon onto his back and kneel between his legs. He took his time exploring every inch of his lover's now damp skin, licking and sucking at his nipples, biting the skin that stretched over his jutting hip bones and following every intriguing line of taut muscle he could find.

Beneath him, Simon groaned and bucked against his mouth, his cock filling out again and already dripping pre-cum.

Jack licked at that and then leaned forward to kiss Simon. "I missed you."

"We both missed you." Jack grimaced and Simon chuckled. "It's much easier for you to fuck me than it is for you to make love to Mary, isn't it?"

Jack went still. "What makes you say that?"

"Because we know we are just enjoying ourselves. When you introduce *emotions* to the experience, I suspect you and Mary are equally terrified."

"I don't want to think about her. Is there any oil?"

"On the table beside the bed," Simon answered him. "You want to fuck me because you think you can't have her."

Jack retrieved the oil and dripped some on two of his fingers. "Will you be quiet about your damned sister? This is hardly the place to be discussing her when I'm about to make you scream with ecstasy."

"You'd like it even better if she was here, watching you fuck me, and breathlessly awaiting her turn."

Trying desperately to ignore Simon's banter, Jack eased one oiled finger inside and then another and pumped them in and out. He leaned forward and licked the crown of Simon's cock with every thrust until his lover was lifting his hips to encourage Jack to take more.

"Please fuck me."

"Only if you stop talking about Mary."

Simon's answering smile was wicked. "I'll stop, but I know you're thinking about her now anyway."

Jack gripped the base of his shaft and pressed the head against Simon's well-oiled hole. "Enough." He pushed inward, enjoying the other man's gasps and the tightness of his passage. "Hold your cock, but don't come unless I tell you."

He concentrated on the thrust and withdrawal of his shaft, using his full length to give his lover the most pleasure. Simon writhed beneath him as Jack kissed and sucked his nipples, his throat, and ultimately drove his tongue into Simon's mouth, replicating the movement of his cock. It was blissful but Jack couldn't quite shake off the sense that Mary was indeed watching him and waiting for him to turn to her.

The urge to climax grew and his thrusts shortened until he was slamming into Simon. He reached down to add his hand to Simon's and interlaced their fingers.

"Come with me, now."

With a groan, Simon obliged and Jack closed his eyes and followed him into pleasure. After a while, he pulled out and remained lying over Simon, his face buried in the crook of the other man's neck.

Simon's hand came to rest in his hair. "It's all right, Jack."

"No, it isn't." He was too tired to dissemble. "I've bedded you when—"

"—when you're in love with Mary."

Jack levered himself up on one elbow and glared down at Simon's amused face. "Devil take it, I am not!"

"She's in love with you too."

"That's even more ridiculous." Jack moved away from Simon's comforting warmth and sat on the side of the bed, his back turned to his lover. "Are you going to let me leave now?"

"I don't have the energy to stop you." Simon hesitated. "Why does it frighten you so much?"

Jack shot to his feet and took a hasty wash using the icy water in the basin on the table. He found his shirt, disentangled his satin pantaloons from Simon's breeches, and sat back on the bed to get dressed again. His cravat seemed to have disappeared, but he shrugged into his coat and stood to leave.

Simon hadn't moved from the bed and lay there in all his naked glory, one hand absently cupping his balls, his thumb playing with his cock. Jack looked away from the tempting sight.

"I'm sorry, Simon."

"For fucking me? I wanted you."

"I could've stopped."

"Why?"

"Because I've recently learned that using a person for sex isn't a good idea."

Simon stretched luxuriously. "I liked being used. That's why the Earl of Storr bought me."

"And Mary."

"Do you think I should've left her here?"

"No, I'm sure you did the best you could at the time." Jack hesitated. "In truth, I wish you both well. You may reassure her that I will never try to get out of the obligations of the late Earl of Storr's will."

"I told her you wouldn't."

"I'm not quite that vindictive. If only she hadn't—" He

stopped himself just in time and headed for the door. "Good night, Simon, and thank you for everything."

He heard Simon sigh and softly closed the door. He managed to reach the exit of the brothel without having to deal with Mrs. Picoult, which was lucky because he doubted he could meet the woman with any civility at all. She might claim that her son went willingly with the Earl of Storr, but he found such cold-blooded behavior appalling. It reminded him too much of his own father.

18

Ignoring the dangers, Jack walked back to the Sinners from Whitechapel, his mind too unsettled to contemplate company of any kind. Tomorrow night, as resident host, he would have to attend the social event on the second floor. Watching sexual antics had never been difficult for him. He didn't expect anyone to ask about his *feelings* like Simon did, only to perform as vigorously and inventively as possible.

He didn't even want to participate, but all it required was the ability to maintain an erection and he was more than capable of that. He turned in to the square where the Sinners was located and headed down the steps to the basement. Despite his worries, he was hungry, and he knew the cook would've left something out for his return. He'd eat there and then take the backstairs up to bed.

One of the kitchen maids ladled a big bowl of soup out for him and he sat at the scarred table and ate it with some cheese and fresh bread. Feeling immeasurably better, he thanked the maid and made his way up to his apartment, which was warm and blessedly silent.

With a groan, he dropped his clothes on the floor and filled the bath with hot water. When he finally took possession of Pinchbeck Hall, whatever the cost, he was going to install one of these marvels in the dressing room next to the earl's bedchamber. He sighed and sank deeper into the tub, allowing his head to go under the surface. When he resurfaced he pushed his hair out of his eyes and then almost jumped out of his skin.

"How in God's name did you get in here?"

Mary waited for Jack to stop spluttering and handed him one of the towels warming by the fire. He wiped his face, threw the towel to the floor and stood up. Water ran in rivulets down his magnificent, lean body following the lines of his muscles and the curve of his hip.

"I'm sorry if I startled you."

He stepped out of the bath, grabbed the largest towel, and wrapped it around his hips. "I asked you a question."

There was nothing welcoming in his voice, but she had expected that. Had braced herself to deal with his contempt, even if it hurt.

"The butler let me in."

"Damn him." Jack ran a hand through his wet hair. "That's all I need to make this the perfect evening."

"You saw Simon."

He turned away from her and picked up the other towel. "And what if I did? Are you jealous? Have I become some kind of prize in a competition between you both?" When he swung around he wore the smile she'd learned to hate. "Do you want to fuck me too? Will it be before or after your latest confession?" He rubbed at his hair. "There's no need. Simon did an excellent job of defending you."

"Do you think I asked him to do that?"

"I don't know, did you?"

She forced herself to meet his gaze. "You really don't like me, do you?"

"On the contrary. How could I not admire a woman who is ruthless enough to get what she wants? If you were a man, you would probably be extremely rich, or extremely powerful by now." He bowed. "Now would you mind going away? I'm extremely tired, and I have an orgy to organize here for tomorrow night."

"But—"

He grabbed her by the elbow. "As I've already explained, Simon told me everything that needed to be said."

"Did he tell you about his relationship with Jasper?"

"Yes, he did, thank you. I now understand that you weren't the earl's first choice, and that you were only brought along because Simon insisted."

She shrugged out of his hold. "Did he tell you he went *willingly?*"

"Yes. Aren't you pleased?" His smile was cool. "At least, I can't blame you for that. In fact, he did you a favor by bringing you along, didn't he?"

She pressed a hand to her mouth to stop herself from screaming.

"What's wrong?"

Despite her best efforts, she couldn't stop the tears from falling.

"He hated it." She swallowed hard. "He *loathed* what that man did to him. The only reason he agreed to go with him was to save *me.*"

Jack frowned. "Why would he lie?"

"Because, as usual, he's trying to protect me, to insist that everything was fine. I even believed him myself at first, until I found him shivering and crying and hiding from the damned man, so badly beaten and bruised that—" She gulped in air. "Why do you think I made Jasper marry me?"

"To safeguard your future." Jack had retreated to safety and was searching for something in one of his drawers.

"No! To safeguard *Simon's!*" She actually stamped her foot. "Why shouldn't he receive something in return for all those years of servitude? The earl didn't even leave him the smallest of legacies in his will. How could he be so *ignorant*, so *ungrateful?*" She glared at Jack. "What is that for?"

He gave her a clean handkerchief. "To wipe your beautiful face."

"I don't care about my beautiful face. All it's done has brought me misery." She dabbed at her tears anyway, and defiantly blew her nose. "When I see Simon I'm going to kill him!"

"I think he knows that."

"I never meant things to become so *complicated*. Originally, we were just trying to put George off the scent, and then you turned up, and everything became too much, but it was too late to pull back, and I just *hoped* . . . I never imagined I'd come to feel so *guilty*. . . ."

Jack steered her into one of the chairs by the fireside. Shock obviously turned her into a chattering, weeping fool. Her knees were shaking and her hands were fisted so tightly that her nails dug into her palms.

He handed her a glass. "Drink this."

She obeyed because it was easier not to think, or to argue. The brandy seared down her throat and pooled like lava in her stomach. He took the seat opposite her and sipped his own drink.

She glared at him over her glass. "Don't worry. I'll leave in a minute."

"There's no hurry."

"A few moments ago you were practically throwing me out!"

He regarded her for a long while, his head angled to one side. "I must confess, it's almost refreshing to see you with a red nose and eyes from crying too hard. I don't think I've ever seen you mar the perfection of your features before with real tears."

She took another swig of her brandy. She felt quite unlike herself. "You would know all about pretending, wouldn't you?"

"About wearing a mask?" He smiled. "Of course."

"And when do we see the real Jack Lennox, or is it John? Or whatever you wish to be called now."

"I don't think you'd want to see him."

"Why not? Haven't you got the guts to tell me to my face how much I hurt you by attempting to steal your birthright?"

Cold fury flashed deep in his blue eyes. "I hardly think—"

"That I lied and deceived you, and that despite everything, you still can't wait to get me back in your bed?"

He came out of his seat so fast that she dropped her glass on the carpet. He caged her in the chair, his hands bracketing her head.

"Now that's an excellent thought. We're both so *good* at fucking, aren't we?"

She cupped his rigid jaw. "Stop it."

"You wanted to see the real Jack." He bent his head, his lips bruising her mouth. "He's as much of a whore as you are."

"I whored to protect my mother, to provide her with a place to die that wasn't on the streets. What's your excuse, Jack? From what I can tell, you just love to fuck anything, and then you run away as fast as you can."

"I couldn't run when I was fourteen, could I?" His breathing hitched. "When my father prostituted my services to any man or woman who wanted me so he could continue to live as he pleased? If I run away now, it's because I damned well *can*."

She shoved at his shoulder. "Then run."

"And if I don't want to?"

"Then you stay, and we do this for each other, not for money, or for obligation, or because we want something from the other. We do it because we both choose to stay and we want each other."

He stared into her eyes, a muscle twitching at the side of his mouth. He looked quite unlike himself, all the charm stripped away to display the hardness beneath. And beneath that . . .

His mouth descended again, and this time she let him in. The kiss wasn't nice or pleasant, it was a tangle of need and anger and . . . God. She whimpered his name against his lips and was rewarded by a sharp nip. He picked her up and she wrapped her legs around his waist, pulling at the towel until it fell free and he was naked, his hard cock pressed against her belly. Her back hit the bedsheets and he was over her instantly.

He didn't bother to strip her, just pulled up her skirts, parted her thighs with one heavy knee and was shoving himself deep inside her. She bucked against him, but he held her still, his body too big to push away, his need to have her just as he wanted too strong.

But she was done with lying passively under any man.

She wiggled one arm free and yanked hard on his wet hair until he yelped and released his iron control over her body. She punched his shoulder until he was forced to look at her. There was none of his usual sensual amusement in his gaze; he looked as lost as she felt.

"No." She punched him again, felt his cock jerk inside her. "*Both* of us."

After a breathless second, he rolled them over until he was on his back and she was astride him. She started to move on him then, grinding her clit against the cradle of his groin, squeezing his cock and releasing it within her until he bucked against her, his hands on her hips trying to slow her down, to hold her steady.

With a growl he rolled them again until she was under him and he was pounding into her, each thrust from root to tip. She dug her fingers into his shoulders and then moved them down his back, scoring his skin, making him work her even harder. She climaxed so suddenly she screamed. He rumbled his approval, his cock still working her, his fingers sliding between their two bodies to circle and play with her clit, sending her off again.

He thrust deep one more time, and held still until she felt the hot pulse of his come at her very center. For a long moment, he lay heavily on her, and she didn't have the energy to do anything except breathe. She fought an impulse to wiggle. Her dress would be ruined and her corset was digging into her side.

As if he'd read her mind, he moved off her and set about unbuttoning her gown and unlacing her corset until she was as naked as he was. He sat her on his lap so that she straddled him and put his hands on her, shaping her breasts, and biting and sucking her nipples until she moaned his name. She touched him, too, her hands roaming his chest and broad shoulders, the myriad of scars and marks that lined his back.

Kisses too, something she'd avoided as a whore but craved from him. She leaned into him, rubbing her aching nipples against his lightly haired chest, her wet sex against the underside of his rapidly growing shaft. Eventually she came up on her knees, and let him slip inside again. He wrapped an arm around her hips and held her impaled on his cock. His thumb and forefinger alighted on her already swollen clit. Still holding her gaze, he played with her until she was straining against him, the pleasure too much, too intense, too . . .

"Jack . . ."

He kissed her as she shuddered through her climax and slipped his hands under her thighs, opening her even wider. He pumped in and out until she was unable to think of anything but his mouth, his cock, his hands on her and what they were doing, that she couldn't live with such intense pleasure, but couldn't imagine not having it ever again.

She gasped as he came up on his knees and laid her down on

her back, moving her ankles to his shoulders and pinning her to the bed with intensely deep thrusts that left her unable to move, just to take and take whatever he wanted to give her. There was no artifice now, just two bodies straining against each other to give pleasure.

He started to shudder and each thrust shortened, as his hips jerked and he fought to stop coming. She didn't use any whore's tricks to hasten his climax. She was transfixed by his face, by the strain of his pleasure, by the delicious sight of him almost biting through his lip in his desire to give her everything he had, everything he was.

"Ah, God . . ."

He climaxed and she held on to him through every shuddering pulse until he collapsed beside her on the bed and buried his face against her shoulder. She tangled her fingers in his hair and held him close.

There was nothing to say.

Words were for clients.

This was for each other.

Mary closed her eyes and went straight to sleep.

Jack stared up at the ceiling and held Mary as she slept. He was usually well on his way out of the door before his bed partners fell asleep. But this was different. It was Mary, and she didn't want anything from him except for him to be himself.

Which was terrifying.

He'd never felt so secure and yet so vulnerable before in his life. What if she didn't like him after all? After tangling with the Lennox family once, didn't she deserve better? But then how was he supposed to live without her?

Reason resurfaced with the faint cold light of the dawn. She was his uncle's wife. As far as he understood it, he couldn't marry her if someone else objected, and he was damned sure that George Mainwaring would object from the very rooftops.

And if he couldn't offer her that legal status, he wouldn't demean her by making her his mistress. She'd fought too long and hard to rediscover her respectability for him to ruin her again.

He eased his arm out from under her and moved to the side of the bed. His heart hurt like a bloodied, clenched fist. He was supposed to be meeting Mr. McEwan this morning to go over the finer points of the late earl's will, and listen in on his interview with George Mainwaring. He understood Mary's choices so much better now. Her desire to protect Simon had driven everything she'd done. But where did the truth lie? Had Simon really hated every moment of his time with the earl as Mary claimed, or had he even enjoyed the beatings? From what he'd seen of Simon in bed, Jack suspected the latter. But even Simon had admitted that in his later years, the earl had become difficult and cruel.

He tiptoed to the door and gathered up an armful of his clothes. By the time Mary woke up, he might know what George's secret was. Would it harm her, or harm him? The only way to find out was to keep moving forward, and pray that everything would turn out for the best. It was a cliché but for once in his life, he sincerely hoped it would come true.

"So, as you see, Mr. Lennox, despite everything the late earl—Mr. Lennox? Are you listening to me?"

With considerable effort, Jack jerked his attention back to Mr. McEwan, who wasn't looking very pleased.

"The late earl, what?"

"Kept his affairs in perfect order. The will was properly witnessed and signed, and is thus a legal document."

"So unless George Mainwaring comes up with something extraordinary, the will stands, and Mary Lennox receives her full widow's pension, plus anything I choose to bestow on her in the way of a dwelling place, or an increase in her allowance."

"Exactly, Mr. Lennox. It appears that you were listening after all." The clock chimed ten times. "Would you care for some refreshment? Mr. Mainwaring is due to arrive here at any moment."

"No thank you." Jack looked dubiously around the cramped office. "Are you sure there is somewhere for me to hide in here?"

Mr. McEwan slowly rose to his feet, walked over to one of the bookcases and pulled out a book. To Jack's surprise, a door opened within the shelving to reveal a small chamber beyond.

Jack joined the portly solicitor and examined the latch on the door to make sure it was in working order, and could be operated from the inside as well as the out.

"There is some natural light and ventilation from the small window."

A loud familiar voice permeated through the thick door of Mr. McEwan's study.

"That sounds like George, perhaps I'll make myself scarce." Jack took up his position in the secret chamber and waited until Mr. McEwan shut the door. He could see into the office through a grille at eye level and could hear quite well too.

The outer door opened, and George Mainwaring entered, his expression that of a sanctimonious nun. "Mr. McEwan, you took your time in seeing me."

"I am a very busy man, Mr. Mainwaring. Now, how may I assist you?"

Mr. McEwan took his usual seat behind his desk giving Jack an excellent view of both the men.

"It's about the earldom of Storr."

"So you said in your letter. I have received a copy of the late earl's last will and testament and everything seems to be in order. May I ask what your concern is?"

"Well, it's like this, you see." George leaned forward confidentially. "When the earl was dying I went to see him. The damned Picoults tried to keep us all away from him, but I knew he'd want to see me."

"And why was that, Mr. Mainwaring?"

"Because I'm of his blood, his true family." He slapped his meaty thigh. "And I was right to go. Jasper was desperate to tell me something."

"Relevant to the earldom?"

"Aye, he told me that he wanted to find out if any relations of a Mr. Desmond Norris were still alive."

Jack frowned. *Now what?*

"And what exactly do Mr. Norris and his family have to do with the earldom of Storr?"

"He told me that he'd known Mr. Norris and his sister in his youth, and that he was anxious to get in touch with them before his death."

"Why was it important for him to do so?"

"He wouldn't quite say, at first, but eventually I wheedled it out of him." George's smile was full of triumphant glee. "He was hoping that Miss Norris was dead because, well, he feared he might still be married to her."

"But he'd recently married Miss Picoult!"

"Exactly." George folded his hands on his vast stomach. "Which means that his second marriage is invalid."

"Did he offer you any proof of this?"

"I asked him where the marriage had taken place and the year. He was a little confused as to the details, but after his death I decided to investigate further. It's taken me all these months to finally discover the truth." He took a document out of his pocket. "I believe what I have here is a copy of their marriage certificate."

"Which obviously predates the earl's second marriage. The more important issue is whether Miss Norris is still alive."

"I met the woman, and she confirmed that she and the earl entered into a clandestine marriage during their early years. She is from farming stock, and seemed to have no idea who Jasper really was when she married him, although he was only a younger son, then with little prospects of advancement. I have a signed letter from her here."

Mr. McEwan took the paper out of George's hand, unfolded it, and slowly read the contents. "As one of the trustees of the Storr estate, I will have to check these details very thoroughly, Mr. Mainwaring, before I reach a final decision as to their validity."

"Do you doubt my word, sir?" George scowled. "I have nothing to gain from this. John Lennox will inherit the title, not me. I just knew that bloody woman didn't deserve to be a countess! All I want is those damn Picoults gone from my ancestral house, and exposed as the thieves and liars that they are."

"Are you suggesting the current dowager knew about the previous marriage?"

"I'll wager she did. It would explain why she tried to keep me away from the earl at the end."

"That is pure conjecture, Mr. Mainwaring, and I deal in fact."

"Then deal with that marriage certificate and letter from Miss Norris, and that upstart John Lennox's son."

"We are still investigating Mr. Lennox's claim too." Mr. McEwan looked up as George rose to his feet. "Thank you for bringing the matter to my attention, Mr. Mainwaring. It certainly throws a new light on the matter."

"I thought you should know before you start believing that woman's lies." George crammed his hat back on his head and picked up his gloves. "I'll wait to hear from you, but don't take too long about it, mind."

Mr. McEwan didn't reply and George finally left. After a few moments, Mr. McEwan opened the door into the secret room and stood back.

"That was rather unexpected."

"I would say it was." Jack took the seat George had recently vacated. "It also complicates matters rather more than I anticipated."

"If the sixth earl was married to Miss Norris and she is still living, then his marriage to Mary Picoult isn't valid."

"I gathered that." Jack pondered the toe of his well-polished boot. "Actually, I wouldn't mind at all if Mary's marriage wasn't valid."

"I beg your pardon?"

Jack offered him a brief smile. "Never mind. I think I'd like to meet this Miss Norris myself. Will you trust me to investigate the matter before you speak to either the Dowager Countess or to George again?"

"As it is in your best interests to find out the truth, I am happy for you to take on this task." Mr. McEwan handed Jack a piece of paper. "Here is Miss Norris's information."

Jack glanced at the paper and nodded. "It isn't that far away. I should be able to make it there and back if I leave now. There is one thing you can do for me. Could you ask my butler, Haddon, to contact a Mr. Nicodemus Theale and have him meet me later tonight at the Sinners?"

"Yes, Mr. Lennox."

Jack shook Mr. McEwan's hand. "Thank you."

The solicitor took off his glasses and sighed. "This has certainly been one of the most interesting cases I've worked on for years."

"Hopefully, all will soon be resolved. Now I must leave, or I'll never make it back to Town for the evening's entertainment."

19

"Did you know about this?" Simon barged into Mary's bedroom, where she was curled up on the bed in a miserable ball, and held out a letter. "It's from Jack. He wants us to meet him at the Sinners Club tonight for a late supper." He frowned. "It is rather short notice."

"He probably wants us to join in the orgy he's planning."

Simon's gaze brightened. "What orgy?"

"How would I know?" She sighed and stared up at the ceiling. "He just mentioned it in passing, although if he's asking us to a late supper he's probably hoping to enjoy that first, and attend to us afterward."

Simon shook his head and tutted. "That man is insatiable."

Mary glared at him. "Don't."

"Don't what?"

"Talk about him like that, as if that's all he's capable of."

"My, you are quite besotted with him, aren't you?"

She raised her chin. "Perhaps I just see him for what he is: a man who was just as damaged by others as we were."

Simon held her gaze for a long moment. "So, do you want to go, or not?"

"I suppose we should." Mary groaned. What if he'd decided that their night together meant nothing to him, and had retreated back into his charming, charismatic, soulless self? Could she bear to see him like that, knowing the complex and vulnerable man beneath?

There was only one way to find out. She had to face him. If he didn't have the courage to be himself, then he wasn't worth caring about anyway. She had her pension from the late earl, and would live out her life very happily without bothering the new Earl of Storr ever again.

"Mary?"

"What?"

"You're woolgathering, my dear." Simon tapped his pocket watch. "If you mean to go, we really should change our dress."

"But it's far too soon!"

He winked at her. "Not if we want to be exceptionally early."

When they arrived at the Sinners Club, the place was already ablaze with lights. Mary was surprised to see that Mrs. Picoult had been correct, and that ladies and gentlemen appeared to be equally welcome within the confines of the club. When the butler saw them come in, he hurried to intercept them.

"My lady, Mr. Picoult, you're rather early. Would you like to wait for Mr. Lennox in his study?"

"He's not finished at the orgy yet?" Simon looked around.

"Not quite, sir. He *is* the host. But I'm sure Mr. Lennox won't be long. He is aware that you are coming."

Simon winked at Mary. "Don't worry, we'll find him ourselves. Where exactly is this orgy taking place?"

"On the second floor, sir, but—"

"Thank you." He took Mary's arm and walked past the butler. "We can find it ourselves."

Mary pinched him hard. "Are you certain you feel like doing this?"

"Why, don't you?"

"I'm not exactly in the mood to throw myself at anyone."

"Even Jack?"

She favored him with her best glare. "Jack is probably busy."

"He *is* the host."

"And he asked us to wait for him in his study. He's hardly going to be pleased to see us up here, is he?"

"Mary, Mary, when did you become such a prude?" Simon patted her hand. "Letting Jack see you enjoy yourself without a care in the world is the best thing you can do at this juncture. That's what you've always told me in the past."

Had she? Mary gazed unseeingly at the bright swirl of colors and people crammed into the large salon on the second floor. She didn't want to do that to Jack. She was so tired of playing games. . . .

"Are you by chance, the Dowager Countess of Storr?"

She half-turned to find an older woman dressed in a beautiful sapphire silk Indian robe smiling at her.

"Yes, I am."

"I thought it must be you. Mr. Lennox told me that you were very beautiful. I'm Lady Westbrook. My husband and I founded the Sinners Club."

"How very brave of you." Mary dropped into a curtsey. "I understand that the club welcomes women. That must have been your doing."

"If a woman has risked her life for her country, why shouldn't she enjoy the same rewards as a man?" Lady Westbrook linked her arm through Mary's and started toward a door concealed in the corner of the salon. "Come along. I'm sure Mr. Picoult can cope without you."

Amused by Lady Westbrook's forceful manner, Mary allowed herself to be led away and ushered into the small book-room adjoining the salon. To her surprise, it was full of people changing into some of the most exotic costumes she had ever seen. Her companion spoke to some of the women in their own language and then smiled at Mary.

"I thought you might enjoy watching the performers dress." She touched her own vivid silk clothing. "At my age, I tend to wear the more modest version of the Indian sari. You, of course, can wear nothing under the wrapped silk but your skin." Her smile was quite wicked. "After being forced to wear a corset, it is a very freeing sensation. And for a man to unwrap you . . ." She sighed as if she had some very happy memories. "It is *quite* extraordinary."

Mary smiled at the young woman who was holding out a long swathe of jade silk to her. "I would love to try. Hopefully someone can show me how to put it on."

"Oh good." Lady Westbrook clapped her hands. "Now take everything off, and Meera here will wrap you up like an exotic silk parcel."

Mary stood still as Meera draped the silk low on her hips, and then around and around. The skirt length was just above the ankle, and felt cool against her skin. She held her breath as the girl deftly made a series of pleats and tucked them inside the waistband.

"Now for the top."

The remaining part of the silk was brought around to the back and then tossed over her right shoulder leaving only one thin layer covering her bosom. Her nipples crinkled against the fabric and were easily visible through it.

"It is rather daring. Perhaps we should pin it at the hip?" Lady Westbrook suggested.

"Is that what the other women do?"

"No."

"Then I won't do it either."

Lady Westbrook smiled. "You need to take your hair down and wear a veil over your face, at least at first."

"Until when?"

"Until dear Jack realizes who you are and allows himself to enjoy the festivities to the fullest. There have already been three dances, and he hasn't taken part in any of them."

Mary bit her lip. "I'm not actually supposed to be here at all."

"I think he'll be pleased to see you."

"Are you sure?"

Lady Westbrook took her hand and walked her over to another door. "Look."

Jack sat on a pile of cushions watching as the dancers filed out into the room. He wore his usually charming smile, but she knew him well enough to recognize the tension in his shoulders and his complete lack of interest in the salacious sights in front of him. One of the women danced over to him and dropped to her knees to kiss his feet, her naked breasts brushing against him. Although he toasted the woman with his glass, he made no move to actually touch her.

Mary found such a sight equally reassuring and also quite foreign. Had she done this to him? Made him as weary of the games as she was?

"Meera will teach you the basic movements of this particular love song, which is about the joys of fellatio. I'm sure you'll pick it up quite quickly; you are naturally graceful."

Mary squeezed the older woman's hand. "Thank you."

"You and Jack deserve all the happiness that you can find in this world. I'm glad to help in any way that I can." She reached up and kissed Mary's cheek. "Now go and cheer him up."

A loud crash on the drums made the rest of the dancers hurry into the main salon. Mary followed Meera and stood behind her at the back of the dance troupe. There were seven women, four men, and her. A group of musicians using instru-

ments she had never seen or heard before were grouped in the
bay window. The women were dressed as she was in a rainbow
of shimmering silk, and the men wore a similar wrapped silk
skirt without the covering over their chests. All of the dancers
had darker skin and hair than she did.

Other performers already mingled with the crowd. She
spotted Simon talking to one of the men, his red head bent low
to listen and his smile wide.

The stringed instrument started up, followed by a flute, and
then someone sang a low chant over the melody. Meera beckoned to her, and Mary went down on her knees behind one of
the men, mirroring her companion's movements. As the beat
intensified the women edged closer and closer to the man, who
was rolling his hips and thrusting his groin to the demanding
rhythm of the drum. Mary followed Meera's lead and swayed
back and forth herself, reaching out her hands to the man when
he turned to face her and licking her lips as if she couldn't wait
to have his cock in her mouth.

The beat intensified and Meera caught her hands so that they
made a circle around the man. He half-turned so that their
joined hands cupped his cock and balls and his tight buttocks.
They both kissed his hips, licking the silk as his cock lengthened and grew beneath the tight silk of his skirt.

Another demanding beat of the drum and Meera turned the
man toward her and licked lavishly at the man's cock, kneeling
up to try and take the head in her mouth. She waved at Mary
and pointed toward Jack, who was still watching the dancers.
Each woman who wasn't currently engaged with one of the
dancers was crawling toward a male member of the audience,
their intent to replicate what was happening in the center of the
stage obvious.

Mary started to crawl too, her gaze fixed on Jack through
her short veil. Even before she reached him, he'd gone still, his

eyes narrowed on the sway of her hips and her breasts, the gold of her hair. She knelt between his thighs and licked her way up the front of his satin pantaloons, mimicking Meera's movements until she tried to suck the head of his cock into her mouth.

"God."

His hand slid under the flimsy silk covering her breasts to fondle and play with her nipples. She shifted even closer, and used her teeth to unbutton his placket and drag it away from the thick straining shaft. With a soft moan, she swallowed him down her throat, sucking him deep to the rhythm of the drum. Her hips undulated as he slipped his fingers between her thighs and stabbed them in and out of her already wet cunt.

The music changed, and Mary carefully pulled away from Jack's cock to see what Meera was going to do next. The male dancers now lay on their backs on the floor, their erect cocks freed from the silk, one hand wrapped around the base to keep them vertical. She pushed at Jack's chest and he went down without a complaint, his fingers slipping out of her. She placed one of his hands around his cock and took another quick look at what was happening in the dance.

The women half-crouched over the men, allowing just the tips of the men's cock to brush against their sex while they played with their own breasts and clit. Mary straddled Jack and followed suit, enjoying his groans as she heightened her own arousal.

Another change in the beat and Meera moved over her partner's face until his tongue emerged to lick her folds and press up inside her. Mary did the same and Jack obliged, his wicked tongue bringing her so close to orgasm that she shivered. She wanted to lower herself even more, make him suck, and lick, and bite her until he could only taste and see her, until he was drowning in her juices. . . .

"Mary, I want . . ."

His plea vibrated against her clit and she almost sobbed as she started to come. He suddenly sat up and grabbed her around the waist, bringing her firmly down over his cock, making her climax. When she remembered to look up again, it seemed the dance had become a melee of writhing bodies and moans of satisfaction. One of the women had a man beneath her, and her back arched to accept the cock of another man in her mouth.

Jack stood up, bringing her with him and headed for the nearest wall where he continued to fuck her hard and fast. She was so wet now that he could slide in and out more easily.

"May I?"

She turned her head to see Simon beside them, his gaze on Jack's pumping arse. His fingers were already dripping with oil.

"Be my guest," Jack groaned with each thrust, "but do it quick, I want to come."

"But you'll wait." Simon pointed at the anteroom. "It's slightly quieter in there and there's more space."

Mary didn't care as long as Jack kept fucking her. He lowered her into a pile of cushions and stayed deep inside her. Simon moved behind him, but leaned over to kiss her on the mouth and lightly lick her nipple. She moaned her appreciation and didn't care what anyone thought of her. She loved having two sets of male hands on her skin.

"Do you want him first, Mary?" Jack murmured against her mouth. "His cock in your mouth or your cunt? My cock in yours while he fucks me?"

"You don't mind?"

"Not if it's what you want." He held her gaze, his shaft a thick, throbbing presence deep inside her. "I love watching you suck and fuck him almost as much as I love you doing those things to me." He kissed her. "If you can allow me to be myself,

surely I can do the same for you. There should be no shame between us, no sexual secrets that we can't indulge in together,
don't you agree?"

She could only nod and stare deep into his beautiful eyes.

Simon's cock nudged her cheek. "Suck me, please? Make me
nice and hard for Jack?"

She willingly obliged, aware of Jack watching every twirl
and lick of her tongue against Simon's crown, of every twitch
of his cock when she did something he found particularly-
arousing. The sense of other people around her faded away and
she simply enjoyed her men.

Jack watched as Mary sucked at Simon's cock and appreciated every salacious second of it. He reached around to touch
Simon's hip.

"How about we both make love to her?"

"I'd like that. Are you sure?"

"I can't think of anything I'd like to see more at this moment than Mary taking us both, can you?"

He loved her sensual nature, he gloried in it, and he would
never become the kind of man who stopped his lover from enjoying herself in bed as much as he did. Of course, he *hoped*
she'd always include him in any games she wanted to play; in
fact he would insist upon it. He was willing to swear that he'd
never touch anyone else without her consent or her participa-
tion.

He stared down at her. Was this what love did to a man?
Made him want to please her more than himself? After what
he'd learned from Miss Norris earlier that day, he could only
pray Mary would linger long enough to listen to his declaration
of love.

Simon eased his cock out of Mary's mouth and turned to
Jack. "Where do you want me?"

Jack pushed aside all his unsettling thoughts and concentrated on the fact that he was with the two people he wanted to fuck more than anyone else in the world. More surprisingly, they seemed to want him too. He wrapped his arm around Mary's hips and brought her up with him, curling her legs around his waist.

"There."

"But, Simon—"

"I'm here, love."

Jack watched over Mary's shoulder as Simon eased an oil-slickened finger inside her, shuddering as Simon deliberately ran the pad of his finger along the thin wall that separated Jack's cock from him.

Mary's nipples hardened against his chest and she gasped Simon's name. Jack waited until Simon nudged the head of his wet, oiled cock against Mary's tight hole and then cupped her breasts, his fingers playing with her nipples until she rocked against him, driving Simon deeper with each roll of her hips. He felt Simon's cock slide against his and fought to hold still and not come until his lover was fully sheathed.

He kissed Mary and then Simon, holding them both, loving them both.

"Do you want more, Mary? Another cock in your mouth, filling you up completely?"

She came and he had to grit his teeth to stop himself from joining her. "There are plenty of men here who'd be more than willing to oblige you." He bit Simon's lower lip. "Next time, maybe even more. Simon and I both in your cunt and two others, would that be enough for you?"

Simon moaned. "Have you ever done that?"

"Yes, it's damned tight."

"Oh God." Simon started to thrust. "I want that one day, I want my cock against yours while we both have her."

Jack couldn't stop his body from responding to Simon's, and he started to move as well in counterpoint. Between them, Mary started to come endlessly, her screams captured in his mouth as he strove to give her everything he was, to become everything she ever needed. . . .

His come exploded deep inside her and he simply gave in to the sensations until he could give nothing else, and felt Simon doing the same.

"Thank you, Mary," he whispered.

He held her tight as Simon kissed them both and moved away to wash. It was too late to change course now. Loving someone was obviously a far more powerful force than he had ever imagined. He had to tell her the truth about everything and hope that, in the end, she would turn to him and not run. He had no intention of running away from her ever again.

After a long soak in Jack's incredibly modern bath, Mary felt remarkably relaxed. It helped that Jack had left her alone while she bathed, because she wasn't sure what to think, or how to deal with him anymore. He hadn't been angry to find her at the orgy. In fact, he'd seemed delighted. Having sex with him and Simon had been incredible and quite unexpected. She trusted them both implicitly.

When had she started to trust Jack?

When had she started to depend on him as much as she depended on Simon?

Pushing such unsettling thoughts away, Mary got out of the bath, dressed with the aid of one of the kitchen maids, and was escorted down the stairs. Simon was waiting for her in the hallway.

When they entered Jack's study, Mary, overcome by a wave of shyness, found it impossible to raise her eyes from the intricate rug on the floor.

"My lady."

Jack's voice and his hand on her bare skin made her jump. "Good evening, sir."

He brought her hand to his lips and kissed it. He'd washed and changed and his dark hair was still damp and curling at the ends.

"I'd like to introduce you to Mr. Nicodemus Theale."

Mary half-turned and noticed for the first time that she and Simon weren't the only people in the study. A slight black-haired man stood up and bowed.

"Good evening, my lady. I'm Mr. Theale."

She nodded and smiled as Jack took her hand again and turned her toward someone else.

"And this is Miss Norris."

Her smile froze as she stared at the older woman dressed in a plain muslin gown that looked twenty years out of fashion. The woman's eyes were brown like her own, and anxiously fixed on her.

"A pleasure." Mary murmured, her heart racing, her thoughts in a terrible jumble of fear and anticipation and—what on earth was Jack Lennox playing at?

"Would you all like to sit down so that we can begin?" Jack asked.

"Begin what?" Mary said, aware that her tone was too high and full of suspicion.

He glanced over at her. "Sorting out this deplorable mess, once and for all."

She sat, mainly because her knees gave way. Simon was on her left. He reached out to pat her shoulder.

Jack remained standing, his hands behind his back, his expression thoughtful.

"George Mainwaring came to see my solicitor, Mr. McEwan, this morning, and offered him an extraordinary tale. I was fortunate enough to overhear every word, and equally determined to see if there was any truth in the story." He bowed to Miss Norris, who looked even more terrified than Mary felt.

"Apparently, on his deathbed, the earl confessed to Mr. Mainwaring that he had contracted a previous marriage. He wanted George to find out if his first wife was still living."

"*What?*" Simon asked. "But—"

Jack continued talking. "The earl mentioned the family name was Norris, which struck me as rather coincidental seeing as I'd recently been informed that the man who paid for Mary's mother, Catherine Miller's, keep was a Mr. *Desmond* Norris." He studied his audience's faces. "Could it be that the earl had married the sister of the man who was the unacknowledged father of his second wife? How bizarre would that be?"

Mary wrapped her fingers together on her lap and stared down at them. No wonder George had been so sure of victory. If he were right, Mary would be left without a feather to fly with. She suddenly felt immensely weary. All her efforts had been for nothing. She was right back in the gutter where she apparently belonged.

She rose to her feet. "I'd rather not hear any more."

"Sit down, Mary."

She glared at Jack. "Are you enjoying this? I'm surprised you didn't invite George along. He would love to be the one who throws me out—or do you want that privilege for yourself?"

"Mary." His gaze was full of compassion, which terrified her even more. "Please let me finish."

Simon tugged at her fisted hand, and she reluctantly sat back down. They might have ruined her, but she'd be damned if they made her cry again.

"After hearing George's story I offered to post down to Hertford and meet Miss Norris for myself." Jack smiled at the older woman. "She was kind enough not only to invite me into her home, but to accompany me back to London."

"So is she Jasper's wife?" Simon interrupted him.

"It appears that she is." Jack held up his hand. "But things are never quite as simple as they seem. George was so eager to confirm the marriage that he forgot to ask any more questions."

"If she's Jasper's wife, then Mary isn't, and that's all there is to it," Simon stated.

"Not quite. If Miss Norris is the Dowager Countess of Storr, why didn't she come forward to claim the title?"

Miss Norris stood up. "Because it would've been a lie." She swallowed hard. "I married Jasper under duress to protect his ungodly relationship with my brother, Desmond. He wanted an excuse to spend time with Desmond, and they used me to get what they wanted. Officially, I kept house for them both." Her mouth twisted. "Oh, we were well paid for it, and Desmond threatened to kill me if I ever breathed a word to anyone, so I kept quiet."

"Even when Jasper became the Earl of Storr?"

"I didn't want all that grandeur, and pretense. It would've choked me. I was much happier where I was, with people who loved me. Eventually, everyone forgot that Jasper had ever been part of my life. Desmond made other arrangements to meet the earl in London, and I was left to myself. In truth, I'd almost forgotten all about it until that unpleasant Mr. Mainwaring came calling and threatened me with the magistrate."

Mary almost wanted to smile. How strange that the earl had married two women to disguise his real interest in another man. It was so very likely that she didn't doubt Miss Norris's story for a second. She cleared her throat with some difficulty.

"One must assume that Desmond Norris continued to meet the earl at the house my mother and I inhabited in Hans Town."

Jack, who was assisting Miss Norris back to her seat, looked up. "Mr. Theale has the answers to that part of the puzzle."

The quiet curly-haired man stood and bowed before producing a notebook. "Mr. Desmond Norris is listed as the owner of the house in Hans Town and was considered to be the protector of your mother, Catherine Miller. However, after some research, it does appear as if all the funding for the house and upkeep actually came from the Earl of Storr."

"So my mother and I were simply a front for the earl's romantic liaison with Desmond Norris?"

Mr. Theale's glance veered over to Jack, who nodded.

"Go ahead."

"I fear it was more than that, my lady."

"Let me guess, Desmond Norris wasn't averse to bedding women, and I am his bastard?"

Mr. Theale hesitated. "From what I understand from Mrs. Picoult, my lady, it wasn't Mr. Norris who bedded your mother but the Earl of Storr."

Mary stood up so fast that she knocked her chair over. She managed to make it to the door and ran toward the entrance of the club, fighting her way through the incoming members with all her strength. But it was no use; she was hauled back from behind and found herself in Jack's arms.

"No, damn you!" She kicked and fought him as hard as she could. "Let me go!"

Without a word, Jack picked her up, slung her over his shoulder, and mounted the stairs at a run, not stopping until he reached his apartment and had her inside. He locked the door and faced her. All the color had leached from her skin, leaving it as pale as the finest porcelain; her eyes were huge and full of pain, her hand jammed over her mouth as she gulped in air through her tears.

"Mary." He held out his hand to her.

She backed away. "Get away from me, I'm going to be sick."

"It doesn't matter. It doesn't change anything."

Her breathing was as uneven as his. "It changes *everything!* Did he know? Did he deliberately take me up, and *marry* me? He made me watch him with Simon, he—" Her chest heaved. "Oh God, I can't—"

She slid down to the floor and he followed her, taking her into his arms and hauling her onto his lap. He wrapped himself around her and just concentrated on holding her shaking form.

"I don't know if he knew. Desmond's death wasn't reported to him. It was Desmond's solicitors who ordered the sale of all his assets and threw you and your mother out of the house."

"But he found us at Mrs. Picoult's. He must have known!" Her voice was muffled against his chest.

"I suppose it's possible that Mrs. Picoult wrote to tell him what had happened to you and your mother. She did know of their relationship." He sighed and kissed her now disheveled hair. "I should imagine she thought it might help."

"In her way of thinking, it probably did. She made a profit and Simon and I got out of the brothel."

He hated the note of defeat in her voice.

She shuddered. "Jasper was a monster."

He couldn't argue about that and concentrated on rubbing her back and kissing her throat and ears.

"Now what am I going to do with myself?"

"There isn't really any other option." He kissed her ear again and took a deep breath. "You're going to have to marry me."

She shoved him away. "I can't do that!"

"Why not?"

"If I'm . . ." She faltered. "Jasper's daughter, we're related."

"Barely, and who is going to know or care about that? We'll unleash the gossip about Jasper's previous marriage to Miss Norris and install her as the Dowager Countess of Storr. Everyone will be terribly sorry for you and feel it only just if I do the right thing and marry you myself."

"But we're practically cousins!"

"Which is a perfectly legitimate connection in this country."
He eased a finger under her chin and raised her head until he
could look into her beautiful brown eyes. "If it makes you feel
any better, my father was quite convinced his mother had a
lover and that he was the result of that liaison. He was born
several years after his siblings, and looked nothing like them.
Naturally, my grandfather either had to accept the child as his
own, or cast doubts on his wife's virtue and the legitimacy of all
of his children. Apparently he chose to put up with the situation, but made my father's life a misery, hence his early departure from the bosom of his family."

"Jack."

He smiled down at her. "What?"

"You are incorrigible."

"I know." He kissed her gently on the mouth. "I'm only talking so much because I'm terrified you haven't actually said yes."

"To what?"

"To marrying me, to loving me for the rest of your life and
keeping me in my place."

She took in a deep, shuddering breath. "Oh, that." She patted his cheek. "Will you let me up?"

"Not until you answer me."

"I'm not convinced everything will work out quite as well as
you believe. What on earth will we do about George?"

"The logistics don't matter." He shoved a hand through his
hair. "I love you."

Her smile was beautiful. "You see, that wasn't so hard to say,
was it?"

"I've never said it before and meant it." He swallowed hard.
"Now I think I'm the one who wants to be sick."

She climbed off his lap and straightened her crumpled gown.
Her hair was falling down, her eyes were red from crying, and
yet she'd never looked more beautiful to him.

"I love you, Jack."

For a heartbeat, her image blurred in front of him and he hastily blinked. "Good, then." He managed to get off the floor and offered her his arm. "Are you ready to face them with the good news of your upcoming marriage?"

She gave him a severe look. "I haven't agreed to that yet."

He flung the door open and escorted her through it. "Oh, but you definitely will."